# OTHER PEOPLE'S MONEY

## ALSO BY ARTHUR LYONS

# ARTHUR LYONS

# OTHER PEOPLE'S MONEY

**THE MYSTERIOUS PRESS**

**New York • London • Tokyo • Sweden**

The Mysterious Press, 129 West 56th Street, New York, N.Y. 10019

Printed in the United States of America

First Printing: July 1989

10 9 8 7 6 5 4 3 2 1

Library of Congress Cataloging-in-Publication Data

Lyons, Arthur.
    Other people's money / by Arthur Lyons.
    p.
    ISBN 0-89296-218-6
    I.  Title.
PS3562.Y44608   1989
    813'.54—dc19                               88-34369
                                                       CIP

Once again, for my wife, Marie,
who never lets me get away with anything

# ACKNOWLEDGMENTS

I would like to give special thanks to Dr. Alla Hall of the Armand Hammer Museum and to Tina Oldknow, Nancy Thomas, and Pieter Meyers of the Los Angeles County Museum of Art, for the gracious lending of their knowledge and professional expertise; James W. Grodin and Gerald Petievich, for their friendship and editorial comment; Chuck Coons, for knowing so many people; and Dashiell Hammett, for having written.

# OTHER PEOPLE'S MONEY

# ONE

The wizened, whiskered sentry blocking the door of the restaurant was a prime example of what used to be called a bum but was now commonly referred to as a "street person." As the collective guilt accumulated on society like blackened layers of tarnish, we seemed to compensate by diluting the language. Midgets became "little people." Bums were "street people." Soon, with the changes brought on by Reaganomics, they would probably be transmogrified into the "less tidy." To me, they would still be bums.

The man held out a gnarled, grimy hand and asked, "How about some spare change for a cup of coffee?"

It was a good thing I didn't smoke. He smelled flammable. I shook my head; then, lest it be said that I was indifferent to the suffering of my fellow man, I pointed to the hamburger stand across the street. "You want a cup of coffee? Tell you what. Let's go over there, and I'll buy you one."

Thoughts moved clumsily behind the bloodshot eyes. "No need for you to go to all that trouble. I can get it."

"It's no trouble."

1

A bluish tongue darted out of his toothless mouth. "I'd rather have the money."

"I'll bet."

"Go fuck yourself," he muttered and shuffled off to join a group of his friends occupying the sidewalk a few yards away.

It had been two months since L.A.'s Army of the Homeless had established a beachhead on the sands of Venice as a social statement about what the government was not doing for the nation's poor. Along with the Unfortunate Regulars, however, had come a sizable regiment of winos, hypes, panhandlers, grifters, and other, less classifiable species of derelicti, the result being that those who had once come to the beach for fun and sun had departed for less socially conscious climes. The boardwalk—once jammed with tourists, joggers, bronzed and bikinied girls on roller skates, and Walkman-headed skate-board wizards—was now occupied by the Legion of the Damned.

Business inside the Crab Shell reflected the state of seige. The downstairs was empty, except for the blond hostess and a blue-jeaned waitress who were engaged in bored conversation. They broke it up when I came in, and the hostess asked if she could help me in a tone that seemed to anticipate that I must be lost and in need of directions. She perked up when I said: "I'm supposed to meet someone here. My name is Asch—"

A thickly accented voice behind me said, "You are supposed to meet me, I believe."

I turned to face the voice. The man was short and plump, of swarthy complexion and middle age. His face was very round and his thinning black hair was combed in different directions in an attempt to cover his bald spot, which was most of his head. He wore an expensive-looking blue silk suit over a white shirt that was open at the throat, exposing several thick braids of gold.

"Mr. Saffarian?"

He bowed his head curtly, smiled, and offered his hand, which turned out to be damp and limp. The smile faded quickly and he said, "I was not sure I was going to get in here alive. I thought one of those beggars was going to assault me when I refused to give him money." He regarded me skeptically. "To be truthful, I did not realize that this was that kind of a neighborhood."

"It isn't," I assured him. "These people settled here a couple of months ago. Nobody knows what to do about them."

He scowled darkly. "In my country, we would know what to do with them."

I took the cue. "What is your country, Mr. Saffarian?"

"Turkey. I am from Istanbul."

I was tempted to ask just what they did with their beggars in Istanbul, but said instead: "I could have met you somewhere else, Mr. Saffarian, but you said you were close by and this seemed the most convenient. As I explained on the phone, my office is being redecorated and is in a shambles—"

The rather gaudy diamond on the pinkie of his small brown hand caught the light as he made an impatient gesture. "It is all right. Where can we talk?"

I told the hostess we wanted to sit on the patio, and she led the way upstairs. There were only two other couples on the small, glassed-in terrace overlooking the beach, and we took a table up front. Even though there was a cool, morning sea breeze blowing off the ocean, Saffarian's face was covered by a slick film of perspiration. His small eyes were like two flat black buttons sewn deep into pouches of coarse-pored rubbery skin, his mouth soft and fleshy. In the sunlight, I noticed that the scalp beneath his hair had been darkened with what looked like eyebrow pencil.

We both ordered coffee from the waitress and just to make conversation, I asked, "Have you been in América long, Mr. Saffarian?"

"Three days."

"You speak English very well."

He smiled tightly. "Thank you. I learned through necessity. It is somewhat a prerequisite in my business."

"What business is that?"

"I have a large import-export firm in Istanbul."

"Is this a business trip, or are you here for pleasure?"

"Neither," he said, frowning. "Which brings me to the point of this meeting. I would like to know how much you would charge to follow someone."

"Who?"

"My daughter." He paused, then said, "Perhaps I should give you some background."

"That might be helpful."

He nodded and began. "Seven years ago my wife died, leaving me to care for our only daughter, Naci. I did my best, but it was difficult. My business demanded a lot of my time, and Naci was—how you say?—a wild child? Extremely bright, but rebellious. She had always been that way, but after her mother died she went completely out of control. Repeatedly I caught her sneaking out in the middle of the night to meet boys. I tried talking to her, I threatened to lock her up, but it did no good. Perhaps I should have followed Muslim tradition and beaten some sense into her, but I could not bring myself to do it. I have always prided myself on being a modern man.

"Anyway, Naci seemed to straighten out for a time, and I thought everything was all right. She entered the university in Ankara, and for two years did very well with her studies." He paused, and for a brief moment, his voice swelled with pride. "She wanted to become a doctor."

I smiled sympathetically and nodded for him to go on.

The pride leaked out of his voice and his expression turned sad again. "Four months ago, Naci called from Ankara. She said she had met a man and intended to leave the country with him. Nothing I said could dissuade her. I flew there immediately, but by the time I arrived she was gone. I hired a detective in Istanbul to find out who this man was and where they had gone. Two weeks ago, he reported to me that the man was named Dimitrios Papadoupoulous. He worked as a furnace worker in a tile factory in Ankara. The detective had traced him to an address in Los Angeles."

He handed me a piece of paper on which was handwritten a Santa Monica address.

"You've checked this out?"

He nodded. "Naci is there. The man is with her."

"Have you talked with her?"

He shook his head ruefully. "No. If she knew I knew she was there, she would only run away again."

"What else do you know about this Papadoupoulous?"

"Only that he comes from Izmir." He paused and added meaningfully, "And that he is Greek."

"You have something against Greeks?"

He smiled strangely. "If you knew anything about Turkish history, Mr. Asch, you would not ask that question. The Turks and Greeks have been murdering each other for hundreds of years. My own grandfather was slaughtered by Greek soldiers in the Turkish-Greek War of 1921."

"As long as you don't intend to perpetuate the hostilities."

His dark eyes twinkled with amusement. "I can assure you, I abhor violence, Mr. Asch. I intend no harm to anyone. I do not even intend to contact my daughter. I only want to make sure she is not getting herself into any trouble."

"Any particular kind of trouble you have in mind?"

He shook his head, then hesitated. "I do not wish to insult your country, but I believe it can be safely said that the moral values here are, shall we say, lax? Temptations abound. It would be all too easy for a young person—especially an impressionable young person—to be led astray in such an environment."

"And as long as your daughter is behaving herself and this Papadoupoulous character is kosher, you're willing to let her stay with him and not interfere?"

"Kosher?" His expression grew puzzled, then cleared. He grinned. "Ah, I see. Yes, as long as he's kosher, as you put it." The grin faded and he sighed heavily. "My daughter is very headstrong. She would only try harder to spite me if I tried to interfere. God knows what she would run away with next time. I do not wish my daughter's enmity, Mr. Asch. I love her. I am convinced she will come to her senses eventually."

That sounded reasonable enough to me. In a way, it was comforting to know that the problems of parenthood were the same the world over. I looked at the sunlight dappling the surface of the ocean. Out on the pier, a couple of kids dangled fishing lines in the water and waited for a bite. Farther out, red and orange sails tacked in the wind. The only thing marring the painting was the huge canvas awning directly below us, where a television field reporter was doing a standup in front of a soup line, trying to make degradation a newsworthy event. "What exactly do you want me to do, Mr. Saffarian?"

His dark eyes narrowed. "I want to know who Naci is seeing and what she is doing. And I want to know what this

Papadoupoulous is up to. I want them both followed twenty-four hours a day."

"How long do you want them tailed?"

"Until I tell you to stop," he replied flatly, then pulled out a pack of unfiltered Turkish cigarettes from the inside breast pocket of his jacket. He extracted one and asked, "Do you mind if I smoke?"

"No."

He held the cigarette European-style, pinched between his thumb and stubby forefinger. He inhaled deeply and blew the smoke out courteously, away from me.

"May I ask how you happened to pick me for this job, Mr. Saffarian?"

He sat back and smiled pleasantly. "We Muslims are great believers in destiny."

"*Kismet*," I said.

His expression seemed to light up. "Precisely. You are familiar with the Muslim concept?"

I shook my head. "No. The movie. Howard Keel, 1955. Great songs. 'Baubles, Bangles, and Beads'?"

He smiled uncertainly, as if not quite sure if I'd been making a joke. "I'm afraid I did not see it."

"You didn't miss much. It wasn't very good. Getting back to how you picked me for this job—"

His dark eyes turned shrewd. "To tell you the truth, Mr. Asch, I picked your name from the telephone directory. I wanted someone who was from this area. I thought it would be easier keeping an eye on my daughter that way. Now that I've met you, I am confident that my choice was correct.

I decided to test the depth of his belief in kismet. "My fee is three hundred dollars a day plus expenses. For the kind of surveillance you want, I'll have to pull in three other men besides myself. They will cost you twenty dollars an hour each."

One of his black eyebrows lifted in surprise. "Three?"

I nodded. "One man on Papadoupoulous, one man on your daughter. Breaking it down into two twelve-hour shifts, that comes out to four men. If I'm one of the men, that leaves three."

His expression grew momentarily troubled. He probably hadn't anticipated that a skid row detective would be that expensive. Before I lost him, I asked, "May I make a suggestion?"

"By all means."

"The chances are that if your daughter and her boyfriend are at home after midnight, they are going to be staying in. If we eliminate midnight to six, we can eliminate one man entirely and use one of the others primarily for relief. Also, I think I can get them for a little less, perhaps sixteen an hour. Not the men I would have liked, but competent ones."

He smiled gratefully. "That will be satisfactory. You see? I told you it was destiny. When can you begin?"

"As soon as I get a retainer."

"Certainly. How much would you require?"

"One thousand dollars."

Without batting an eye, he pulled out a fat wallet and counted out ten crisp one-hundred-dollar bills. I pocketed the money before he could change his mind, and scribbled out a receipt.

"Would you happen to have a picture of your daughter, Mr. Saffarian?"

He grimaced. "Unfortunately, no. I did have one in my suitcase, but as luck would have it, that piece of luggage was lost by the airline on the trip over."

"How about a description?"

"Certainly. She is twenty years old, five-foot-five, slim in build, with dark eyes and long black hair. She is very pretty."

"How about Papadoupoulous?"

"I have only seen him from a distance. He looks to be about thirty. Tall—over six feet—muscular, black hair, Mediterranean complexion."

They sounded like a good-looking couple. I didn't say so, considering how he felt about Greeks. "Are they the only two living at this address?"

"As far as I know." He mashed out his cigarette and said, "I would like a report every day."

"That shouldn't be a problem. Will a taped report be all right?"

"That will be satisfactory. I am staying at the Holiday Inn Bayshore in Santa Monica, room twelve-thirteen. Do you know it?"

I nodded. "It's very close to your daughter's address."

"That is why I chose it," he said flatly.

"I'll drop off a standard contract for your signature with the first report."

He nodded curtly. "You will start immediately, then?"

"As soon as I leave here."

"Excellent."

In a magnanimous gesture, I used a bit of his thousand to pick up the check, and we went outside, where an old woman in a filthy, moth-eaten sweater and red knit stocking cap stood on the curb muttering an obscene mantra at passersby.

"That woman is obviously insane," Saffarian said. "Surely you have a place you put such people?"

"Unfortunately, we have a president who thinks insanity is just a state of mind."

He nodded as if he understood that, said his car was parked down the street, and scurried off just as a younger version of the bum who had stopped me earlier sidled up. He walked alongside me as I headed away from the beach and said in a whining voice, "Hey, mister, how about some spare change?"

I rattled my pockets and kept going. "Sorry, no change."

"I'll take paper. You got a twenty?"

I had to laugh as I lengthened my stride. He kept up for a while, but after a block or so he got the hint. Like a pilot fish, he dropped off me and attached himself to a camera-laden couple strolling back toward the beach.

# TWO

I walked the two blocks to the office, made some calls, and sat back to wait. While I waited, I glanced around the room.

I'd lied to Saffarian about the place being redecorated. It was the same small, shabby affair it had been for the past four years and would be, in all likelihood, for as many as I chose to occupy it. I leased the place because of the combination of price and proximity to my apartment. It was strictly a mail drop and a repository for my files, not a place where I usually entertained clients, so I'd never seen the necessity of expending a lot of money I could put in an IRA into maintaining a lavish front. When Saffarian had called and said he was nearby and wanted to come over, I'd given him the redecorating ruse and arranged to meet him at the first place that came to mind, figuring there was no sense in his losing confidence in me before he hired me. There would be plenty of time for that later.

The ploy had almost backfired, however. I'd thought so fast, I'd forgotten about Tent City. If a political solution wasn't found soon, I would have to remember to arrange to meet all prospective clients outside the area. Otherwise, I might be forced to *really* redecorate.

I had my feet up on the desk and was looking the place over, trying to work up some economical ideas for sprucing up the place, when Dave Bick limped in.

Bick was a grizzled, forty-seven-year-old ex-LAPD undercover narc who had retired on a disability after being run over by a panicked speed dealer who was being popped for sales. Bick's right knee had been shattered to the point where he could not bend it past a thirty-degree angle, but he could sit all right, which was what he did most of the time nowadays, in front of his TV. In the eight years he had been retired from the force, he had become a full-time soap opera junkie. I threw an occasional surveillance job his way and, although for the most part the work was not as stimulating as *All My Children*, he was usually happy to have it. At least it got him out of the tiny one-bedroom apartment where he lived alone since his divorce.

He lowered himself into a chair and asked: "What do you got, Bunky?"

It wasn't a term of endearment; Bick called everybody Bunky. Once I asked him why, and he just shrugged and said he'd heard it on a record a long time ago and it had stuck with him. You remember the record, where the guy intones in a sad voice, "What's the matter with you, Bunky? You say you put a dime in the hot chocolate machine and you got a cup, right on your new shoes?" Bick said his luck ran like that. He also said it saved him from having to remember names. I'd often wondered if at an unconscious level, it had something to do with the fact that it rhymed with *junkie*, a word he had used a lot in his twenty-odd years on the force.

"Routine tail job," I said. "I'll lay it out in detail when the other guy gets here."

He scratched his head. "A three-man job?"

I nodded. "We have two people to shadow, two shifts."

"Who you using?"

"Greg MacPherson. You know him?"

"No." He grimaced and shifted his leg uncomfortably.

"Leg bothering you?"

"The fucking thing *always* bothers me," he said sourly. "The past couple of days it's been really bad, though."

"Can't the doctors do anything about it?"

He shook his head. "I've been to the best orthopod in the city. Too many pieces to work with. I've been thinking of trying to find that doctor from the *Six Million Dollar Man*, see if he can replace the whole fucking leg with a bionic one, like he did with Lee Majors." He paused thoughtfully. "What was his name?"

"Who?"

"The doctor from the *Six Million Dollar Man*."

"Somehow, it has slipped my mind."

"Rudy!" he said as it came to him.

It was encouraging at least to know that his taste in daytime programming was expanding.

He looked around the office, made a face, and said, "You should do something with this place, Bunky. It's a shitbox."

"You must be psychic. I was just thinking the same thing. Got any ideas?"

His gaze floated, analyzed. "A few plants. Plants are always nice. Fake ones, so you don't have to water 'em. They make stuff today you can't tell from the real ones."

"Bionic plants," I said. "When you get in touch with Rudy, maybe you can ask him if he can make me up a couple."

He ignored that and went on with his evaluation. "Some paint, definitely. New carpet. A new desk, some chairs—"

I stopped him before he got to the Mr. Coffee. "Why don't I just burn the place down and start from scratch?"

"That's a thought," he said seriously. He pointed at the oil painting of the Midnight Skulker from "B.C." hanging behind the desk. "For starters, you could get rid of that thing."

I tried to get the proper indignation in my voice. "That piece has great sentimental value. It was painted by a portrait painter I used to date. I had to sit three days for it."

He was still thinking that one over when Greg MacPherson entered.

MacPherson was a twenty-four-year-old ex–frozen-food salesman who had seen too many Rockford reruns and wanted to be a P.I. in the worst way, which was about the only way there was. He thought it was glamorous. I had used him on a couple of stakeouts and he had done okay and, miraculously, he still thought the job was glamorous.

I introduced him to Bick, then proceeded to lay out what I

knew about the job. I was to take the split-shift, working six
A.M. to four P.M., then coming back on at six P.M. and working
until midnight. Bick would work the twelve hours from six to
six, and MacPherson would take the shorter shift, from four to
twelve. If either Papadoupoulous or the Saffarian girl were
still out somewhere at midnight, it was understood that
surveillance would be maintained until they both went home.

They both agreed to the twelve-per-hour rate, then Bick
asked, "We got a picture of these people?"

"No."

He looked skeptical. "The guy comes all that way in search
of his wayward daughter and he doesn't bring a picture of her
along?"

I had to admit I'd had trouble with that one, too. I repeated
the lost luggage story, but Bick still looked skeptical, perhaps
because he hadn't had the opportunity to travel much on a
cop's salary. "How in the hell are we supposed to know what
they look like?"

I passed on Saffarian's descriptions and gave them the
address. "We'll drive over separately and each of us will get
ideas of the layout. There's a Denny's on Lincoln by the
freeway. We'll meet there after and compare notes."

Bick suddenly looked troubled. "How long do you think
this job is gonna last?"

"I don't know. Why?"

"I'll be missing *General Hospital*. Scorpio's ex-wife is being
held prisoner by a psycho with a man-eating Rottweiler. It's
touch and go."

"I'll throw a *Soap Opera Digest* into the deal," I told him.

He didn't look pleased, but he knew that was the best he
was going to do, so he let it go. Before we left, I gave them
both HTs so we could communicate with each other and
called Santa Monica P.D. dispatch to notify them of what we
were doing, in case they received a call from a nervous
neighbor about strange men parked on their street.

Bick drove a five-year-old green Datsun 4×4, Greg had a
new blue Ford Escort, and I followed in my 1984 black
Mustang GT convertible. I'd bought it three months ago after
my '67 Plymouth decided to play Polaris submarine and
launched a piston through its hood.

The War Wagon had been long overdue for the scrap heap,

but its demise had come at a bad time; I took it as a symbol of what was happening to me.

Every since my forty-first birthday in January, everything seemed to be falling apart. Another bad romance had left me dumped and down, a couple of bouts of impotence—while short-termed—had scared the hell out of me, new gray hairs appeared in my mirror every morning with disturbing regularity, and my back had been giving me fits to the point where I'd had to quit jogging. After receiving word that an old friend had dropped dead of a heart attack at the age of thirty-nine while playing basketball, I'd begun to ponder my own obituary. It certainly wouldn't make *Newsweek*, but I figured it would rate a couple of lines in the *Chronicle:* "He worked here for a while."

That could probably sum up my earthly existence. He worked here for a while. Only the work had lost its flavor, and for the past six months I'd felt like a man at an awards banquet trying to look happy dining on one of those prefabricated cardboard meals they serve at those affairs. My body was checking computer records, but my mind was in Pago Pago. I was in the middle of an existential crisis, searching for some meaning in my life, and although my accountant had tried to convince me a Mustang GT and all its glorious depreciation was it, the conviction had not yet sunk in.

Maybe this job would make me enough to get to Pago Pago, I thought as I drove up Pacific. I would sell the Mustang, fly to American Samoa, and *find myself.* It had to be easier there—I mean, it was a *small* goddamned island. Maybe I'd write a best-selling book—*Island Therapy* or *Self-Actualization on the Tropic of Capricorn.* That thought lifted my spirits as I turned onto Ocean Park.

I dropped back and took up the rear as we spread out to make our individual passes. The address was on Second, a narrow, one-way street that in many ways was typical of all of Santa Monica. Once a boom area, strict rent control laws had stifled development and discouraged landlords from making any improvements on their rental properties. Entire neighborhoods were frozen in time, only to be worn away by the forces of weather and decay. From one side of Second, newer, blocky apartment buildings faced old, tiny, matchbox houses, decayed remnants from the thirties. Number 3314 was one of these, a pink clapboard affair with a tar-paper roof and a weed-choked front yard. A green Acura Legend was parked in the driveway and I took down the license number as I passed.

The house was crowded between a prairie-style house, whose front yard was a graveyard of rusted cars, and a dirty Spanish-style bungalow. A sign outside the bungalow said NO CARES DAY SCHOOL. The driveway was a hazardous-looking congestion of swings, slides, and jungle gyms. No children were playing on them and there seemed to be no activity in the school. That was okay by me; all I needed was for some concerned parent to spot me sitting across the street and peg me for a child molester looking for prey.

Across the street, next to a three-story stucco apartment building, a gnarled, lifeless tree leaned against an abandoned church that stood like lost hope, its white spire peeling paint and its stained-glass windows smashed out. I circled back to Ocean Park and drove over to Denny's. Bick and MacPherson already had a booth. I slid in and ordered coffee.

"Not too many places to stay unnoticed for very long on that street," Bick said, echoing my own thoughts.

I nodded and opened the map book on the table. "I figure one man on Ashland, between Second and Third. The house is visible from there, but it's out of line of the windows, in case anybody happens to be looking out."

Bick tapped the map with a finger and said, "I'll take the northeast corner, here. The one-way runs south. Anybody leaves, I'll be behind him."

I nodded my approval.

"That Acura theirs?" Bick asked.

"I don't know. I'm going to check it out."

The waitress came back and we all ordered lunch. Bick and I ordered cheeseburgers and fries, and MacPherson ordered a club. When she had departed for the stainless-steel recesses of the kitchen, Bick asked, "How long you have the Mustang?"

"Couple of months."

"Nice little car," he remarked casually. "Business must be good."

I didn't want him thinking it had been *too* good; he would just pressure me for the four dollars an hour of his I was pocketing. "Actually, I won it."

That raised his eyebrows. "No shit."

"It was first prize in a 'Draw Your Favorite Nazi' contest."

MacPherson chuckled, but Bick's expression remained dead-pan. "Who'd you draw?"

"Goebbels."

His head bobbed approvingly, as if he thought that was a good choice, then said in a matter-of-fact tone, "Hitler's still alive, you know."

"Really?"

He nodded. "I saw him three weeks ago in Hussong's in Ensenada."

I scrutinized his face trying to determine if he was putting me on, but he gave away nothing. With Bick, you never could tell. His views of history tended to be conspiratorial, views that had only been exaggerated by two years of soap opera saturation. "What was he doing there?"

He looked at me as if I were the dumbest man on earth. "Drinking," he said. "What the hell does *anybody* do in a bar?"

# THREE

The Acura was still in the driveway when I settled into a space across from the abandoned church. The neighborhood was quiet. I sipped coffee from my to-go cup and waited. After that, I waited some more. Nothing happened very slowly.

Two teen-age girls in short-shorts wandered up the street, chewing gum and chattering noisily. A Mexican woman pushed a baby stroller in the sunshine. Some cars drove by. The most exciting thing that happened was when an old man shuffled up the block, put a finger against one side of his nose, and blew out a big one on the sidewalk next to the car.

Anyone who thinks detective work is exciting should sit on a stakeout for half an hour. If he still thinks it's exciting, he should try it for six hours. After that, if he still thinks it was exciting, he should see a good shrink. I was starting to worry about MacPherson.

At 2:14 the HT on the front seat sputtered and Bick's voice said, "Movement in the house. Someone is coming out."

I sat up and looked through my binoculars. A tall, lean man who matched Papadoupoulous's general description came through the front door and down the steps. He was dressed in dirty jeans and a blue workshirt, with the sleeves rolled up to the elbows. He got into the car alone and backed out of the driveway. "That's our man," I told Bick.

"I'm on him," he said.

I slouched down in the seat as the Acura drove by, then got up to see the back of Bick's car disappear around the corner. After that, it was a thrill a minute. A few more cars drove by. Across the street from the house a couple of kids slammed the front door of a small, ramshackle dwelling, got on their bikes, and peddled off gleefully down the street. Two mockingbirds had a noisy territorial dispute going over the dead tree outside the church. Neither of them probably would have wanted it if it had been in any other place, but this was the beach.

At 3:10 a young, dark-haired girl emerged from the house. I watched through the binoculars as she came down the front walk and turned to walk toward Ocean Park. She might have been Turkish but she dressed American, in a white sleeveless blouse, tight jeans, and white running shoes. I followed her on foot down Ocean Park, keeping a good two blocks between us. She was small and trim, but her stride was deceptively long, and I had to push myself to keep up with her.

She was pretty, all right, with large dark eyes, a wide mouth, and fine bone structure. Her body was small but had a durable look to it, with pronounced muscular definition in her brown arms.

At Main, a street lined with trendy boutiques and restaurants, she turned left. She took her time window-shopping, stopping in one or two of the stores to try things on. She didn't buy anything. She went into a frozen yogurt store and killed twenty minutes eating a cup of some flavor at a table by the window. I hung out across the street, trying to look inconspicuous waiting for her to finish. At 4:17 she came out, looked around without seeming to notice me, and strolled at a slower pace down to the sea.

As I followed her across the asphalt parking lot that used to be Pacific Ocean Park, I was hit by a sudden wave of nostalgia. I used to come down here a lot before they tore down the old fun park, to ride the rickety dinosaur of a roller coaster and throw baseballs at metal milk bottles. As I crossed what was once the midway I could almost smell the aroma of the corndogs that used to fill the air like a thick, invisible mist.

I watched from a distance as the girl walked to the end of the cement stub of a pier that pointed out at the ocean like an amputated finger. She stopped there, put her hands in her pockets, and stared out at the sea, which lay like a silvery sheet in the afternoon sun. As I watched her, for some reason, I thought of Oscar the Movie Penguin.

Many years ago, Oscar had occupied a cement igloo at the bottom of the old pier, which had been torn down even before POP, and I used to come down to talk to him on those lucky days my father would allow me to accompany him deep-sea fishing. He would stand outside his house, erect and dignified in his formal black and white dinner suit, and stare with indifferent eyes at foolish gawkers like me who would try to get him to perform. No matter how vociferous the entreaties, however, Oscar would merely stare at the crowd with haughty indifference. Oscar was a star; he only performed for the cameras.

I saw Oscar the other night at three A.M. in an old Ritz Brothers movie, roller-skating through a haunted mansion, and I had wondered then, as I did now, where he was. In all likelihood he was only alive in my mind, but that was better than nowhere, I supposed.

The girl stood looking out at the ocean for another ten minutes, then turned slowly and walked back up to Ocean Park. She never once looked back to see if she was being followed. Either she suspected nothing, or she knew I was there and didn't want me to know she knew.

The Acura was still not back when she went inside at 4:50 but MacPherson was. I contacted him on the HT and told him I would see him at 6:00 and to tell Bick when he got back to stay there until I returned.

It wasn't worth going home, so I spent the hour respite back in Denny's consuming a patty melt and four cups of coffee over a copy of the *Times*.

A few minutes after six o'clock I pulled into a space half a block behind Bick's Datsun and hoofed it up the street. Bick greeted me with a yawn as I opened the door of the truck and slid in. "When did you get back?"

He shrugged. "A little after five."

"Where did he go?"

He flipped open his spiral notebook and read, "The subject proceeded directly to Hermosa Beach, One-four-five East Fifth street. It's an outfit called Deep Six Diving. He waited outside the building for twenty minutes, at which time, a Chevy van, red, license 2GHN315, pulled up and parked. The occupant of the van, a Caucasian male, six-foot-one, two hundred pounds, shaggy blond hair, greeted the subject and unlocked the door of Deep Six Diving, and the two went inside. They remained inside until three thirty-six, at which time they both emerged. The subject was carrying an envelope."

"What kind of an envelope?"

"A plain white business-sized envelope." Bick continued in his typical stilted cop-ese. "The driver of the van locked the place up and the two men got back into their cars. They proceeded to King Harbor, to the Port Royal Marina. They parked and went aboard the boat moored in slip B-forty-three. At four-twelve Papadoupoulous emerged alone and returned to his car. He drove back here without stopping, arriving at five-sixteen."

He ripped out the page and handed it to me. I asked, "Any idea what was in the envelope?"

"No, but it was fat."

"Money?"

He shrugged.

I chewed on that one for a moment. "Saffarian said Papadoupoulous is a furnace worker, not a scuba diver."

"Maybe he's taking up a new trade." He hesitated meaningfully. "I'll tell you one thing—there's something wrong with that blond guy."

"What do you mean?"

"There's something off about him. I can feel it."

Like most good cops, Bick had an uncanny sense for spotting who was into illegal activities and who was not. It was an intuitive knack with which he had probably been born but which he had refined through years of working the street, where accurate snap judgments were often the key to survival. "Can you check him out?"

"I'll make a call tonight. How about the girl?"

"She did a little window-shopping, took a walk down to the ocean, then came back."

He nodded and said, "Guess I'll go home and see if the timer on my VCR worked."

"Maybe the Rottweiler ate Scorpio's ex-wife."

"I hope so," he said seriously. "I can't stand that bitch. A British chief of police in America. And a *woman* yet." He intoned it as if it were his worst nightmare.

I told him I would see him in the morning, and then went back to my car. When he left, I pulled into his space and settled back into the routine of waiting. During the next hour a few cars pulled in and out of driveways, but nothing much else happened.

I tuned in the Laker game on the transistor radio I'd brought. It was halfway through the second quarter and they were trailing Houston by fourteen. Jabbar was oh-for-six. That was what happened when you turned forty. I turned it off. The dull ache was starting up again at the base of my spine and I washed down three generic acetomenophin with some coffee from the Thermos.

At 8:20 a black-and-white cruised by slowly. I waved at the two young cops in the car, but they didn't wave back. I didn't mind that as long as they didn't stop, which they didn't. I turned the game back on. Jabbar had gone on a rampage in the last quarter, hitting six of seven skyhooks, and with a minute and a half left to go, the Lakers were up by eleven. My spirits buoyed. Maybe it wasn't too late for me after all.

At 9:10 Greg contacted me on the HT and said he had to relieve his bladder and would be out of position for fifteen or so. Inevitably, that would be the time both subjects would decide to move, I thought. It was pretty bad when going to the bathroom became the most suspenseful part of one's day.

My fears, this time at least, turned out to be unfounded. After Greg got back I took my turn and drove down to the gas station on the corner of Pico.

Nobody had moved from the house while I was gone. Nobody moved from the house during the rest of the night. A little before midnight, I pulled out and stopped by Greg's car and asked him to spot me in the morning for a couple of hours, between ten and noon. He said no problem, and I told him good night and drove the half-dozen blocks to the Holiday Inn.

The open, high-ceilinged lobby was deserted and my heels

clacked loudly on the pink tile floor as I walked to the front desk. I dropped off the cassette and the contract for Saffarian and drove home.

It took me about ten minutes to get to sleep. I spent the night roller-skating around POP, chasing Oscar. I never caught him.

# FOUR

I woke up tired and in pain. My back hurt. So did my feet. Probably from my nocturnal recreation. I hadn't skated in years.

After a hot shower and a shave, I headed down empty streets toward Santa Monica. It was still dark and the Acura was in the driveway as I drove by the house at 6:06. I took my position on Ashland and five minutes later, Bick knocked on my window. I unlocked the passenger door and he got in. He was holding a bag that said MOON DONUTS. "Good morning, Bunky," he said cheerfully. "Sleep well?"

"No, as a matter of fact. I chased fucking penguins all night long."

"Huh?"

"Never mind." I took a sip from the twenty-ounce 7-Eleven cup of coffee I'd procured on the way over.

He opened the bag and pulled out a glazed and his own, smaller, cup of coffee. "Want one? I bought extra."

I took the doughnut. It looked like a normal earth doughnut. I bit into it. Certain things seemed to be the same no matter where you went in the universe.

22

"What about the van?" I asked.

"I couldn't get hold of anybody last night."

"That's okay. I can check it out today." I facetiously asked how *General Hospital* had come out, a move I immediately regretted as he mistook my inquiry for genuine interest and began to give me a blow-by-blow description of the perils of Scorpio's ex-wife. She had apparently escaped the slavering jaws of the Rottweiler, only to be severely beaten by the dog's demented owner. Bick sounded positively happy as he re-counted the violence done to the poor woman; I think he saw something of his own ex in her.

Soon it got light, and up and down the street men and women got into their cars and went to work. Shortly before eight, Bick walked back to his own car. Other than a few mothers dropping their toddlers off at the No Cares Day School, nothing eventful happened until Greg showed up at ten. I gave him my space and drove downtown to the offices of Greenberg Bail Bonds.

Hymie Fein, owner of Greenberg Bail Bonds, had been an out-of-work actor in 1956 when he had gone to work for Martin Greenberg to supplement his meager bit-part income, and in the nine years he had worked for the old man, Greenberg—who had no children of his own—had come to look upon Hymie with paternal eyes. Still, when the old man died and left Hymie the business, Hymie had been totally surprised. He saw now that he shouldn't have been. It was all part of the curse.

In deference to his benefactor Hymie didn't change the name of the company, or even its slogan—"Our Bond Is Our Word"—even though he hated it. At the time he inherited the business, Greenberg had been writing up six million dollars' worth of bonds a year, of which ten percent was gross profit. Twenty-three years later, that figure was down to five million, due to the fact that the county was letting more defendants out on their own recognizance and because of the personal surety bonds issued by the federal courts, which allowed defendants to pay bail directly to the courts without going through a bondsman. The whole bail bond business was going right down the toilet, Hymie was wont to remind anyone who would listen, but that was all right with Hymie. It was the "shittiest business in the world" and he wouldn't miss it a bit when it was gone. The only thing that bothered him was thinking about what dismal practical joke God had in store for him when the inevitable happened.

I did an odd job for Hymie every once in a while, skip-tracing bail jumpers and such. As a token of his appreciation Hymie, for his cost, permitted me access to his computer. The computer was hooked into the National Information Resource Center, a national computer information pool, and although the stuff in it was generally not as accurate as good old-fashioned legwork, it could save a lot of steps at times. I figured this could be one of those times.

Hymie was behind his desk, on the phone, when I walked into the office. He was dressed conservatively as usual, in a pink sports jacket, red shirt, white tie, and maroon slacks with a white belt. I couldn't see his shoes, but no matter what color they were I wouldn't be surprised. He stopped stroking his white walrus-mustache long enough to wave me into a chair with a diamonded pinkie, then said petulantly into the phone, "What are you, a man or a woman? Oh. I couldn't tell there for a minute. So what are you trying to tell me here? Okay, don't get excited. Come into the office in an hour and I'll take you over and you can turn yourself in. Right."

He hung up and shook his white head. "A transvestite hooker. First it's Georgette, then it's George. See what I have to deal with here? Nobody's fucking normal anymore." He shook his head again and slapped the sizable paunch that pushed persistently against his belt. "Whores and drunks, they're the worst. They'll stiff you every time. A whore's got something between her legs she can sell wherever she goes, know what I mean?"

I said I knew what he meant.

"The shittiest business in the world." His sad, heavily bagged blue eyes perked up. "Not for much longer, though. Another year, it'll just be a bad memory. You want in Jake? I'll make you rich."

For lack of something better to do, I smiled. Hymie's hatred of the bail bond business and his view of its inevitable future collapse inspired him to come up with a never-ending litany of get-rich-quick schemes, for which he was constantly searching out partners. Desperation, in Hymie's case, was not the mother of invention, however; in the past he had had considerable difficulty locating partners whose enthusiasm for his ideas matched his own. The last one had been a pineapple plantation in Idaho. He had checked it out and found that there was no competition up there. He figured he could make a killing. "What is it this time, Hymie?"

He leaned forward and lowered his voice conspiratorially. "Two little words. Juke balls."

"You're sure it's not one word?" I asked.

He looked troubled. "No. I'm not." The momentary cloud passed from his features and he said, "Doesn't matter. However many words, it spells M-O-N-E-Y."

I sighed and asked the mandatory question. "All right. What are juke balls?"

"You know how prisoners at the county jail are fed?" he asked excitedly.

"Through the bars."

"Funny," he said, grimacing. "The meals are served on little foil plates with the salad, main course, and dessert divided up, like they are in TV dinners, know what I mean?"

I said I knew what he meant.

"When a prisoner causes problems and is thrown into solitary, they don't serve him the same meals the other prisoners get."

"No?"

"They do and they don't," he said cryptically. He paused, his eyes gleaming with significance. "What the cooks do is take the dinners and throw them into a meat grinder and grind all the stuff up together. What comes out is a round ball, about the size of a softball."

"Juke balls."

He slammed his fist down on the desk and jabbed a finger at me as if I'd just responded correctly to the Daily Double on *Jeopardy.* "Right! And in that one juke ball a prisoner is getting a balanced meal, complete with all the vitamins and minerals he needs." He paused to let me ponder that, then painted a picture in the air with his palms. "Now, as you well know, there are a lot of busy people in the world who can't take time to sit down in a restaurant for a meal, so they just grab some greasy junk food and go. Why should they have to do that, when they could put a few quarters in a machine and get a completely balanced, nutritious meal? That could even be the

slogan on the commercials." His voice turned religious as he
recited, "'Juke Balls—For People on the Go.' What do you
think?"

"What do they taste like?"

"I don't know. I haven't had one yet. I'm arranging with a
friend of mine over at the jail to get one. You want in?"

I wanted in that computer. "When the sample comes in, let
me know. In the meantime, I need to run a couple of things
through your computer."

He tossed up his hands and grinned broadly. "Anything for
my future partner. Rose!"

Rose Spivak, Hymie's trusted secretary for the past ten
years, answered the summons.

"Run a few things for Jake, will you, Rose?"

She led the way into the back room and fed the information
I gave her into the computer. I had her run the plate numbers
of the van and the Acura for ownership, then checked county
property records for the address on Second. After that, I had
her do a credit check and preliminary asset check on Papadoupoulous, as well as run him for civil suits and county,
state, and federal priors. Since he was not a citizen, I doubted
there would be anything on him, but it was worth a shot. I
had her do a credit check on Deep Six Diving, but since it was
a DBA, it didn't come up in the data bank. I had her run it
through the Fictitious Business Filings Index. She told me
that would take forty-eight hours; all the rest of the information should be in tomorrow.

When I came out, Hymie was on the phone again. His face
was red and he was obviously having trouble trying to keep
the anger out of his voice. "It's all the same to me. I ain't got
time to hold your fucking hand. If your ass isn't in court
tomorrow morning at nine, your gray-haired mama is out on
the street. *She put up her house, you understand?*"

He slammed down the receiver and looked up at me.
"Goddamn hype. He's panicked they'll put him away if he
shows up in court and he won't get his fix." He shook his
head. "The shittiest business in the world. You get what you
need?"

"Tomorrow."

He nodded. "I should have one by then."

"One what?"

"A juke ball."

"I'm salivating already."

He nodded empathetically. "I have a feeling about this one, Jake. It's the ship that's going to carry me out of this." He shook his head thoughtfully. "Hookers, drunks, and hypes. They're the worst."

The phone rang again and as he picked it up, I had the feeling that the list of the "worst" would soon be longer.

# FIVE

---

The Acura and Bick were both gone when I drove by the house shortly after noon. I pulled up alongside MacPherson and asked, "Who left?"

"The guy. A few minutes ago. The girl is still inside."

He said he would see me at four and took off, and I backed into his vacated space. I dug into the bag I'd picked up at Sam's Deli downtown, pulled out a rare roast beef on rye and a dill pickle, and munched while I watched.

At 12:39 a late-model red Chevy van pulled into the driveway of the house. The plates matched the numbers of the vehicle Bick had seen at Deep Six Diving, and so did the driver's description. He stepped out of the car, and I picked up the binoculars for a better look.

The man was blond and heartthrob-handsome, with a wide chiseled jaw and a prominent brow. He was muscularly built, wide through the shoulders and narrow in the hips, and looked as if he worked a lot outdoors. Either that, or he had a lot of free time to spend at tanning salons. He was dressed in a purple short-sleeved form-fitting shirt, white chinos, and white tennies, no socks. I tried to determine just what it was about him that Bick found so ominous, but my radar must not have been as finely tuned as his. To me, he looked like just another bronzed beach bum with a Ph. D. in volleyball.

He started up the front walk and was met by Naci Saffarian, who stepped out onto the porch, smiling widely. They embraced and kissed, a long kiss that looked like it had some tongue in it. They broke and she glanced around sheepishly, then took his hand and led him inside. It appeared that Mr. Saffarian's "Wild Thing" might be just that. I jotted down the time and went back to my sandwich.

At 2:43 the blond man came out of the house, got back in the van, and drove away. I considered following him but decided against it. I could find out about him later; the girl was my target. Who knew what other visitors she might be entertaining today?

It turned out to be none. At 4:19 the Acura pulled into the driveway and Papadoupoulous got out. I watched him go into the house, then contacted Bick on the HT. He strolled over and got into the car.

"You're looking at a man who's got culture," he said. "We spent the day at the L.A. County Museum of Art."

"Doing what?"

"Looking at statues and old pots. What else do you do at museums?"

"That's all? He didn't meet anybody?"

He shook his head. "He drove there, spent two and a half hours walking around, stopped for a sandwich at a coffee shop, then drove back here."

"You able to get anything on the owner of the van?"

"I'll be able to get in touch with somebody tonight for sure," he said, and went back to his car.

MacPherson showed up at four on the dot and I drove back to the apartment. I fixed my evening meal—a tuna fish sandwich on whole wheat—while listening to Oprah Winfrey and her female audience go through their daily whining litany of what was wrong with men. By the time I'd bagged the sandwich and an apple and made a Thermos full of coffee, the stunning realization had set in just what a selfish, insensitive lout I really was. Violent, too. The paring knife in my hand trembled as I fantasized diving through the TV screen and

ridding Oprah of a pound or two of flesh her liquid protein
diet hadn't taken.

I rolled up behind Bick a little before six and he waved and
took off. As dusk fell like a blanket of sooty ash across the
windows of the car, lights winked on behind windows up and
down the street. At 7:20 I started on my tuna sandwich, the
thrill for the hour.

At 8:20 Naci and Papadoupoulous came out of the house.
They were arguing heatedly and loudly, but I was too far
away to hear what they were saying. Even if I could have, I
would have needed an interpreter to translate. I had to wonder
if it could have been about the afternoon visitor.

They got into the car and slammed the doors. Papadoupoulous gunned the motor and laid a patch of rubber on the
way out of the driveway. He sped off down the street ahead of
me and I picked up the HT. "Coming your way, Greg."

"Got 'em."

"Leapfrog," I said. "I'll go first."

"Right."

I waited until the Acura was around the corner and past
Macpherson before I turned on my lights. In my rear-view
mirror, I saw Greg's headlights making a U-turn and falling in
behind me.

The Acura made a left on Lincoln, then a right on Olympic,
heading east. I tailed loosely. They didn't seem to have any
idea they were being followed, and I didn't want to give them
one. After a mile or so, I raised MacPherson on the HT and
dropped back to let him take over a while.

We drove past the lighted towers of Century City, skirted
the poorer side of Beverly Hills, headed toward downtown.
At Robertson, I took the lead back from MacPherson. Two
blocks later, he notified me that he'd caught a red light.

At La Cienega, the Acura signaled right and turned just as
the intersection light was changing to yellow. I speeded up
and got into the right lane, but a station wagon was stopped
ahead of me at the corner. The driver had on his right blinker,
but in spite of the fact that the coast was clear and that he
could legally make a right turn on a red, he refused to budge.
To give him a little incentive, I leaned on my horn until he
moved. The driver must have been eighty if he was a day. As

I passed, I waved to show there were no hard feelings. He glared and flipped me off.

Four or five blocks ahead of me, the street was clear. The Acura was nowhere in sight. I gunned the Mustang, scoping out the side streets as I passed, but couldn't spot it. I hit the steering wheel with my palm, hard. Two on one and we still lost them. I was about to turn around and head back when I glanced over at the parking lot of a motel across the street and saw Naci and Papadoupoulous getting out of the Acura.

I braked hard, pulled over to the curb, and backed up. I watched through the binoculars as Papadoupoulous unlocked the trunk and he and Naci each lifted out what looked like cardboard shoe boxes. Naci closed the trunk and the two of them went across the lot to one of the doors and knocked. After a moment the door was opened, I could not see by whom, and they went inside.

Macpherson pulled up behind me and we both got out of our cars. I told him to stay on the car and follow them if they came out, that I was going across the street to do some recon.

The motel was 1950s Characterless—twin, two-story stucco buildings that faced each other across the parking lot. The name—Starlite Motor Lodge—was surrounded by multicolored neon stars that blinked on and off. At least half the stars were burned out. Below that, buzzing pink neon read: V CA CY.

Guarding the driveway entrance was a tiny, doorless office fronted by slotted, bullet-proof glass through which money and keys could be exchanged. There was nobody inside. A button beside the glass told prospective clients to ring for service. I went by without ringing.

There were twenty or so cars in the lot, most of them older models. I fished my car keys out of my pocket and fumbled with them as I walked past the room into which Naci and her boyfriend had gone. The number on the door was 16. Curtains were pulled tightly across the window. I jogged back across the street and waited in the car.

Twenty minutes later, Naci and Papadoupoulous came out. Naci was carrying one of the shoe boxes under her arm, but Papadoupoulous was empty-handed. They got into the Acura and started it up. They backed out of the space and made a right out of the driveway, heading back toward Olympic.

MacPherson, who had positioned himself across the street, took off after them.

I waited, keeping my binoculars trained on the door of 16, and three minutes later the door opened and a dark-haired woman emerged, carrying the other shoe box. She appeared to be young and slim, dressed in a dark, conservatively cut suit. In the dimming light I couldn't make out much else.

The woman walked to the glass cage and deposited the room key, then walked briskly over to a new silver Dodge 600 ES convertible. She pulled out onto La Cienega, heading north, and I had to wait for a break in traffic to hang a U. I broke some speeding laws catching up with her, but I finally did, at San Vicente. She hit the red there and I nosed in behind her. It was closer than I would have liked, but I wanted to get her license number in case I lost her in traffic. The light changed and I dropped back a bit as we took off.

She drove in no particular hurry up to Sunset and hung a right onto the Strip. I followed her through Hollywood, and whatever glamour that name conjured up soon wore off as the buildings became smaller and grimier and the signs changed from English to Spanish. At Glendale she turned left and headed into Silver Lake.

Silver Lake, named after the reservoir in the hills directly above it, was a compact neighborhood of twisted streets that had been chic in the thirties and forties but whose exclusive reputation had suffered since its encirclement by the mass Chicano immigrations of the sixties and seventies. The area had not lost all of its charm, however, and architecturally it was still one of the most interesting in L.A., showcasing houses by Neutra, Schindler, Lautner, and other past giants in the field.

She turned onto a small side street that wound tortuously up a steep hill crowded with houses stacked one behind the other, like a giant wave of stucco. Halfway up the hill she signaled and pulled into the driveway of a modest, flat-roofed split-level that was almost hidden behind sprays of magenta bougainvillaea and two large century plants. I slowed down while she got out of the car and hung right onto a narrow street half a block up. By the time I turned around and started back down, she was at the front door.

She held the shoe box under her arm while she fiddled with

her keys, opened the door, and went inside. The lights went on behind the shuttered windows. I took down the address and waited around across the street for a few more minutes, then took the freeway back to Santa Monica. It was 10:55 when I found a space a block away from the house.

MacPherson nearly hit the car's headliner when I yanked open his door. "Jesus Christ! You scared the piss out of me."

"Lucky you have vinyl seats. What's been happening?"

"Nothing," he said, running a hand through his long, sandy-colored hair. "They came straight back here and that's it. What was that bit at the motel all about?"

"I don't know." I told him about the woman and the shoe box.

"Kinda weird, don't you think?" He sounded hopeful.

"I don't know if it is or not," I said truthfully. "You might as well knock off. I don't think they're going anywhere else tonight."

"You're the boss."

Saffarian had left the signed contract for me at the Holiday Inn desk. I exchanged it for the new tape and drove home.

# SIX

The alarm rudely rousted me out of bed at five. I dragged myself into the bathroom for my morning ablutions and stared blankly at the puffy face in the mirror. My shortened sleep schedule was starting to take its toll. I'd read about people who got along just fine on one or two hours of sleep. I heard the chief engineer at Chernobyl was one. The secret was not having anything taxing to do during the day, I decided. I had the bases covered on that score.

I made a Thermos of extra-strong coffee and stopped at an AM/PM on the way into Santa Monica for a cinnamon roll. The headline on the tabloid by the checkout counter proclaimed: EXPERT SAYS MANY CONTROLLED BY THE DEAD: HOW TO TELL IF YOU'RE POSSESSED. I was tempted to buy it, just to see if my symptoms matched up, but decided on a copy of the Santa Monica *Messenger* instead.

Bick was already on the job when I took my spot by the church. As he got into the car, I asked, "Find out anything?"

He nodded. "The van is owned by Deep Six Diving, same address."

I offered Bick some of my coffee and we sipped it silently.

34

I didn't make the same mistake as yesterday and ask him about *General Hospital*. It was getting light. Bick took the sports page from the paper and I looked over the front page. Tent City was the headline story. Tensions in the community over the settlement were building and several citizens' groups had formed to vocalize concern about the continued presence of the homeless in Venice. Merchants complained that business had gone to hell; residents complained that gardening tools and anything else left unattended had been disappearing from yards with annoying regularity. Some had come home to find Tent City dwellers sleeping it off on their doorsteps, even in their living rooms, and more than some had gone outside in the morning to fetch their morning papers only to step in excremental gifts dropped off anonymously during the night by their thoughtful new neighbors.

The political response to the complaints was, for the most part, underwhelming. Nobody on the County Board of Supervisors or the City Council were about to go on the record as being anti-poor, but nobody was going to cut loose any funds for low-cost housing, either. So the irate citizenry had begun to take things into their own hands.

Over the past week, in three different incidents, half a dozen Tent City residents had been hospitalized with serious injuries after being beaten by gangs of unidentified marauding youths. And the violence was not all one-sided. Several tourists reported being punched out by panhandlers after turning down appeals for funding. Last night one homeless woman, angry at being repeatedly run out of a beachfront restaurant, drove a stolen car through the establishment's front doors. The situation was growing hot, and something was going to have to be done before it boiled over.

Bick and I traded sections, and I was reading the player stats from the Lakers' latest win when Bick sneered, "This is bullshit."

"What?"

"This says it's estimated that there are fifty thousand homeless in L.A."

"So?"

"That's bullshit. The L.A.P.D. knows exactly how many homeless there are in L.A."

"How many?"

"Nineteen."

I looked at him closely. There was no hint of sarcasm in his voice, no trace of a smile. "You're kidding."

He shook his head vehemently. "They know 'em all by name, for chrissakes."

"Who are all those people on the beach, then?"

"Agitators. Outsiders. Fucking snowbirds. Where would you rather be, on Venice Beach, lulled to sleep by the sound of the surf, or in Oshkosh, Wisconsin, watching your ass turn blue?"

"I've always been in favor of the optional snow plan, no doubt about it," I admitted.

"Fucking-A. It's all a big scam. This guy who's leading this whole thing, stirring everybody up—what's his name, Cummings?—he's the biggest scam artist of them all."

"Your radar working again?"

"You wait and see," he said confidently. "He's full of shit, I'm telling you. He's in it for the bread."

"What bread?"

"This guy knows that media exposure means money. He's the Jimmy Swaggart of the homeless. He's pulled all these people together to use them. Parade 'em on TV and show the people how you're saving their poor raggedy-assed souls. It's the same old evangelism gaff. Make 'em feel guilty enough and they'll pay. That's okay by me. I don't give a goddamn what anybody does, as long as it's with his own money. But the scary thing is that these dumb fucks in Washington are starting to fall for it, too. When they start taking my disability checks to line this con man's pockets and keep a bunch of winos in muscatel, that's when I draw the line."

I looked into his eyes and knew that he was totally sincere. "You're serious about there being only nineteen homeless people in L.A.?"

"Absolutely."

All I could do was shake my head, but he seemed unfazed by my obvious skepticism. After expounding on his social theories for twenty minutes or so, he went back to his car and I went back to the paper. Half an hour later, I was wishing I'd brought a book. *War and Peace.*

At 1:10 Papadoupoulous came out of the house, got into the Acura, and drove off. Bick pulled out and I continued to wait expectantly for nothing to happen. I wasn't disappointed. Today, she didn't even go for a walk. By 2:30 I found myself searching the trees for a good bird fight, but as luck would have it a peace treaty had been signed in Birdland and all the feathered residents of the street were abiding by the territorial boundaries laid out forthwith. Tomorrow I'd have to bring some bird seed and see if I could shake up the political situation. One could learn a lot about human behavior by watching birds, I decided. One thing was that you could go a little crazy if you watched too long.

At four, I was saved by the cavalry in the form of MacPherson. I drove to my apartment, popped the tab on a Bud Lite, and called my answering service. There were several messages, all from Saffarian and all saying the same thing: that it was important that I get in touch with him as soon as possible. I tried his room, but he didn't answer, so I left a message with the front desk that I'd called, just so he wouldn't feel ignored. I called Rose. The stuff had come in and I told her to read it to me.

As expected, Dimitrios Papadoupoulous had no credit, listed assets, lawsuits pending, or prior arrests, at least in L.A. County. The house he and Naci were living in was owned by one Morris Drexel, 17411 Stamford Court, L.A. The Acura was a rental registered to Budget Rent-A-Car, and as Bick had already found out, the van was registered to Deep Six. I took it all down and asked her to add a DMV check on the Dodge ES to my bill. She didn't sound happy about it, but she told me to check with her tomorrow, same time, same station.

Drexel's number was listed in the phone book. He wasn't home. I finished my beer and was on my way to the refrigerator for another when the phone rang. I recognized the accented voice immediately. "I need to see you as soon as possible," Saffarian said.

Something in his tone made me ask, "Is something the matter?"

"No. I would just like to talk to you. Can you come to the hotel?"

"Twenty minutes?"

"That will be fine. You know my room number."

The Holiday Inn sat on its hilltop rise on Pico like an Aztec pyramid, stained blood-red by the setting sun. I let the valet

park my Mustang and took the elevator up to the twelfth floor.
Saffarian opened the door when I knocked and stood back to
let me enter. He was dressed casually, in a white terry-cloth
shirt, the buttons of which were strained at the waist, baggy
brown slacks, and brown leather slippers, no socks. He had
just showered and he had not yet re-eyebrow-penciled his
scalp, so his wet hair looked even sparser than it had yesterday
morning.

The twin-bedded room was good-sized. He showed me to a
table in front of a sliding glass door that led out onto a small
patio. A small patch of the blue Pacific was visible just over
the tops of the adjacent buildings. Saffarian sat opposite me at
the table and said, "I would like to hear about this meeting at
the motel last night."

"I put it all in the tape."

He pondered that. "You haven't learned the identity of the
woman?"

"Not yet. I should by tomorrow."

"Did you get a good look at her?"

"Not really." I described her as best I could, then asked,
"You think you might know her?"

"No," he replied with finality. "You have no idea what was
in the box they left with her?"

"As far as I know, it could have been filled with Styrofoam
peanuts."

His    brow    knitted    incomprehendingly.    "Styrofoam
peanuts?"

"Never mind."

He rubbed his chin. "What about this blond man in the
van?"

"The van is registered to Deep Six Diving. I don't know
who the blond man is yet, but I should soon."

He listened intently, then said, "I wish you to discontinue
your surveillance."

That took me by surprise. "Pardon me?"

He cleared his throat. "I received a call last night from my
office in Istanbul. An urgent business matter there requires
my immediate attention. I will be returning to Turkey in the
morning."

"Will you be coming back soon?"

He folded his fat hands across his stomach. "I don't know."

"Would you like me to keep tabs on your daughter while you're away?"

He shook his head. "That will not be necessary. I am convinced Naci is all right." I wondered what I'd said to make him believe that. He cleared his throat and smiled inappropriately. "If Naci ever found out I was having her followed, however, she would never come home. I do not wish to take that risk. I am just going to have to trust her good judgment. I have to believe that she will realize the error of her ways and return home of her own accord."

He had not trusted it up until now and I found his abrupt change of mind bewildering. He seemed to sense my growing suspicion and added, "There is the matter of your bill—"

There wasn't much I could do to keep the golden goose penned up. I wasn't, however, about to let him take his eggs with him. I made some calculations on a piece of hotel stationery, then looked up. "My men clocked a total of forty-six hours between them. At sixteen dollars an hour, that comes out to seven hundred and thirty-six dollars. Miscellaneous expenses, gas and all that, one hundred and fifty dollars. I can get you itemized receipts, but that will be tomorrow—"

He waved a hand in the air impatiently. "I trust you."

"You have a hundred coming back from your retainer from my fee, which makes a balance owed of seven hundred and eighty-six dollars."

He raised an eyebrow. "A hundred dollars? You did not work three full days. The first day, I hired you at noon. And it is only six o'clock now—"

The rug merchant in him was coming out now. I smiled at him. "I work by the day, Mr. Saffarian. Whatever time you want to terminate me is okay by me, but my fee is still three hundred dollars."

He didn't like that. A scowl darkened his face, then was quickly banished as he willfully regained his composure. He smiled stiffly. "Of course. Let's not quibble." He went to the bureau and opened the top drawer. He pulled out a money belt, unzipped it, and counted out some bills. "Here is eight hundred dollars. You may keep the change."

I couldn't tell by his amiable grin whether he was trying to be magnanimous or surreptitiously insulting. It didn't matter much to me, either way. I did my own count and pocketed the bills while he put away the money belt. "You always carry around that much cash, Mr. Saffarian?" I asked, standing up.

He smiled. "I have found that business transactions are always facilitated by cash."

"Be careful," I admonished. "Los Angeles can be a dangerous city."

"I always try to be careful," he assured me, still smiling.

I took the hand he held out, and he maintained the grip as he steered me toward the door. I felt the unmistakable breeze from the bum's rush. At the door, he released my hand and I asked, "By the way, Mr. Saffarian, what is the name of your company in Istanbul?"

"Mid-Orient Import-Export," he said without hesitation. He opened the door. "Well, good-bye, Mr. Asch. And thank you. I am grateful for your efforts."

"I'm afraid I didn't do much," I protested.

His smile turned enigmatic. "On the contrary, you've done a great deal. You've taken a great load off my mind."

His wide white smile seemed to hang in the air, like the Cheshire cat's, after the door closed. I stood for a moment in the quiet hallway, trying to figure out what had just happened. I was pretty sure whatever it was wasn't what Saffarian had tried to convince me had, and I wondered if the money in my pocket made that all right. On my way down in the elevator I took the parking stub from my pocket, thought about the next payment on the Mustang, and decided it did.

It was five after six when I drove past the house on Second Street. The Acura was in the driveway. I told Bick and MacPherson to follow me and drove to Denny's. They pulled into the lot behind me and we all got out of our cars.

"What's up?" Bick asked.

"Nothing anymore," I informed them. "My client is returning to Turkey and has decided to dispense with our services."

Bick frowned, displeased. "Kind of sudden, isn't it?"

"He said something came up, a business matter that needed his urgent attention."

"You don't sound as if you believe him," MacPherson observed sagely.

I shrugged. "It doesn't matter what I believe. The only thing that matters is that we're no longer being paid. And I can't think of another reason for getting up at five in the morning and sitting in my car all day."

I dug the piece of scrap paper I'd doodled on out of my pocket. I counted out $240 to MacPherson, $312 to Bick, and threw in another $50 each for gas. They pocketed the money and Bick said, "Papadoupoulous went out to Deep Six again. He and the blond guy had a nice argument about something. I thought for a while they were going to punch each other out."

"They can kill each other as far as I'm concerned."

He scowled unhappily. "I'm telling you, something is going on with those two. There's something wrong with this whole setup."

His radar was working again. I wished he would shut it down. "It's none of our business."

He shrugged and said, a little too quickly, "I guess not. You get any more work, give me a call."

I drove home, my mind buffeted by vague, shapeless thoughts. Bick was right; something was going on, and I had a bad feeling about it. "Don't worry about it," I said out loud, to nobody. "Whatever it is, you're out of it."

As nuts as he had been, Hitler had been amazingly discerning about some aspects of human nature. Like his observation that the bigger the lie, the easier it is to get people to believe it. Even yourself.

# SEVEN

I had Rose mail me the computer printouts I'd asked her for, not because I wanted them, but because I didn't want her to think I'd put her to all that bother for nothing. I filed the sheets after barely glancing at them and was busy forgetting about the whole affair when Tony Bruenig called.

Bruenig was Dave Bick's ex-partner. When he had gotten too old to work undercover he had been transferred to the L.A.P.D. narcotics detail at LAX, and now he sat around the airport dressed in Hawaiian shirts, watching passengers disembark from the flights arriving from Miami, Atlanta, and Dallas. Those cities were the three major transit points on the cocaine pipelines from South America, and it was Tony's job to pick three individuals at random from each flight that he thought looked "suspicious" and ask them to open their luggage. If the process sounded rather arbitrary and unscientific, that was because it was. Besides being a keen observer of human behavior, Bruenig, like Bick, relied heavily on his cop's intuition to tell him who was dirty, and it worked an amazingly high percentage of the time.

"You going to see Dave today?" he asked.

I cradled the telephone receiver between my chin and shoulder as I glanced over the mail on my office desk. "Bick? No, why?"

"Isn't he working on something for you?" Bruenig asked.

"He was. But that was finished up four days ago."

"That's funny," he said. "I talked to him yesterday. He said he was working a case for you, tailing some joker around."

I stopped shuffling the mail around. "What joker, did he say?"

"Yeah. Some guy named Fox. Justin T. Fox. He had me run him for priors."

The name rang a vague bell. "Anything come back?"

"Two arrests. One in 1983 for possession of narcotics for resale. A pound of hash. It was thrown out on a search and seizure technicality. In 1986 he was pulled in on an aggravated assault beef. The case was dropped before it got to court."

I scowled at the top of my desk. "You say Dave called *yesterday?*"

"Yeah. That's why I'm calling. The putz was supposed to meet me for a drink at Charlie Brown's last night and he didn't show. I waited for over an hour. I figured he was moving around, tailing the guy, and couldn't call. I tried him later at home, but his answering machine was on."

"He never called you back?"

"Nope. I tried him again this morning but got the machine again."

"Maybe he's just not picking up the phone," I said.

"He'd call me back." He paused. "You say he's not working for you?"

"Not right now. Bick was helping me with a case, but my client dropped it." There was a moment of uncomfortable silence as we each thought over what the other had said. "Let me call you back, Tony."

I went to the filing cabinet and pulled the Saffarian file. The two computer printouts Rose had sent were right on top when I opened the folder. The Dodge ES was registered to a Heather Piccard, 2346 Berkeley Street, L.A., which was the Silver Lake address. But it was the second report that I was more interested in. Deep Six Diving was a DBA for Justin T. Fox, whose address was a P.O. Box in Redondo Beach. The bell suddenly had the shrill ring of a fire alarm.

I picked up the phone and tried Bick's apartment. I got the recording and, at the beep, identified myself and waited in case he was there listening. Either he wasn't, or he didn't want to talk to me. I left the message for him to call me, then sat staring at the phone. Why would Bick tell Bruenig that he was working for me? Unless he had gotten tired of soap operas and longed for a little real-life drama. Cops-and-robbers type drama, with Justin T. Fox playing the robber.

I pocketed the two printouts, then sorted rapidly through the rest of the mail. Most of it was junk or bills, but one had a Wanderly Ford logo on it and I ripped it open eagerly.

A little over a month ago, Wayne Wanderly, the owner of Wanderly Ford, had hired me to find out where the AM-FM cassette units were going that had been disappearing out of his new models with disturbing regularity over the past six months. So I had put on my white belt and plaid sports coat and gone to work for Wanderly Ford as a salesman, with the understanding that I would get my regular per diem, plus the normal salesman's commission on whatever cars I sold.

Wanderly had become visibly angry when I informed him that the thief was none other than his service manager, Wayne Wanderly, Jr., who also happened to be the silent partner in an auto audio store a few blocks away. The anger had drained from his face, however, when I told him about the loan-sharking operation his credit manager was running out of his office and like, Saffarian, he had courteously and respectfully terminated my employment, saying he knew all about it and would take care of it himself. That confirmed my suspicions that the credit manager's partner was the elder Wanderly himself. It also guaranteed that I would receive the commissions he owed me for the two Bronco IIs I had sold.

There were two checks in the envelope, one for $1,467.98, for the balance billed, and a commission check for $946.34. I smiled as I slipped the two checks into my wallet, relieved that I would not be forced to resort to extortion to get my money.

I locked up the office and went down the stairs. When I hit the sidewalk, I was stopped by a loud, irregular, grating sound, like a dull chain saw trying to cut through a knotty tree stump. I peeked behind the stairs.

Sleeping there, on a flattened-out cardboard box, was a filthy, tattered refugee from Tent City. They had established a firm hold on the beach, and were now moving steadily inland. I'd seen it before in *The Longest Day*.

On the ground beside him was a pile of burned pork chop bones, a bottle of Heinz Ketchup, and a can of Sterno. Welcome to the Hotel California.

I went back upstairs, rolled a piece of paper into my Selectric, and typed out:

## EVICTION NOTICE

Violation. Safety Code 413A Sub. 78b. No cooking in the rooms by order of the Fire Marshal.

I took it back down and he continued to snore steadily as I tacked it up under the stair above his head. He should be used to little jokes by now, I thought as I went to the car. After all, life had been playing them on him for some time now.

# EIGHT

The plans of the Torrance city fathers had obviously called for architectural uniformity, and from the look of things, they were well on their way to achieving that noble goal. All the commercial buildings on both sides of Torrance Boulevard had terra-cotta tile roofs, arched windows, and fake brick and stucco facades—what architects liked to call Mission Revival, and what I called Late Del Taco. The three-story apartment building in which Bick had lived for the six years since his divorce was on a small street running off the wide boulevard and was a paragon of the style.

I parked around back in a space marked for visitors. The swimming pool in the courtyard was lined with gas barbeques—a prep school for future suburban life. It was too early for class and the lounge chairs were deserted. I located the elevator and rode up to the second floor.

I knocked on the door of 219, waited, then knocked again. When I could raise no response I made sure the hallway was clear, then took out my set of picks and went to work. For a cop, Bick was not very security-conscious. He hadn't bothered to lock his deadbolt, and the main Schlage lock took me thirty seconds to crack. I scanned the hallway again and slipped inside.

For someone so quick to critique my office decor, Bick's apartment was a sight. Dirty socks and shirts lay over the arms of the tweedy living room chairs, and a pair of scuffed brown shoes were parked under the coffee table. On top of the table, two opened cans of Anchor Steam stood next to an open box of Domino pizza containing one piece of pepperoni that had lost its battle with the Noid. On the couch was a two-day old sports section from the *Times*. Directly across from the couch, on a caster-bottomed trolley, was a twenty-seven-inch Zenith TV and a Philco VHS unit.

I walked around the flimsy breakfast table into the adjoining kitchen. On the crumb-littered counter by the sink was an opened box of Ritz crackers and an assortment of dirty dishes. A caravan of ants moved around the box, transporting the crumbs to an unknown location behind the refrigerator.

The bedroom was just as messy as the living room and just as empty. A Browning Hi-Power was in the drawer of the end table beside the unmade bed. I closed the drawer and peeked in the closet, then went back out to the living room.

His message recorder was on a small table at the end of the kitchen counter, below the phone. I rewound it and played back the messages. There were four messages—three from Bruenig and one from me—and three dial tones where people had called and hung up. I left the machine on and started to leave, then noticed the red light on the VCR.

I went over to the unit and hit the eject button and a tape slid out. I pushed it back in, and while it rewound, looked over some of Bick's tape titles. *Rambo. Love Story*. At least his taste was eclectic. Bad, but eclectic. When the tape finished rewinding, I turned on the TV and ran the tape. The credits for *All My Children* appeared on the screen. I picked up the *TV Guide* and found out that *All My Children* didn't come on until noon, which meant in all likelihood that the episode on the tape was yesterday's. Bick could have come home, watched what he had timer-taped, then left again, remembering to turn off the TV but forgetting to turn off the VCR. Or he could have not come home at all last night. Being a great believer in Occam's Razor, I gravitated toward less complex theorems.

The problem was that in this case, I didn't like the possible corollaries.

At the door, I paused to take one last look at the room and felt suddenly depressed, not only for Bick, but for myself. I was only a few years behind Bick, and I had about as much to show for my years of living as he did. Some video cassettes to temporarily make yourself forget, a cold pizza, too much booze to kill the lonely hours—it would have been enough to get Ralph Edwards canceled after half a season. It also made it easy to understand why Bick would have wanted to play cop again.

I let myself out and took the elevator down to the underground garage. The parking space for 219 was empty. As I rode back up to the street level, I told myself that I was making something out of nothing. Bick had probably gone out with some drinking buddies, taken in too much of the grape, and flopped somewhere. It wouldn't be the first time. He was probably sitting on a couch right now, trying to come up with what Western science had not been able to achieve in three thousand years—a hangover cure.

Simple. Good old Occam, I knew he'd come through. I just wondered why I couldn't shake the feeling that his razor was pressing against my throat.

# NINE

---

After fattening my checking account with Wanderly's money, I drove downtown, stopping at a liquor store on the way. Rose was diligently banging away at her typewriter when I walked into Greenberg Bail Bonds with the Saffarian file and a gift-boxed bottle of Chivas Regal tucked under my arm. She stopped and eyed the scotch suspiciously as I set it on the edge of her desk. "Chivas. What's that for?"

"For you. In appreciation for all your trouble."

"Well," she said, smiling a little. "Thanks. You owe the kitty thirty-four bucks, by the way."

"You'll have a check before I leave," I promised.

She went back to the forms she was typing. I stopped reading and leaned on the desk. "You look very nice today, by the way."

She went on typing without looking up. "Thanks."

"That blue dress looks great on you. You should wear blue more often. It brings out the blue in your eyes."

She grunted as her fingers flew over the keys.

"Have you done something with your makeup?"

"No, why?"

"You look ten years younger."

That got her. Rose had the mottled, doughy face of a middle-aged woman who liked to tipple a few stiff ones when she got home to the bachelor apartment she shared with two cats. She was not unpleasant-looking, but there wasn't much there that could be improved by makeup or a blue dress and we both knew it. She looked up, and said, a bit harshly, I thought, "What do you want now?"

"What do you mean?" I asked dumbly.

"Liquor, flattery. I have more trouble seeing through the windows of my apartment."

I shook my head sadly. "I'm truly hurt, Rose. This job has soured you on the human condition. It's making you hard and cynical, and frankly, I hate to see it."

"Then you don't want anything?"

"Certainly not."

"Good, because I'm busy," she said, and went back to her typing.

I stood around for a moment, then said, "Now that you mention it, there is something—"

"I knew it," she said disgustedly.

"I promise this will be the last time."

Above the fleshy pouches, her eyes were icy. "You always promise that."

"Yeah, but this time, I *mean* it." I paused, for effect. "It'd be a real favor. I swear I wouldn't ask unless it was important."

She sighed heavily and I knew I had her. I pulled the computer printouts from my pocket. "Credit checks on these two people."

She took the papers and said in a stony voice, "Tomorrow."

I winced and bit my lip. "I realize how busy you are, Rose, but this is really important—"

"So is this," she said, flicking the paper in the typewriter with her middle finger.

I leaned across the desk and glanced at the sheet rolled up in the typewriter. "So the guy gets out ten minutes later. He'll still have plenty of time to get over to the junior high and molest a couple of kids before school lets out."

She rubbed the back of her neck and stood up. "Jesus Christ. All right. I guess the faster I get the stuff, the faster you'll get out of here and leave me alone."

"You've got a great heart, Rose."

Hymie looked exceptionally agitated, even for Hymie, when I walked into his office. In his green and red houndstooth jacket, he looked like a disgruntled Heywood Hayle Broun. He grunted a greeting, and I sat down and asked, "Something the matter?"

"Yeah. We have problems."

"*We?* What kind of problems?"

"Juke balls."

"What about them?"

"My contact brought one over this morning."

"So?"

He wrinkled his nose. "They taste terrible. I can't understand it. Normally, when you eat a meal, things get mixed up on your plate, and they still taste good, right?"

I had to admit that tended to happen.

He nodded, as if that proved his case. "I can't understand how just mashing it all up and compressing it a little can make it taste so bad. I mean, all we're doing is taking the process one step further, right?"

I conceded the point with a nod.

He handed me a piece of paper. "This was the menu for last night that went into the sample."

I glanced it over. "I might mix up some things on my plate," I said, "but I at least make an attempt to keep my salad with Italian dressing out of my apple pie."

He tapped on the desk top with a forefinger. "Maybe you're right. Maybe I'll have Leonard make up a batch without the dessert."

"Sure," I said, trying to sound optimistic. "Try different combinations, see what the prisoners' response is. How do they like them, by the way?"

"Leonard says they refuse to eat them for the first couple of days, but after that, they wolf 'em down."

"There's your problem," I told him. "All you have to do is aim for a different market—the hungry. Ethiopia, Mozambique—"

His eyes lighted up. "You might have something there."

"Sure. You could drop them from planes, like bombs."

"The vending machine idea was penny ante compared to

this," he exclaimed excitedly. "We're talking government contracts here."

"I even know a place we can try them out, not far from my apartment." As I pictured Tent City being pounded flat by payload after merciless payload of juke balls, I suddenly realized that I may have stumbled upon a politically viable solution to the city's problem. It would certainly give the expression "killing them with kindness" a new and more literal meaning. I made a mental note to call the mayor.

Hymie smiled hugely. "Jake, you're a genius." It was good to be recognized finally for one's true talents. Rose came in with the printouts. "That'll be fifty-four dollars now," she said, and walked out.

According to Fox's credit sheet, he had started up Deep Six in 1988. He apparently had had some problems with an earlier business venture in 1986, as there were five civil suits listed, in three different court jurisdictions. The parties filing the suits had all been awarded settlements, totaling some $4,650. Since then, things seemed to have settled down for him, and he had been regular with the payments for his automobile and his boat, CF #557698, which he had purchased back in 1981. His current listed address was the same post office box in Redondo.

My curiosity started to work overtime when I saw that Heather Piccard's employer was the L.A. County Museum of Art. Papadoupoulous had spent the day in the museum, but Bick said he hadn't met anyone. Apparently he preferred his meetings at night in sleazy motel rooms. One thing was for sure: he and Naci certainly did have a diverse group of acquaintances, especially for being in the country such a short time.

The Piccard file went back to 1974, and she was clean all the way through to the present. Her Dodge was two years old and paid for, and she showed only one large outstanding loan. The loan was for thirty years, a mortgage I assumed, on the house in Silver Lake.

I went into the outer office and used one of the phones to call the museum. The receptionist had a thick Chicano accent and she seemed to have as much trouble understanding me as I did her. Bilingual education was a wonderful thing. She didn't know who Heather Piccard was or what department she was in, and after a two-minute Abbott and Costello routine in broken English, I asked to speak with someone else and she disconnected me.

I called back and was relieved to hear a different female voice, one that had a semi-command of the language. I explained all over again, and thankfully this one seemed to grasp my request. She searched a list of the museum employees and told me that Ms. Piccard was a curator in Greek and ancient art, and asked if I wished to be connected. I told her no thank you, and hung up.

I sat for a moment, wondering what had been in that shoe box to bring a curator of ancient art to a cheap motel room on La Cienega. I was still wondering when I tried Bick.

His machine answered and told me to leave my message at the beep. I didn't bother, figuring I'd already left enough.

I was writing out a check for fifty-four dollars when Hymie stepped out of his office, his face glowing with a zeal usually only seen on the faces of saints or corporate raiders. "We could tie this thing in with a record deal. Get all the big rock stars to participate, like in that Africa record a couple of years ago. What do you think?"

I said it sounded like a good idea to me.

He looked past me as if he were seeing a double rainbow with pots of gold at each end. "The subsidiary rights on this thing could be worth millions. T-shirts, records, the works. And you're in on the ground floor, Jakie-boy."

I put the check down on Rose's desk. "Consider this my first infusion of capital into the project," I said, and left him with his visions of playing world savior for fun and profit.

# TEN

Two of the court cases listed in Justin Fox's credit printout had been filed downtown, in small claims. As I was close by, I drove there. I gave the clerk the docket numbers and she pulled the files.

Both cases had been filed against Fox as owner and operator of Underwater Expeditions, a company specializing in locating and recovering sunken treasure. The plaintiffs had claimed that Fox had taken $750 from each of them as a deposit on a scuba-diving treasure hunt for pre-Columbian artifacts off the coast of Costa Rica.

Both plaintiffs claimed they had been lured into taking the trip by a brochure put out by Fox stating that they would be taken to Central America aboard a "fifty-foot luxury yacht." When they had arrived in San Pedro, they'd discovered to their dismay that the yacht was twenty-five feet shy of its advertised length. They also found that they would be cramped in the sleeping quarters with six other people, and that they would have to do their own cooking. Still, seized by the spirit of adventure, the two decided to go through with the venture and paid the balance of the $900.

The expedition sailed south and got as far as San Blas, on the Mexican coast, where the boat developed engine troubles. After two days, the expedition members were told that necessary repairs would force them to return to San Diego, and that the trip would be delayed one week. When they docked in San Diego, the boat was boarded by the Coast Guard and DEA agents, who detained the passengers while they went through the boat from stem to stern, looking for drugs. None were found, but that humiliation proved to be the last straw for the plaintiffs and three other passengers, who mutinied and demanded their money back. When Fox refused to give it to them, they got off the ship, stopped payment on their checks, and sued for their deposit money. The judge decided for the plaintiffs and ordered Fox to repay the money plus court costs.

In my mind I went over some of the details in the court files as I drove the freeway to Hermosa Beach.

Hermosa was typical of the beachfront bungalow communities that grew up south of L.A. during the thirties. Its main drag was a wide, divided street lined with two-story stucco apartment buildings, fast-food restaurants, surf shops, and clothing stores. Tanned and healthy-looking kids swarmed like locusts over the area, walking, on bicycles, or piled three too many in topless Suzuki Samarais. I was the object of their dirty looks and their car horns as I drove slowly, scanning the street signs for Fifth.

I finally spotted it and turned right. It was a narrow residential street that ran up the hill between rows of small, clapboard houses. After two blocks, the street dead-ended in a condo complex and continued half a block over as commercial zoning.

Deep-Six was a small, pink converted house that sat next to the fenced-in yard of an automobile body shop. The red van was parked out front and I pulled up behind it and got out of the car. The front door of the place was open, and as I walked toward it the blond man I'd seen with Naci came out, carrying a cardboard box. His eyes widened when he saw me, then narrowed quickly. He loaded the box quickly into the side of the van and faced me.

He was dressed in jeans and running shoes and a green T-shirt with a circular college insignia on the front. The

letters around the insignia said: CATATONIC STATE. He ran a
hand through his bleached hair and asked in a truculent tone,
"Can I do something for you?"

"Maybe," I said. "If your name is Fox."

His shoulders tensed. "Who are you?"

I smiled easily. "My name is Sterne. Laurence Sterne. I'm
interested in getting on a treasure-hunting expedition. I hear
you run 'em."

His eyes relaxed. They were the color of dirty pennies and
had about as much depth. "Not anymore, pal. I'm getting out
of the business."

"That's too bad. Can you recommend anybody else who
runs trips like that?"

"You might try Fathom in Venice."

I pointed at the open door. "Need any help loading up?"

He looked like he'd been moving some heavy stuff. Beads of
perspiration stood out on his head. "No, thanks."

I approached him until I was able to see in the van. It was
loaded with diving equipment and boxes. He slammed the
door of the van and said, "If you'll excuse me, I'm kind of
busy—"

"The reason I came to you first is that a friend of mine said
you'd know everything there was to know about diving for
treasure." I paused. "Actually, he isn't my friend. I met him
through Naci."

His expression tightened again. He tried to sound casual.
"Naci? I don't know anybody by that name."

"Naci Saffarian."

He shook his head again and tried to look bewildered. "I'd
remember if I ever met any guy with that name—"

"Naci is a girl."

He shrugged casually, but the muscles under the smooth
skin of his jaw bulged like two pigeon eggs. "Guy, girl, I still
don't know anyone named Naci."

I ignored his denial. "The guy's name is Dave Bick. Naci's
friend, I mean. About fifty, gray hair, walks with a limp?"

He smiled and turned up his palms. "Sorry, pal, but like I
said, I don't know the guy or this Naci." The smile remained
falsely on his face. "You a cop?"

"Why do you ask that?"

"You look like a cop."

"I'm not."

His features relaxed. He nodded, apparently satisfied, and kicked me right in the balls. The pain seared through my gut and I immediately assumed the fetal position standing up, only to meet a fist coming up from the other direction. It met the point of my jaw and white light exploded behind my eyes. Another blow landed on my temple and all sense of equilibrium was gone. I felt as if I were floating, and then the back of my head rebounded off the pavement, and I wasn't floating anymore, but felt as if I were in one of those centrifuges at the fun park, plastered against the wall and unable to move. Good old Oscar the Movie Penguin should have seen me now.

Hands tugged and pulled at me, and I was vaguely aware of someone hovering above me, but I didn't know who it was. The hands let go of me and footsteps walked away. I managed to roll over onto my stomach. The engine of the van started up and the thought struck me dimly that it might be a good idea to get out of the road. I might have been stupid, but I was no fool.

I tried to push myself up but was overcome by a wave of dizziness and nausea. I rolled back over onto my back, groaning. Rolling seemed like a viable option, perhaps not the fastest means of locomotion, or even the most efficient, but at least a possibility. I came to rest against the cyclone fence of the body shop as the van took off, its spinning tires pelting me with bits of gravel and rock.

The van turned right at the end of the street and disappeared. I grabbed a handful of fence and pulled myself to my feet. "Dumb, real fucking dumb," I heard myself say. I didn't really have to remind myself; the pain was reminder enough.

The ground was no longer tilting arbitrarily and I shuffled, bent over like an old man with osteoporosis, to my car. I eased myself down onto the front seat, taking great care not to sit on my nuts, which felt as if they were the size of baseballs, and waited for the sickness to sweat out of me. After ten minutes or so my insides had stabilized enough for me to get out of the car.

I went to the door of Deep Six and tried the handle. In his haste, Fox had neglected to lock up. I went inside and switched on the light.

The bright red carpet jumped up and snapped at me. The

white walls were covered with Mexican travel posters. Fox
had left the office furniture behind—a gray metal desk, two
black naugahyde chairs, and a gray three-drawer filing
cabinet—but not much else. The drawers of the filing cabinet
were open and empty.

Across the room an open bathroom door invited me in. I
accepted the invitation and surveyed the damage to my face in
the streaked medicine cabinet mirror. I looked like Charles
Laughton in *The Hunchback of Notre Dame*. My lip was cut, my
right eye was closing, and there was a distinct bluing lump on
the left side of my jaw, but there was nothing that would
require stitches. I splashed cold water on my face and patted
it off with a paper towel from a roll that sat on the back of the
dirty toilet, then wetted another towel and went to work on
the bloodstains on my collar.

After successfully putting my laundering talents to the test,
I went back out. I opened the closed door next to the
bathroom. The room beyond was small and bare. I went over
to the desk. Aside from miscellaneous paper clips, rubber
bands and the like, and an accumulation of rubbed-off bits of
dirty eraser rubber, the drawers were empty. The wastebasket
was not, however. In it was a stack of color brochures. I
plucked one out.

Above a photograph of a stone Aztec idol sticking its tongue
out, was written in bold letters:

## ARCHAEOLOGICAL TREASURES!

He had me hooked. I opened it up and read on.

Not only can archaeological artifacts bring HUGE profits, their financial benefits are two-fold. First, they are a
hedge against inflation. Since the supply is growing
SMALLER, and the demand is growing steadily
HIGHER, their price will only go UP. Second, they are
a TAX SHELTER. You may deduct one hundred
percent of the finds you make from your income.

If you are a diver and love adventure, come along with us
on an exciting, TAX DEDUCTIBLE vacation. Our last

trip to Central America netted over 2,000 pieces of pre-Columbian stone, jade, and gold. Aside from diving, we will be dealing directly with the Indians, purchasing items, and excavating artifacts from various sites in Central America. Incan, Aztecan, and Mayan treasures are waiting for you to discover them!

Contact Underwater Expeditions, P.O. Box 6646, Long Beach 90867.

On the back page was a photograph of a sleek and beautiful yacht, its while paint gleaming immaculately in the sun. Next to it was a photo of a horde of golden Spanish doubloons. It made me wonder why I'd been wasting time in the detective business all these years.

A quick check of the rest of the wastebasket failed to come up with anything else of interest. I pocketed the brochure and drove the mile from Deep Six to the Port Royal marina. That was long enough for me to work up a good case of mad thinking about what Fox had done to me—and sufficient recovery time to make me want to do something about it. I pulled into a wide lot and parked next to a Red Onion Mexican restaurant that sat on the water's edge. I pulled the Uwara stick out of the glove compartment and dropped it in my coat pocket.

A Uwara is a heavy, rolled piece of metal, about six inches long. It is too short to be considered a lethal weapon—which made it convenient in case one was stopped by the cops—but held in a fist it put crunch in your punch, and its knobbed ends were very handy for shattering things, like elbows and eye orbits. I thought of a few of Fox's bones I would like to try it out on as I walked down the marina promenade.

A gray wet haze covered the late afternoon sun, chilling the air. The marina was not large, but it was packed with pleasure craft, their spearlike masts jutting row upon row into the sky. I could have used a spear, but one had to make do.

The gate to the B slips was unlocked. My grip tightened on the Uwara in my pocket as I pushed it open and walked down the pontoon. There was a slight chop and the water made rhythmic, lonely sounds as it slapped against the keels of the boats. It sounded even lonelier when I found slip B43. It was empty.

I limped back to the marina clubhouse like a born-again eunuch and talked to the manager, a crusty old salt named Traynor. He told me that Fox lived on his boat, a thirty-seven-foot Tartan Blackwatch named, surprisingly, *Deep Six*, and had been renting the slip there for the past year and a half. He had pulled out yesterday morning about ten without saying where he was going or when he would be back. He hadn't said anything about giving up the slip, and since his fees were paid up for the month, Traynor guessed he had just gone for a sail. The manager had seen Fox several times in the company of a girl who matched Naci's description, but he didn't know if she or anyone else besides Fox had been on board yesterday morning.

I called Bick's number from the pay phone at the end of the dock and got the same old message. Nobody had left any new ones with my answering service, either. I walked very carefully back to the car, planning my next move. If it turned out to be as good as my last, I figured it would be good for at least a week in intensive care.

Ten years ago the traffic rush hours on the freeways in and out of L.A. used to total four per day, two in the morning and two in the evening. Now there were only four hours during the work day when the traffic was not bumper-to-bumper. The trip back to Santa Monica was not during one of the four.

The driveway of the house on Second Street was empty, the house itself was still. I parked across the street and watched the house for a few minutes before deciding on a course of action. Actually, there weren't many choices.

The enervating drive back, the irritation I felt with myself for the way I'd handled Fox, the nagging worry I felt about Bick, and the too-recent memory of the three days' stakeout on this house, all teamed up to make the thought of sitting there for any length of time intolerable. I was through with the subtle approach; it was time for some straight answers.

I didn't get any when I rang the front doorbell. I didn't get anything at all. I rang again and a voice like a creaking shutter said, "They moved out."

A disheveled woman in a dirty green smock and a face like a Kadota fig stood among the front-yard rubble of the No

Cares Day School next door, staring at me over the fence. She held the hands of two little boys of preschool age.

"The couple who lived here?" I asked.

She nodded. "Night before last. Late. Packed up everything in their cars and left."

"Do you know where they went?"

"No. They weren't very social. They friends of yours?"

"Not really."

One of the children started to whine, and she let go of the other one's hand to bop him on top of the head. "Shut up."

The technique didn't work. The kid started sniffling and squirming and she gave him a look that foretold ominous things to come once they were out of the public eye.

I stepped off the porch and walked closer to the fence. "You said *cars*. There was more than one?"

She nodded. "A guy in a red van was helping."

"A blond man? Looks like a weightlifter?"

"Yeah, that's him." The kid started whining again. She glared down at him angrily, then, realizing she was being watched, consciously changed her scowl into a tolerant smile. "That's okay, Jimmie. In just a few minutes, we'll go inside and have some ice cream, okay?"

The kid must have heard that one before, because he broke into a low wail. *Ice cream* must have been code for *the rack*.

"What time was that?"

She shrugged. "After midnight. I couldn't sleep. I got home late and they were loading up. I asked the blond guy if they were moving, and he said yeah."

After midnight. A strange time to be moving. Unless you were in a hurry.

"You a bill collector or something?" she asked.

"Something," I affirmed, and went back to the car. I wanted in the house, but not while her prying eyes were around.

I drove down to Pico, stopped at the first pay phone I spotted, and dialed the County Museum of Art.

I was transferred to the proper extension. A rather deep voice answered, "Ancient art, Heather Piccard."

"Ms. Piccard, you don't know me. My name is Jacob Asch. I'm a private detective. I would very much like to talk to you if you have a few minutes to spare sometime this afternoon."

"Private detective?" she asked with a hint of surprise.

"That's right."

"What is this concerning?"

"The Starlite Motor Lodge."

"How did you know about that?" she asked uneasily.

"I was following the couple you met."

There was a thoughtful pause.

Her tone grew suspicious. "Who are you working for?"

"Nobody right now," I said vaguely. "I'll be glad to explain, but I'd rather do it in person."

There was a four- or five-second gap of silence. "I can see you at five o'clock. Come to the front desk in the Ahmanson building and ask for me. I'll come up and get you."

I hung up and dialed the Child Abuse Hotline and told the woman who answered the phone that she might want to look into the operation of the No Cares Day School and gave her the address.

# ELEVEN

She was younger than I had expected. Despite the shock of white in the front of her dark brown hair, she could not have been more than thirty-five. Her hair was long and coarse, pulled back and fixed with an ornate ivory comb that looked quite old. She wore a brown wool sweater over a loose-fitting green calf-length dress and high brown leather boots. A green scarf was knotted loosely around her long, graceful neck. "Mr. Asch? I'm Heather Piccard."

I said I was glad to meet her and she asked in a businesslike tone to see some identification. I showed her my driver's and investigator's licenses, and while she looked them over I looked her over.

She was not really pretty, but there was something compellingly attractive about her, particularly in the large, intelligent gray eyes and the wide, full-lipped mouth. Her skin was smooth and white, like polished ivory. She wore no earrings or makeup and I had to wonder to what extent the lack of cosmetics was cosmetic in itself. The image she projected was scholarly, resolved, mature, just what a museum curator should look like, and I wondered how much of that was intentional. I somehow doubted that a woman who looked like Jayne Mansfield would be taken seriously enough to be promoted to the head of a department of ancient art.

She was looking at me strangely, and it took me a few seconds to realize why. That was what a good beating will do for you—slows you down a tick. "Roller-skating accident," I explained.

"It must have been a good one."

"The Law of Selective Gravity."

"Pardon?"

"'A body will always fall as to do the most damage.' Actually, I was doing quite well until that stupid penguin skated in front of me."

I was digging myself a hole. She was looking at me even more strangely now. "Penguin?"

"Private joke."

Her expression told me she didn't want to be let in on it. She turned and led the way to a door at the end of the high-ceilinged hall, and down a set of stairs. At the bottom of the stairs, a uniformed armed guard went over me with a hand-held metal detector. When it was determined that I was clean, I was given a plastic security badge that I was told to pin to my coat, and resumed following Heather Piccard through a labyrinth of hallways.

We entered a wide corridor in which men were moving large crates on fork lifts, and she pushed open a heavy metal door and led the way into a well-lighted room filled with worktables.

"This is the conservation department, where we test for age and authenticity," she said nonchalantly as she passed through the room. I could say nothing; all I could do was stare.

I could see now the reason for the security check. There must have been twenty million dollars worth of ancient art sitting out on the tables being fussed over by aproned technicians. There were small pre-Columbian idols, a huge stone Egyptian head from the time of the pharaohs, a black-figure Greek crater that had been in someone's home around the time Sparta and Athens were duking it out, and in a glass vacuum chamber, a small Byzantine painting of the Madonna. A panorama of history lay before me, open for inspection, and

its proximity—without a glass barrier between it and me—
made it doubly awesome.

We went out another door and down a short hallway to a
spacious office. Mini-blinds covered the window behind the
large oak desk. The wall to the right of the desk had
floor-to-ceiling shelves crammed with books. On the left hung
framed posters advertising art exhibitions at the museum. One
of them, an exhibit of Scythian gold, was still here and would
be for the next three weeks.

Heather Piccard sat behind the desk and asked me to sit on
the olive-green couch opposite. Before I could do that, a tall,
thin, silver-haired man stepped through the open doorway.
He was dapperly attired in an expensive-looking gray worsted
suit, pale yellow dress shirt with a gray and yellow striped tie,
and immaculately buffed gray wingtips. "Have I missed
anything?" he asked with a barely noticeable German accent.

"No," Heather Piccard said. "We just got here. Mr. Asch,
this is the director of the museum, Dr. Pieter Gros. I took the
liberty of telling him about your call, and since the museum
could possibly be involved he wanted to listen in."

"Certainly."

Gros's pale blue eyes went over me alertly as we shook
hands. His long face was devoid of humor or color. Everybody around here could have used some sun. He waited until
I sat down, then perched himself on the edge of the desk and
looked down at me. It was an old trick, intended to establish
dominance by asserting height, but it only worked if the
trickee didn't know what the tricker was doing.

"You used to work for the *Chronicle*," he said.

"That's right."

He nodded. "The name sounded familiar when Heather
mentioned it, so I made a few calls. You went to jail for
contempt a few years ago, for refusing to reveal your source
on a story you wrote."

I wondered who he had called. Not that it mattered much.
"That's me."

"I followed it in the newspapers at the time. I greatly
admired your stand. There are few men who would be willing
to give up their freedom for something as outdated as principle. You never went back to reporting?"

"No."

He nodded as if he understood. "It looks like your new line of work is a bit rougher than working for a newspaper."

I involuntarily touched my face. "Sometimes. Actually, detective work is pretty dull most of the time."

"How well I know," he said, offering up an ingratiating smile. "To be a successful museum director, you have to be a bit of a detective. You have to be an 'eye' as they say in the museum trade. In the hunt for objects one has to be able to put bits and pieces together, to follow the trail of things that have been long lost. The tracking is often slow, involving a lot of tedious footwork, slogging through old records, but the hunt can be thrilling, too."

I wondered where he was heading now that we were one consanguineous group. I didn't have to wait long to find out. "So what brings you here, Mr. Asch?"

I took a breath and began. "Last week, I was hired by a man named Garo Saffarian to keep an eye on his daughter, Naci. The girl had allegedly run away from home in Istanbul with a man named Dimitrios Papadoupoulous and come to the United States. They were living in a house in Santa Monica. Saffarian didn't trust his daughter's taste in men and wanted the two of them watched to make sure they weren't up to anything.

"On Tuesday night, I tailed them to a motel on La Cienega, where they met Ms. Piccard. They entered a room carrying two shoe boxes. When Ms. Piccard left, she had one of the boxes."

I paused and looked from Gros to Heather Piccard. Neither of them said anything. I went on. "The next day, Saffarian called and said he wanted to see me. He was very curious about the identity of Ms. Piccard and the contents of the box. Then, out of the clear blue, he said he had decided to dispense with my services. He said he was going back to Turkey and he had changed his mind about having his daughter watched. I thought it was kind of funny at the time, but there wasn't anything I could do about it. He paid me off and that was that.

"Only that wasn't that. Today I learned that a friend of mine who had been helping with the surveillance on Papadoupoulous has disappeared. He's an ex-cop and he'd developed an interest in one of Papadoupoulous's acquaintances, a man named Justin T. Fox. Ever heard of him?"

Both of them gave an unequivocal "No."

I went on. "Fox ran a business called Deep Six Diving in Redondo Beach, specializing in underwater treasure hunts. From his observations of Fox, Bick—that's my friend—had become convinced that Fox was into some sort of illicit activity. I went down to Redondo this morning to talk to Fox, to see if he had seen Bick. He became very nervous when I started asking questions. He assaulted me and bolted."

"I thought you tripped over a penguin," Heather Piccard said caustically.

I shrugged and smiled. "When I went to the marina where Fox kept his boat, I found out he had pulled up anchor and sailed."

"What has all this got to do with Ms. Piccard?" Gros asked impatiently. "Neither of us has ever met this Fox fellow."

"Fox isn't the only one who has bolted. Papadoupoulous and the girl have also gone. Packed up and moved out in the middle of the night, two days ago. Fox helped them move."

Gros shook his head, mystified. "I still don't know exactly how you think we can help you."

"What was in that shoe box?"

Heather Piccard shifted in her chair uncomfortably.

"Nothing that could possibly have anything to do with your friend's disappearance," Gros said.

"I'd like to be convinced of that."

He thought it over and shrugged. "A potsherd."

"A what?"

"A piece of a clay pot, about two centimeters square."

"That's all?"

He smiled wryly. "That's *less* than all."

"Excuse me?"

Gros glanced at Heather Piccard. "Tell him about it."

She looked at him and cleared her throat. "About ten days ago, I was contacted by the man you call Papadoupoulous. He refused to give me his name but said he had some very old objects he wanted to sell. Pre-Hittite, from an excavation near Hacilar, in Turkey. I asked him how he had come by them, and he said that he'd acquired them from a dealer in Switzerland."

"You have to realize this sort of thing goes on all the time," Gros broke in. "The museum is contacted every day by people claiming to have valuable old pieces for sale. Some of them are genuine, but more often than not the stuff is worthless or forgeries. Still, we have to investigate calls like that. We would be remiss in our duties if we passed up an acquisition and it turned out to be a major find. It does happen."

"Go on," I told her.

She did, hesitantly. "I told the man that before any decision could be made about the purchase of any artifact, its authenticity had to be verified. He told me to take the room at the Starlite Motor Lodge and he would bring a sample I could test."

"That was the potsherd?"

"Yes."

"You tested it?"

"Yes," Gros said. "We ran a thermoluminescence test on a sample of the clay. The material tested out at forty-eight thousand years old."

I shook my head. "I'm no expert on the history of kitchen utensils, but isn't that kind of *old*?"

He smiled indulgently. "Much too old. The piece was obviously a fake."

He must have correctly interpreted my blinking as incomprehension, because he asked, "Do you know anything about thermoluminescence testing?"

"About as much as I know about the mating habits of New Guinea tree shrews."

He ignored that and assumed a tutorial tone. "All clays and most ceramics contain certain amounts of natural radioactivity. Some of the minerals present in ceramics absorb radiation and store it. This stored energy can be released in the form of light, by heating the minerals up to approximately five hundred degrees centigrade. When a clay is fired, to make a pot, say, it is heated to well over five hundred degrees, which releases the energy—the thermoluminescence—and sets the energy clock back to zero. The thermoluminescence then starts accumulating again. By reheating the sample to five hundred degrees and measuring the accumulation, we can date the time it was fired. One way to foil the results of the test is to bombard the ceramic with Xrays. That is what the forger did in this case. What the test was measuring was not naturally stored radiation, but a large, artificially administered dose of radiation. Thus, the sample tested much older than was claimed by your Mr. Papadoupoulous."

"Did you hear from him again?"

Heather Piccard glanced at Gros, but he was looking at me. "Two days later. He called and wanted to know how the test came out. I told him and he hung up."

"So you see," Gros interrupted, "the mystery is solved. The meeting could not possibly be connected to the disappearance of your friend."

"It doesn't seem so," I admitted. I took out a card and jotted my home number on it. "In case Papadoupoulous or the girl happens to call again—"

"That isn't likely," he cut me off. "There would be no reason for them to. We made it clear that we knew they were crooks."

I put the card down on the desk. "In case they do, I'd appreciate it if you'd let me know. You can reach me at one of these numbers at any time. Thank you for seeing me."

I started to leave, but Gros stopped me. "Just a moment, Mr. Asch. Your coming along at this time could be a fortuitous coincidence."

"How is that?"

"I—or rather, the museum—is in need of someone with your experience and discretion. There is a small job I would like you to do."

"What kind of a job?"

"I need to locate a man."

"Who?"

"His name is Arbogast," Gros said. "Benjamin Arbogast. He's an archaeologist with the Oriental Institute in Chicago. He called four days ago, but I was out of town. He told my secretary he would be visiting in L.A. for a week and gave her the number of the hotel where he was staying, but unfortunately she somehow misplaced it."

I shrugged. "He'll probably call back."

"I'm afraid I can't take that chance. He probably already thinks I'm not interested."

"Interested in what?"

He took a deep breath. "Professor Arbogast is in possession of certain artifacts I am very interested in purchasing for the museum. That is why he is on the West Coast. I am not the only one interested in the artifacts. If I don't get in touch with Arbogast, he will certainly sell them to the competition. Time is of the utmost importance in the matter."

"Have you called the Institute in Chicago? Maybe they know where he is staying."

He shook his head. "They don't. All they know is that he is on a two-week holiday. They didn't even know he was in Los Angeles."

"What do you want me to do once I find him?"

"Report back to me. I'll take it from there."

I nodded. "My fee is three hundred dollars a day, plus expenses."

"How long do you think it will take you to find him?"

"A day, maybe. Unless he's using an alias."

He smiled tolerantly. "I doubt that very much." He got off the desk. "That will be satisfactory, then. If you're interested in taking on the job, of course."

I couldn't think of a good reason not to take his money. In all likelihood, I would be able to find the guy and never have to leave my living room. "I'll require a retainer of one day, in advance."

Gros's smile turned paternal. "Certainly. If you come with me up to my office, I'll write you out a cheek."

I said good-bye to Heather Piccard, who had been quiet as a dormouse since her recounting of the great motel caper. Her gray eyes regarded me coolly. "Good-bye."

# TWELVE

On the way back to the beach, I stopped off at Zucky's on Wilshire to kill whatever was left of the daylight over a turkey on rye. I finished the sandwich, had a third cup of coffee, and watched the light dim through the deli windows. When it was dim enough, I paid my check and left.

Except for the barking of a couple of dogs halfway down the block, Second Street was quiet as I parked and stepped out of the car. It was the dinner hour, a time for families to be together indoors, eating their Kraft macaroni and cheese dinners in front of the tube, which was why I'd picked it. The other reason was that the dusky light, while dim, was still strong enough to see by. I didn't want to have to turn on any lights in the house, just in case fig-face had her nose over the fence again.

I went down the weed-cracked concrete driveway, around to the back of the house. As I rounded the corner, I was startled by a sudden movement in the weeds on the far side of the tiny backyard, and I glanced there quickly enough to catch the black tail of a cat disappearing through a gap in the

wood-slat fence. At least it hadn't crossed my path. I didn't
need any more bad luck than I already had.

The pungent, acidic smell of fertilizer was very strong,
almost overpowering, in the yard. That struck me as odd,
since although almost every imaginable species of weed was
rampant in the fenced-in plot, there was no grass or any other
identifiable plant or flower that anyone would intentionally
attempt to grow. The place looked like the experimental
laboratory of some mad allergist.

I shrugged it off and went up the two concrete steps to the
back door and tried it. It was locked, but the door was old and
flimsy with a lot of clearance between the lock and jamb, and
my plastic library card opened it easily.

The kitchen, too, was pervaded by the smell of decaying
organic matter; this time, food. The cupboard doors were all
open, which I thought a bit strange, and I located the source
of the smell behind one of them, under the sink. The plastic
wastebasket there was filled to the brim with rotten vegeta-
bles, chicken bones, and foil trays that contained the remains
of partially eaten frozen dinners.

Some dirty glasses stood on the countertop by the sink, one
of them with a smudge of lipstick on the rim. There were
more nonmatching glasses in the cupboards, along with some
plastic plates and boxes of dry foodstuffs. I went through the
open door that led into the living room and stopped, my
stomach tightening into a small, hard knot.

It had snowed in the room. The snow was the stuffing from
the cushions and backs of the two old easy chairs and couch,
which had been sliced open and gutted. The Uwara was still
in my pocket, but not for long.

The twilight that filtered weakly through the gauzy curtain
inner-liners across the windows seemed to thicken as I listened
to the house for a noise, any noise, to tell me that whoever had
done this was still around. There was none. I tried not to add
too much to the silence as I moved slowly through the room.

The man who stepped out of the hallway hadn't added
much to it, either. He was short and thin, with a narrow
swarthy face, shiny black hair, and a mustache so thin that it
looked as if it had been drawn on with an auditor's point pen.
He had a long, narrow nose and two small black chinks for

eyes and a large black mole on his right cheek. He wore an inexpensive tan suit, a white shirt, and a wrinkled green tie.

We stood for a moment staring at each other, and then he asked in a thick Middle Eastern accent, "Who are you?"

"I was about to ask you the same question."

"I'm looking for the people who live in this house."

"Ditto."

His dark eyebrows knitted together. "Pardon me?"

"So am I."

"You are friends of theirs?"

"Never met them in my life," I said. I waved at the room. "What did you think, they were hiding in the couch?"

Again, his look became uncomprehending. "I do not . . ." Then it hit him and he shook his head. "I had nothing to do with this."

"Uh-huh."

"The place was like this when I entered."

"How *did* you enter, anyway?"

He gave a slight bow and smiled whitely. "If you will excuse me, I will be going. Nobody seems to be at home."

He started to move forward, but I put up my left hand and hefted the Uwara in my other, making sure he noticed it. "I think maybe you'd better stick around."

"What is that in your hand?" he asked curiously.

"It's called a Uwara stick. It's good for breaking bones. If you don't want any of yours broken, just stand there."

I spotted the phone on a stand by the couch and went over to it. As I lifted the receiver, he asked, "Who are you calling?"

"The police."

His smile grew friendlier. "That will not be necessary." He reached into his jacket. "I will show you who I am and then you will understand."

The wallet he came out with looked a lot like a gun. A small, short-barreled automatic, a .32 or maybe a .25. Bores tend to look bigger when you're staring into them. "You will put the phone down, please, and put that stick down, also."

I complied with both requests.

"Put your hands on your head, please, and turn around."

"What are you going to do?" My voice was a high-strung twang.

"I am not going to harm you, don't worry." He stepped up

behind me and kept the gun barrel pressed in my back as he patted me down.

I thought about what Sam Spade would have done in this situation. Drop his elbow and spin to the right, at the same time smashing a hand down on the pistol. Easy. I rehearsed the moves in my mind three or four times, then stood very still. Psychologists who advocate "Knowing yourself" should point a gun at their patients. The pointee becomes very intimate with himself at that instant in time. Everything becomes focused and immediate, nobody else's opinions matter, and one becomes very inner-directed. At that moment I *knew* without a doubt that I was not Sam Spade. He lifted my wallet from my breast pocket and the gun went away.

"Look, buddy, take the money, but I'd appreciate it if you left the I.D. That stuff is a pain in the ass to replace—"

"I have no intention of taking your money," he said indignantly. "I am no thief. You are a private detective?"

"Yeah."

"You may turn around." I did, and he asked, "Who are you working for?"

"Nobody right now."

"What are you doing here?"

"Looking for a friend. Dave Bick. You know him?"

"No. Why are you looking for him here?"

"It seemed as good a place as any."

"That is a joke?"

"No."

He looked confused. He glanced at the stainless-steel watch on his wrist and waved the gun away from the front door. "You will stand over there, please, and keep your hands on your head."

I took three giant steps toward the kitchen to give him a wide berth, and he moved cautiously to the front door, keeping the gun on me. "Do not try to follow me."

"I wouldn't think of it."

He put his hand on the door handle. "Just remain inside."

"Sure, Abdul."

He opened the door and went out, closing it behind him, and I let out the breath I was holding. I went to the window and pulled back the sheer inner-liner. He was walking briskly up the block, then passed out of sight. I grabbed my wallet and Uwara and went outside, but by the time I hit the sidewalk he was nowhere. I went back inside to finish what I'd come there for.

The place hadn't been much before it had been operated on. The walls were the color of unhealthy flesh and adorned with Penny Saver seascape prints; the beige, hi-lo carpeting that showed through the snow was soiled and threadbare. I was almost across the room when my eye was caught by one area more badly soiled than the rest. I bent down and pushed aside the stuffing to get a better look.

The stain was a dark circle with a two-foot diameter that someone had unsuccessfully tried to wipe away. I could still smell the solvent. Blood is a bitch to clean up, especially after it has had some time to soak in, which it looked like this had. I touched it. It was dry and crystalline, probably several days old. The big question was who and where the donor was. If he or she was still alive he had to be in bad shape, considering the size of the stain.

I snicked on my flash and ran the beam slowly over the area. It landed on the end of a cylindrical object protruding from beneath the couch and I duck-walked the two steps over to take a look. I used a ball-point pen to ease the object from beneath the skirt of the couch.

It was an empty plastic bottle of Schilling meat tenderizer. Maybe the blood on the floor was from a steer that had been slaughtered in the living room and prepared for a barbeque, but somehow I doubted it. All sorts of thoughts crowded my mind, none of them nice. A lot of them had to do with Bick.

I left the bottle there and stood up. A breeze stirred the curtain liners, throwing gossamer shadows across the floor. The patterns reminded me of the quiverings of a spider's web when disturbed by a trapped fly. Since flies and I were both persistent pests, I threw myself into the role, and went down the hallway to the single bedroom.

A similar job had been done there. The mattress on the queen-size bed had been pulled off and disemboweled, the box spring cut open, its skeleton exposed. The drawers of the two scarred maple end tables were open and empty, as were those of the flimsy maple dresser against the wall.

The closet had been cleaned out, and so had the adjoining bathroom, except for some long, dark hairs in the sink and dirty bathtub. The pink plastic wastebasket beside the toilet was filled with trash. I closed the bathroom door and turned on the light, then set the wastebasket on the closed lid of the toilet. It may not live up to the public's romantic ideas of detective work, but cases are broken by garbage all the time. An intensive search of the basket produced two tampon wrappers, six used Q-Tips, one discarded toilet-paper roll, and an unknown number of used tissues.

I went back out through the rapidly darkening gloom of the living room to the back door. I eyed the stinking garbage under the sink and immediately put the thought from my mind. As I stepped outside, a noise made me flick on my flash and wave it toward the back fence. The beam caught the green eyes of the black cat, who had returned and was crouched over a dirt clearing in the weeds.

The cat froze in the light, its startled eyes wide, then its ears went back and it opened its mouth and hissed a territorial warning. Undaunted, I moved toward it, and it turned suddenly and slithered through its escape hatch in the fence. The cat's reaction made me curious, and I went over to see what the attraction was that had brought it back.

The territory the cat had reluctantly relinquished was a slightly elevated mound of loosely packed earth, about five feet by four feet and darker than the surrounding dirt. The humus smell was particularly strong there, and it tried to smother the other smell, but could not completely. It was still there, disguised, but distinct. I moved the flash slowly over the mound and then saw the prize the cat had been guarding so jealously. Poking out of the mixture of earth and mulch were two blue-white fingers, chewed almost to the bone.

# THIRTEEN

I watched apprehensively as the jump-suited forensics team dug a wide pit around the body, then carefully cleared the remaining dirt away with gloved hands to make sure a shovel did not accidentally puncture the corpse and confuse the autopsy findings. When they had finished, the body was resting on a pedestal of earth surrounded by a moat three feet deep. I didn't envy them their work; the smell was bad enough from ten feet away.

The body lay on its side, doubled up, the hands tied by rope behind the back. It was fully clothed in a T-shirt, jeans, and running shoes. The face was a bloated lump of ground chuck and the maggots were busy working on the cheeks, which had been flayed to the bone. The end of a filthy rag hung out of the open mouth and there was a small, neat hole in the middle of his forehead.

"Papadoupoulous," I said, letting out a long breath. At least it wasn't Bick.

"The guy you say you were tailing for this"—Hyde paused to consult his notes—"Saffarian?"

"Right."

He was tall and less than thirty, heavy-set, with black wavy
hair and a black mustache. His face was round with pudgy,
baby-fat cheeks, but that was the only thing babyish about it;
the scrapbook containing memories of those carefree days of
innocence and irresponsibility had long ago been put away
and had accumulated a thick layer of dust. The expression was
blank, the eyes were boarded up and padlocked, the mouth
was a tightly compressed line. It was the face I'd seen on a lot
of cops who had donned heavy armor in preparation for
combat, and who had worn it so long they slept in it.

Hyde's partner, a leanly built jock type with short brown
hair named Gamble, came up and looked at the body. "Jesus."

"Yeah," Hyde said. "Whoever killed him really did a
number on him first." We moved back toward the driveway to
get away from the smell, but I still had to breath through my
mouth. "You talk to the woman next door?" he asked Gamble.

"Yeah. She didn't want to let me in at first. Thought I was
from social services." He shook his head in disgust. "The place
is a fucking pigsty. I don't know how parents could leave their
kids in a place like that."

"That's somebody else's problem," Hyde said impatiently.
"What did she say?"

Gamble shrugged. "She pretty much confirms his story.
Said he came by about three, asking questions. I called the
station, too. He called dispatch on the sixth and said he would
be house-sitting the address."

Hyde scratched his head, puzzled. "One thing I still don't
get. If the woman told you Papadoupoulous and the girl had
moved out, why did you come back?"

I'd already explained it to him twice. I figured the story was
good for at least two more tellings before he got as tired of
hearing it as I was telling it. I took a deep breath and said, "I
told you, I thought she might have been mistaken."

Hyde glanced at his notes. "You went to the front door and
rang the bell."

"That's right."

"So then you went around back and broke in—"

I sighed in exasperation. "I went around back and knocked.
The door was ajar, so I pushed it open and went in."

"Right," he said doubtfully. He wasn't buying it, but there

was nothing he could do about it and we both knew it. "Tell me about this Arab again."

"I've already told you everything I know. Anyway, I'm not even sure he was an Arab. He was dark and had Semitic features, but for all I know he could have been Israeli. Or a Turk. Or Iranian."

"He didn't say why he was looking for Papadoupoulous?"

"He didn't even say he was looking for Papadoupoulous. He said he was looking for the people who lived in the house. He never said a name. Anyway, I doubt he did this."

Hyde raised an eyebrow. "Why?"

I shrugged. "Because this man was obviously buried more than an hour ago. And killers only return to the scene of the crime in the movies."

"Maybe he came back to look for something."

"Why didn't he look for it when he killed him?"

He either didn't have an answer or didn't feel like sharing it with me. Both cops transferred their attention to the tall, lean man coming down the driveway carrying a large black attaché case. The man had brush-cut gray hair and a neatly trimmed gray mustache under a prominent Teutonic nose. Unlike the two Santa Monica cops, who looked uncomfortable in their suits and ties, he looked at ease in his neatly pressed charcoal-gray suit, crisp white shirt, and gray and pink striped tie.

"Voss," Gamble said. "How's business?"

"Dead," came the inevitable answer. "Where's the stiff?"

Hyde jerked a thumb behind him. "Over there, ready and waiting."

"Since when do you work the night shift, Voss?" Gamble asked.

"I don't. I was on my way home when the call came in. We're short of men and it was on my way, so I told them I'd take it. These fucking budget cuts are killing us."

Gamble grinned and winked at Hyde. "Hey, Voss, you know why they buried Liberace with his ass sticking out of the ground?"

Voss' eyes rolled skyward and he sighed with forbearance. "No, why?"

"So his friends could come over for a cold one." Gamble got off a good belly-laugh at his own joke.

"Funny," Voss said again, not cracking a smile. "You guys

might have nothing to do but stand around and crack jokes all night, but I have places to go, things to do, and people to see."

"*Dead* people." As Voss walked over to greet the forensics crew, Gamble said to Hyde, "That guy is one strange duck. You know he raises roses as a hobby? Wins all sorts of flower shows with them. He told me once his secret is that he uses human blood for fertilizer. He has the docs save it from the autopsies and he takes it home in jars."

The coroner's investigator began pulling on a jump suit and surgical gloves. Hyde said, "Let's get back to what you know about Papadoupoulous."

"I don't know much."

"You knew he was Greek."

"I was *told* he was Greek."

"By this Saffarian."

"Right."

"You say he went back to Turkey?"

"That's what he told me he was going to do."

He turned to Gamble. "Check the Holiday Inn, just in case."

Gamble nodded and went into the house.

Hyde turned back to me. "While you were watching the house, did you see anybody visit except for this Justin Fox?"

"No."

"You say the guy was having an affair with Papadoupoulous's girlfriend?"

"That's what it looked like."

He rubbed his chin. "Maybe they had a little confrontation about it and things got out of hand—"

I shook my head. "This wasn't any crime of passion. The man was tortured. And why would they tear up the place?"

"You say this Fox was busted once for sales. Maybe he and Papadoupoulous were in a dope deal together and Papadoupoulous ripped him off. Where does your friend Bick fit into this?"

"I wish I knew," I said truthfully.

I considered telling him about the potsherd, but it wasn't likely that that would have had anything to do with murder. Not if Gros had been telling the truth about it.

Gamble came out the back door and said: "Saffarian checked out four days ago, just like he said."

Voss instructed the forensics crew to make sure they transported the body to the Forensics Science Center in the position it lay. While they bagged the body and carefully worked wooden planks underneath it to lift it from its resting place, he packed up his samples, snapped the lid of the attaché case shut, and walked over to us, holding a large manila envelope. "Got a wallet here."

"Let's see," Hyde said.

Voss opened the envelope and dropped the wallet out into a surgical-gloved hand. He went through it. There were twenty dollars in ones and fives, some credit cards and an international driver's license made out to Dimitrios Papadoupoulous, and in one of the plastic picture slots, a small color snapshot of three people standing together, smiling happily in the sunshine. I leaned forward for a better look.

In the picture, Papadoupoulous, Naci, and Fox stood in front of an ornate metal railing of a bridge. Behind the bridge was a dark blue body of water, and in the distance beyond, a city. Whatever city it was, one thing was for sure: it wasn't L.A. The skyline was delineated by domes and needlelike minarets.

"It looks like they were all friends before they got to the States," I said.

"Where was this taken?" Hyde asked.

"I'm not sure," I replied. "Could be Istanbul."

He pondered that, then dropped the wallet back into the investigator's envelope. "When you get through with that, send it over. How about a cause of death?"

"Most probable cause is gunshot," Voss said. "There's a small caliber bullet hole in his head. He could have died from shock before that, though. Whoever did it sliced up his face pretty good." His brow furrowed. "Looks like they used some sort of chemical, too. The skin is strange, almost like mush."

"Meat tenderizer," Hyde said. "We found an empty jar of it in the living room."

The trouble in Voss's face cleared. "That'd do it."

"I read about a case in New York where the KGB did that to a guy," Gamble said.

"We got enough to worry about without bringing the fucking KGB into it," Hyde snapped, then turned back to Voss. "Can you give us a time of death?"

Voss shook his head. "The rate of decomposition varies greatly with buried bodies. Since he was buried in humus, I wouldn't even venture a guess. Rigor has gone, which means he died at least thirty-four hours ago. I've taken a liver temperature, as well as a soil temperature. Even after the autopsy, unless you can give us an exact time for his last meal, it's doubtful we can give you any more than an approximation."

"Why would they bury him in fertilizer?" I asked.

Voss shrugged. "Maybe they were growing something there and had already dug up the area. The ground around that pit is pretty hard. If they were in a hurry to plant the body, which they probably were, that could have been the easiest place to dig."

Gamble couldn't pass that up. "I'll bet roses would grow real good there now," he said, winking at Hyde.

Hyde seemed oblivious. He said to Voss, "There's a lot of blood in the living room. That's where we figure he got it."

Voss checked his watch and sighed. "I'll take a look."

Hyde said, "Okay, Asch. Go on home. We'll be in touch."

"I've got to scoot, too," Voss said. "My wife fixed a special dinner and I'm already late."

Gamble smirked and asked, "What is it, brains?"

"Nothing gourmet," the coroner's investigator said, shaking his head. "Just a little colon tartare."

Gamble's smirk faded and his face turned ashen. Voss turned and whistled happily as he went into the house.

# FOURTEEN

I woke up the next morning with the whirlies, courtesy of the three strong vodka see-throughs I'd downed in rapid succession last night on my return home. After a pot of coffee and a hot shower, the ride had slowed down enough for me to let go of the couch and pick up the phone.

Locating Arbogast was a simple matter of legwork, or perhaps I should say fingerwork; I let them do the walking. I started with the L.A. Central Yellow Pages and worked west, toward Beverly Hills. Two and a half hours and forty-seven phone calls later, I scored. He was staying at the Beverly Wilshire, which was a bit of a surprise. The Beverly Wilshire didn't share the show-biz glitz-and-glamour reputation of its cross-town competition, the Beverly Hills Hotel. It catered to an older, more sedate crowd, but it was just as overpriced, its room rates starting at $275 a night. Which meant that either Arbogast had another source of income, or archaeologists made a hell of a lot more than I thought they did.

I called Gros's extension at the County Museum, but his secretary told me he had not come in yet. I left my number and had her transfer me to Heather Piccard's line. Another woman picked up and said Ms. Piccard was not in her office, but was in the building somewhere, and suggested I call back.

After trying Bick and getting the same old story, I sat down on the couch with a cold beer and turned on the tube. When I landed on *Mid Morning L.A.* I stopped flipping the channels.

Seated opposite the host was a study in contrasts—Garrett Bronson, the young, slick-haired yuppie Santa Monica city attorney, and goateed and long-haired Lyle Cummings, organizer and mayor of Tent City, looking particularly scruffy this morning in a dirty stocking cap and soiled gray sweatshirt.

"How do you reconcile your public pronouncement yesterday," the host was asking Bronson, "that you would not enforce Santa Monica's vagrancy statutes against the homeless with your responsibilities as the city's chief legal representative?"

"He can't, you putz," I said out loud.

He was obviously going to try, though. Bronson smoothed down his already smoothed hair, and said: "The issue here is not vagrancy. The issue is social justice as well as the public welfare. These people have been victimized enough. It would not serve the public interest to waste police manpower and logjam the courts, which are already overburdened, to prosecute them."

The host turned to Cummings. "What is your reaction to that, Mr. Cummings?"

Cummings tugged on his goatee. "I applaud Mr. Bronson's decision. This, however, is just a beginning. The homeless of this country need more than inaction on the part of the police. They need positive action. They need housing, food, clothing, medical care—"

The speech was interrupted by the phone. I snatched it up. "Mr. Asch, this is Pieter Gros. You called?"

"Are you going to be around this morning?"

"Yes, why?"

"There has been a development I'd like to discuss with you and Ms. Piccard as soon as possible."

"Is something the matter?"

"As a matter of fact, yes."

"What is it?"

"I'd rather not discuss it over the phone."

"Very well," he said, sounding a bit peeved. "It's a little after eleven now. Say about noon?"

I said that would be fine, and rang off. Bronson was talking again and I turned off the set before I could hear what he was saying and got too mad. For all his bleeding-heart pronouncements, I didn't hear the man offering to relocate Tent City to Santa Monica beach. The more I thought of that idea, the more appropriate I thought it was. If these people truly wanted to get the public's attention, this could be the way to do it. Tent City could be the new rallying symbol for Santa Monica's liberal-minded city council. Jane Fonda could do an inspirational exercise tape with the residents of Tent City and donate the profits to the homeless. This could be the first destitute group to have its own personal physical fitness trainer. Only in L.A.

On the way to the museum, I stopped by a paper stand and grabbed a copy of the *Chronicle*. Papadoupoulous's murder had been relegated to the second page of the Metro section. It said that Santa Monica police detectives had discovered the body of a thirty-year-old man buried in a fertilizer pit in the backyard of a residence on Second Street in Santa Monica last night. According to Det. John Hyde, the cause of death had not yet been determined, although "foul play was suspected." That was what I called playing it safe.

Hyde went on to say that the identity of the man, who had apparently been dead for several days, had not been positively determined, although it was believed that he was a foreign national, perhaps Greek or Turkish. Wanted for questioning was the dead man's female companion, who had also been living at the rented house and who was now missing. Neighbors knew little about the "mystery couple" except that they had moved into the house two months ago, were "quiet," and "kept to themselves pretty much." The girl was described as small, early twenties, with long black hair and a dark complexion. There was no mention of me in the article, which was okay by me. That kind of spotlight I didn't need.

Gros and Heather Piccard were in his upstairs office when I came in. He was meticulously dressed, as usual, this time in a navy-blue pin-striped suit with a pink shirt and a gray silk tie. Heather Piccard, who was seated in one of the chairs, wore a mocha-colored dress cinched with a wide, white belt, and an emerald-green scarf knotted loosely and draped over her right shoulder. Gros stood behind the desk and after the obligatory greetings, told me to sit down.

The office was quite a bit larger, and considerably more plush, than Heather Piccard's. The dark green carpet was thicker, the chairs and sofa were covered in soft brown leather, the top of the large mahogany desk was polished to a mirrorlike sheen, and the framed paintings on the walls were original oils, not posters of museum exhibits.

Gros steepled his fingers in front of his mouth. "So what is so important that it could not be discussed on the telephone?"

Tap-dancing time was over. I handed him the newspaper folded over to the article about the murder. He read it impassively and said, "So?"

"That 'unidentified foreign national' is Papadoupoulous."

Gros bit his lip. "How do you know?"

"Because I'm the one who found him. I went over there last night after I left here. Somebody shot him and buried him."

"Papadoupoulous was *murdered*?" Heather Piccard gasped.

"That's right. Whoever did it was looking for something. The house was torn apart."

"Do the police have any idea who did it?" Heather Piccard asked.

"Ideas, but that's about all. They're looking for Naci Saffarian and Justin Fox, the man I asked you about."

Gros looked troubled. "Did you tell the police about Papadoupoulous contacting us, or about the potsherd?"

"No. I wanted to talk to you first."

He nodded relievedly. "Good."

"I'm going to have to, though."

His forehead pleated. "Why?"

"This is a homicide investigation, Dr. Gros. If I withheld information, it would be considered misprision of a felony. At the least, I could lose my license. At the worst, I could go to jail."

He turned up his hands. "What information? The police are looking for this Fox and Papadoupoulous's girlfriend. We don't know where they are and, as I've told you, it isn't likely that they will attempt to contact us again. If they do, I would certainly inform the police."

"What if they didn't do it?" I asked. "What if Papadoupoulous's death had to do with the forgeries they were trying to peddle?"

"Why would anybody kill him over some worthless pieces of clay?"

"Maybe the murderer didn't know the stuff was worthless."

Gros shook his head. "If they had been real, the items Papadoupoulous had described would have commanded a moderate price, but solely for their archaeological interest, not from any intrinsic value. The only buyers who would have been interested in purchasing them would have been a few individual collectors, or an institution like the museum, and we don't kill to make acquisitions."

I didn't say anything, but looked at Heather Piccard, who frowned worriedly and looked away.

Gros must have interpreted my silence as reluctance, because he sighed and said, "The truth of the matter is that police prying into the museum's business affairs at this time could seriously jeopardize certain current negotiations on which I have worked very hard for the past year. A very wealthy collector has been considering donating his entire collection to the museum. We have gotten board approval for a new wing to house it, and he is going over the plans right now. The man has been running hot and cold, between giving us the collection and building his own museum to house it. All he would have to hear is a hint that the museum is being investigated in connection with a murder, and his mind would be made up."

"Why, if the museum is not involved? Anyway, there's no reason he should hear about it. The police are usually pretty discreet about these things."

He shook his head grimly. "I'm afraid your trust in the police is greater than mine. I can't take a chance of a leak at this stage. It could ruin a year's work. It would be different if we had information that would help them, but we don't." He hesitated and asked in a tone that sounded slightly officious, "Aren't the disclosures of your clients considered to be privileged information?"

It was my turn to look amused. "That's only in the movies, Dr. Gros. A private detective is not a doctor or a lawyer. Anyway, you aren't my client anymore."

His look turned quizzical. "What do you mean?"

"You paid me and I found Arbogast. The job is over."

He came forward in his chair. "Where is he?"

"The Beverly Wilshire, room ten-oh-two."

"The Beverly Wilshire?" he asked, surprised.

"Yeah," I said, nodding. "Pretty ritzy for a professor of archaeology."

"He has to have a sponsor," he muttered to himself, then his eyes turned shrewd. "What if the museum was still your client? Would you feel more of an obligation to protect its interests?"

"You mean by not telling the police about Ms. Piccard's meeting with Papadoupoulous?"

"Not just that, but if it came down to it . . ." He didn't finish.

I thought about it and shrugged. "It probably wouldn't make any difference to the cops, but it would to me." That must have sounded pretty bad, as if I could be bought. Sounding bad was sometimes the price you paid for being honest.

Gros pulled a checkbook out of the middle drawer of his desk, scribbled in it, ripped out a check, and handed it to me. It was made out to me, in the amount of two thousand dollars. "What's this for?"

"It isn't a bribe, if that's what you're thinking," he said. "I want you to find out who Arbogast is dealing with besides us."

Heather Piccard came forward in her chair. "Are you sure you want to do that, Pieter?"

He scowled at her imperiously. "If we're going to be in a bidding war, I want to know who we're bidding against." He turned back to me. "How about it, Mr. Asch?"

I looked past him, out the window. His office looked down on the La Brea Tar Pits, the natural oil pit where mastodons and saber-tooth cats had once come for a drink of water, only to unwittingly wind up getting caught and sinking into the oozing, black mire. I knew just how they must have felt. I had a nagging suspicion I was soon going to be reliving prehistory. "As long as you understand that I have to be able to use my own judgment when dealing with the police."

He smiled. "Certainly. As I told you before, Mr. Asch, I trust your discretion." He rose. "You are doing me and the community a great service. After all, the museum exists for the cultural enrichment of all the people. What helps the museum, helps the entire community."

"Sort of like General Motors," I observed.

He looked puzzled. "Pardon me?"

"'What's good for General Motors is good for the country.' Do you know who said that?"

He frowned. "No."

"I don't either," I said. "But I'd lay two to one that it was the president of General Motors."

I said good-bye and Heather Piccard showed me out. As we stepped into the elevator, I asked her, "Did you want to say something to me?"

She blinked. "Like what?"

"I don't know. It just seemed as if you wanted to say something in there."

She considered it, then looked down self-consciously. "No." The elevator doors opened and she smiled coldly as I said good-bye. I was getting used to that look from her.

# FIFTEEN

The Beverly Wilshire Hotel had long been suffering from a bad case of split personality. One of its buildings had the look and ambience of an old luxury hotel, with muted lighting and red carpets and dark wood paneling on the walls, while its twin across the mutually shared driveway was all bright chandeliers and marble and glass and cold hard surfaces. For the past two years, the old wing had been shut down for renovation, to bring it into line with its more modern counterpart, but the hotel management didn't seem to be in any hurry to make that happen. Frankly, neither was I. I was a sucker for nostalgia.

I went through the cold and sterile lobby to the elevators and rode up to the tenth floor. The door of 1002 was opened by a short, soft-looking man in a summer undershirt and baggy slacks. He was fifty or so, with ruddy, mottled face and wavy brown-gray hair that was receding, like a monk's, from his wide forehead. He had a short, wide nose and a thin, straight mouth like the slash of a pen. The questioning look in his brown eyes was magnified by the thick lenses of his dark-rimmed glasses. "Yes?"

I tried to look confused. "Is this Phil Levine's room?"

"No."

"I'm terribly sorry," I said, backing away in embarrassment. "I must have the wrong room."

"That's all right," he said in a preoccupied tone, and closed the door.

I went back downstairs and found a men's room. In one of the toilet stalls I took off the glasses and fake mustache I'd been wearing, combed the part out of my hair, and took off my sports jacket. I carried the jacket out into the gift shop adjacent to the lobby, where I bought a *Discover*, thinking I might as well learn something while I waited.

I sat on a settee across from the elevators and cracked the magazine. An hour later I'd learned that the Big Bang might never have happened, and that while lactating, female prairie dogs—cute, playful, cuddly prairie dogs—often cannibalized the babies of their kin. After I read that, I put the magazine down, not wanting to run the risk of further disillusionment. I was cynical enough; I didn't need any more unpleasant surprises in my life at the moment.

A little after five Arbogast stepped out of the elevator and headed for the doors that led out to the valet parking area. He crossed the driveway to the cashier's booth and handed the man his parking stub. Not wanting him to get too much of a jump on me, I edged by him and did the same. Arbogast didn't seem to notice me. Jacob Asch, master of disguise.

I paid the cashier two bucks and stood behind Arbogast, who fidgeted as he waited on the curb. A new gray Olds Cutlass roared up the ramp to the underground lot and squealed to a stop and a young, pimply faced attendant hopped out. Arbogast slipped something into his hand, but whatever it was, the kid didn't look too impressed. Arbogast drove carefully out of the driveway and turned left, heading toward Wilshire.

It was my turn to fidget. After what seemed like half an hour, my Mustang came up the ramp and I stuffed a buck into the hand of the attendant, jumped in, and peeled out. Fortunately, the light at Wilshire had been red. It changed and Arbogast turned left. I gunned it and sailed through the light just as it turned yellow.

Traffic on Wilshire was heavy. The Cutlass passed over the

old Santa Monica railroad tracks, then, at Whittier Drive, on
the western edge of Beverly Hills, made a right. The street
skirted the eucalyptus-lined border of the Los Angeles Country Club on one side and million-dollar homes fronted by
perfectly manicured front lawns on the other, up to Sunset,
where Arbogast made another left.

I kept my distance as we wound through the hills, past
more big houses sitting in beds of ivy, past lonely-looking
roadside vendors selling maps of the movie stars' homes, past
the sprawling UCLA campus. The road dipped, and he
signaled right and drove through the gated entrance to Bel
Air.

He took a series of lefts and rights onto narrow, twisted
streets, and I had to close the gap between us to make sure I
didn't lose him. The homes that graced the hills here were not
ordinary houses but estates fronted by fifteen-foot walls and
dense foliage. The occasional glimpse one could get of them
through the wrought-iron gates across the driveways made the
houses in Beverly Hills look pauperish by comparison. Arbogast turned into the driveway of one and honked his horn and
waited for the gates to open. I drove on by to the top of the hill
and turned around. When I drove by the house, the ornamen-
tal iron gates were closed and the Cutlass was nowhere to be
seen.

The house was not visible from the street, hidden by the
wall and the tops of tall oak trees. Closed-circuit television
cameras were mounted on the brick wall on each side of the
driveway. I pulled over to the curb across the street, out of the
camera's range, and killed my engine. I jotted down the
address of the house and sat back to wait.

I didn't get to wait long. Ten minutes later, the gates
opened and a new black Mark VII pulled out onto the street.
It pulled up behind me and stopped, and I watched in the
rear-view mirror as two men stepped out. They were both
dressed in dark suits, both in their late thirties and clean-cut.
So clean, in fact, they were almost sterile.

They came up alongside my car and bent down to take a
good look at my face. I reciprocated and took a good look at
theirs. The one on my side had a square jaw and taut skin and
short brown hair. His brown eyes were deep set and expressionless. He looked like the type who would have lettered in

every sport in school and would have been lauded for his "leadership abilities," but whose intelligence was suspect, and was definitely on the unimaginative side. The type perfectly geared for a position in government—Secret Service or CIA. The other one was heavier, with a wide, crew-cut head and pale eyes and a dimple in his chin the size of a thimble. If the intelligence of the one was suspect, this guy's wasn't. There wasn't any reason to suspect that he had any.

"You having some sort of problem?" the one on my side asked.

"Me?" I asked, wide-eyed.

"You."

"You mean aside from not being able to get a girl?"

"You trying to be funny?" dimple-chin asked in a pronounced Texas accent.

"Not me."

"What are you doing here?" the one on my side asked.

I smiled ingenuously. "Waiting for Burt and Loni."

He looked at me strangely. "Burt who?"

"Reynolds." I pointed at the house across from the gates through which they had come. "According to the Map of the Stars, he lives here. I figured if I stayed here long enough, I could maybe get a glimpse of him and Loni—"

His expression didn't change. He said to Dimple-chin: "I think you're right, Leroy. I think he's trying to be funny."

Leroy. It figured. "Honest, I'm not—"

Leroy held out his hand. "Let's see the map."

I said sheepishly: "Well, I didn't really *buy* one. I wasn't really interested in any of the other stars, just Burt and Loni, so I couldn't see the point of spending a whole two bucks for it. The guy selling them was real nice about it, though. He gave me the address."

"Well, he screwed you, pal," Mr. CIA said. "So you can buzz on out of here."

I looked at him, shocked. "You mean Burt and Loni don't live here?"

"That's just what I mean."

"Who does?"

"Somebody who doesn't like people hanging around outside his house."

"It's a free country," I said indignantly. "This is a public street—"

"That's right, it is," he said, then pointed up to the sign ten feet away. "And this is a no-parking zone. So shove off."

He started to walk back to his car and I called out, "Would you happen to know where Burt and Loni *do* live?"

"Sure," he called back. "In Beverly Hills, Six-twelve Roxbury Drive."

"Thanks a lot," I said enthusiastically, and drove away. If he wasn't an ex-government man, somebody somewhere had screwed up on his recruiting duties. The guy was perfect. He had just enough imagination to be a decent liar.

# SIXTEEN

The answering service had three messages for me when I returned home, one from Tony Bruenig, the other two from a Det. Louis Janneck with Sheriff's Homicide. Both of them said it was important and both of them wanted me to call them back at the first opportunity. I tried Bruenig first, but the detective who answered the phone said he had gone home for the day. I left word that I'd called back and tried the number Janneck had left with the service.

I apprehensively listened to it ring. I knew that both calls were related to each other, that they both involved Bick. A raspy voice answered, "Homicide, Janneck."

The voice sounded vaguely familiar, but I couldn't quite place it. "This is Jacob Asch, Detective Janneck. You called me?"

"Right. You probably don't remember me, but I met you a couple of times with Al Herrera." He must have heard the cards flipping in my mental Rolodex because he jumped in to help me out. "Louie the Hat."

That stopped me on the right card.

Louie the Hat was one of the old-timers with the Sheriff's

Department, one of the few who could tell you what the mean streets of L.A. had been like in the fifties, when Mickey Cohen and Joe Sica were something other than barely recognizable names in those terminally boring histories of organized crime that someone for some reason writes at least once a year. We had met half a dozen years ago through Al Herrera, a long-time personal friend of mine who also happened to be a robbery-homicide lieutenant with LASO, and since that time I'd run into Louie several times, usually when I'd been with Al, lunching in one of the downtown eateries frequented by the local constabulary. My feeling of trepidation eased somewhat. "Sure, Louie. What can I do for you?"

"Do you know an Ekrem Deveci?"

I did a quick mental inventory and came up with zilch. "No."

"How about a Kemal Alkim?"

"Sorry."

"Garo Saffarian?"

"Yeah."

"What was your relationship with Mr. Saffarian?"

"I did some work for him."

"When?"

"A few days ago."

"What were you doing for him?"

"Keeping an eye on his daughter," I said. "She was a runaway and he was worried about her. What's this about, anyway?"

He ignored my question. "You're no longer working for Mr. Saffarian?"

The feelings of disquietude were starting to return. "No. He had to go back to Turkey."

"When was that?"

"Four days ago."

"You haven't seen him since?"

"How could I?" I asked. "He's in Turkey—"

"That's something you might be able to help us clear up," he said matter-of-factly. "Can you meet me down at the Forensic Science Center?"

"What for?"

"To tell us if the stiff on the gurney upstairs is Garo Saffarian."

# SEVENTEEN

Louie the Hat claimed to have 150 hats, and not one of them looked good on him.

Some of his co-workers on the force conjectured that the source of his sombreral passion was the fact that he was bald as an egg, but Al had told me that Louie wasn't embarrassed in the least by his baldness, that he just simply loved hats. The one he had on today was a green felt Alpine-climber's affair, with a brush stuck on the side. To complete the ensemble, he wore a dark green mohair sports jacket over a crisp white shirt, brown slacks, and a matching brown tie.

He was a small-boned, wispy man with a thin, liver-spotted face and intensely blue eyes that seemed devoid of duplicity. He looked fifty-five, but he had looked fifty-five when I'd first met him, and I wouldn't doubt if he'd looked fifty-five when he was twenty. At least the shock of aging was over for him; he'd had plenty of time to get psychologically adjusted to it.

Louie introduced me to his partner, Leonard Rothko, a heavy-set, middle-aged, ruddy-faced man in a brown polyester suit that had gone out of style about the time someone was composing the tunes for *Hair*. After exchanging the customary "goodtomeetyous" with Rothko, we went to the elevator.

While we waited for its arrival, I asked Louie, "Talk to Al lately?"

"Not for a few weeks. I don't see him much anymore, since I transferred to West Hollywood."

"When did that happen?"

"A year and a half ago. I requested it. It's closer to home and a hell of a lot quieter than downtown. After thirty years I don't need any sudden rushes of adrenaline. In West Hollywood it's mostly junkie ODs, an occasional fag killing. I don't have to worry about some gang punk opening up on me with an Uzi. At my age, I wouldn't be able to move fast enough to get out of the way."

"Actually, I'm surprised you aren't retired by now."

"The wife and I have been talking about it. She wants to travel. Actually, that's one of my dreams, to go around the world and bring back a hat from every country."

"Just what you need," Rothko inserted. "Another fucking hat."

"You can make fun of my hats all you like," Louie told him deadpan, "but I got news for you: if Aeschylus would have worn a hat, he would have lived to write a hell of a lot more plays."

"The Greek dramatist?" I asked, curious where he was going to go with that.

"That's right," Louie said. "He died because he wasn't wearing a hat. An eagle picked up a turtle and was flying around looking for a place to smash its shell. It spied Aeschylus and mistook his bald head for a rock and let go. That was it for old Aeschylus. If he'd been wearing a hat, the eagle never would have made the mistake and who knows what he would have accomplished?"

"You're bullshitting me, right?" Rothko asked uncertainly.

"Look it up," Louie said confidently.

The other cop just shook his head. He knew better than to question Louie about the history of hats, or the lack thereof. I wondered where I would look that up if I wanted to. I wondered if there was a book on ancient Greek trivia. I wondered if there was such a thing as ancient Greek trivia. To the ancient Greeks, *nothing* Greek was trivial.

After wondering all that, I wondered out loud where Saffarian had been found.

"At the Mondrian Hotel, on the Sunset Strip," Louie said. "Room seven-nine-eight. A maid discovered the body at ten this morning when she went to clean the room. He was lying on the floor by the bed in a lot of blood. She ran next door and called downstairs and they called us. The day clerk at the desk identified the dead man as the guest who had been staying in the room for the past two nights, Ekrem Deveci."

"That's one of the names you asked me on the phone," I said.

He nodded. "It's the name he checked in under. And that's the name in his Greek passport."

"Greek? Saffarian was a Turk. At least, that's what he said."

"He could have been," Louie said, shrugging. "That wasn't the only passport he had. In the dresser, there were two others. One Turkish, for Garo Saffarian, the other Egyptian, for a Kemal Alkim. All of them had his picture in them."

"What do you make of that?"

"I don't. I was hoping you could."

I shook my head. "I know very little about the man. I only met him twice, once when he hired me and the second time when he fired me. How did you connect him to me?"

"A piece of paper in his wallet with your phone number and name on it."

"You have a motive?"

He shrugged. "Maybe robbery. We found an empty money belt on the floor. There were a couple of credit cards in the bureau with Deveci's and Saffarian's name on them, but no cash in the room at all, except for some loose change."

"He had a lot of cash when I saw him."

The elevator came and we rode up to the second floor. "How was he killed?"

"Shot once in the heart with a thirty-two auto, close range. We found the cartridge. Winchester Silvertip. Whoever did it wanted to make sure the job stayed done. A lot of stopping power packed into those little fuckers."

I thought about that. "What time did it go down?"

"The doctor who did the post figures it happened between nine and eleven last night."

"Witnesses?"

He shook his head. "The rooms on both sides of him and across the hall were empty. Nobody heard a thing. From the powder burns on the victim's shirt, the muzzle of the gun must have been right on his chest. That would have muffled the sound some."

"It could have been robbery," I said thoughtfully. "It could have been something else, too."

That warranted a raised eyebrow. "What?"

I proceeded to tell him about Papadoupoulous, leaving out Heather Piccard and the museum.

"The gun this Arab pulled on you—you say it was a thirty-two?"

"Could have been. At that point, I was more concerned with what was in his eyes. It wasn't a larger caliber, I know that much."

The elevator doors opened and we stepped out onto the security floor. As always during my visits to the morgue, I felt slightly giddy as I walked along the corridor, as if I were walking through some surreal dreamscape. The place was bustling with activity; frocked doctors and attendants walked by, chatting and joking, paying no heed to the dead who were lined up on gurneys against the wall and who were waiting with stoical silence for their turn in the autopsy room. Louie stopped at the gurney by the open door. "This your client?"

Saffarian had obviously already been inside. He lay naked and uncovered on the gurney. The great sutured Y ran across his chest from shoulder to shoulder, down to his pubic area, where they had opened him up and hollowed him out, making him looked like some grotesque Frankensteinian creation waiting for life. He would be waiting a long time. The round, brown face was blue-white now, his eyes were half-open and covered with a thick glaze, like darkly fired porcelain. "That's him."

Compared to the huge, nasty incision, the neat, black bullet hole in the flabby left pectoral looked small and harmless. It was funny that something so small could cause all this trouble.

I looked up. Through the open door, I could see cadavers lying on stainless-steel tables in various stages of disassembly. Green-frocked pathologists busily cut, weighed, and measured, converting what had once been human lives into a series of statistics to be filed. At one table, the doctor was making the scalp incisions on a dead woman to prepare for the opening of the skull. I watched in horrified fascination as he pulled and the face came away, peeling from the skull like a latex mask.

Rothko chuckled. "That's what you call pulling the wool over your eyes and kissing your forehead good-bye."

"How do you figure it?" Louie asked me.

"I don't at this stage."

"We'll put out an APB on Fox and the girl and see what we come up with. In the meantime, I'll check with Santa Monica P.D. and see what they've got." He paused thoughtfully. "I know Bick, by the way. We interfaced on a couple of cases over the years. You think he might have stumbled onto something this Fox was into and got popped?"

I didn't like that thought, but I couldn't seem to get rid of it. "I don't know. I hope not."

"Drop down to the Hall of Justice sometime tomorrow," Louie said. "I'll want a statement."

I told him I'd be by in the afternoon and left, grateful to be out of there. The morgue had never been my idea of a pleasant place to spend an afternoon, but today the atmosphere was particularly discomfiting. Part of the old mid-life crisis, I supposed. Death had a disquieting proximity I hadn't felt before, and I kept seeing myself on a gurney, pale and thoughtless, staring up sightlessly into the pitiless fluorescent glare. I wondered if that would be the totality of my contingent of mourners—two mildly curious cops trying to figure out whodunit, not because they cared, but because they were getting paid for it.

Who needed mourners, anyway? I told myself as I stepped out into the night. Look at Elvis. He had millions of 'em and he died on the can, alone.

# EIGHTEEN

I needed a drink and I figured the bar in the Beverly Wilshire was as good a place as any to get one. The price of a libation, like the price of the rooms, was exorbitant; but it was close to my quarry and it was all going on the old expense account, so what the hell.

I sat at the bar and nursed a vodka and soda and when that was empty, ordered another and started nursing that. There were only two other people in the lounge, a couple, their faces hovering like yellow moons over the candlelit table in the corner. As they got up and left, I said to the bartender, "Quiet night."

"Yeah," he grunted and went back to wiping glasses. Apparently he didn't want to spoil the mood of the place.

I killed another twenty minutes then drifted out. It was after one and the lobby was deserted, which was just how I'd hoped it would be.

I have always gotten along well with night clerks. As a breed of humanity I have found them to be a very friendly bunch, if not at first, definitely after the first sight of green. The reasons behind this are varied and not difficult to understand. Often they are disgruntled about the hours and the pay. The early-morning hours are lonely and usually not very busy, and are therefore more conducive to friendly conversation. Most important, there is an absence of supervisors around who might object to their supplementing their meager salaries with a little tax-free money.

I stood around for a good three minutes until someone appeared through a doorway behind the desk. "Yes?"

He was a tall, thin young man with a hatchet face. He didn't smile, and I hoped it was because he was unhappy with his job. "I need a little help," I said. "My name is Arbogast, room ten-oh-two. I need a copy of the calls I've made since I checked in."

I didn't really expect that to work, but I felt obliged to give it a try. He eyed me circumspectly. "Do you have your room key?"

I patted my pockets and said, "I must have left it in the room."

He scowled and said in a revelatory tone, "You aren't a guest of the hotel."

"You're too smart for me, pal." I opened my wallet, extracted a fifty, and put it down on the counter.

His hand twitched as he looked at it, a good sign. "What is that?"

"The identical twin of this guy," I said, pulling out another fifty and laying it down alongside the first.

He looked confused. He'd obviously never been bribed before. "Nothing you have to worry about. Mr. Arbogast's employer thinks that he has been padding his expense account lately, and he wants to check up on the calls he's made. That's all."

He licked his lips and looked around. "I don't know. I could get fired if anybody found out—"

"Nobody is going to." I touched the bills and said, "They're not going to become triplets. Say no and they walk with me. No problem."

He snatched up the bills and walked over to the computer. "Ten-oh-two, you said?"

"Right."

He punched some buttons and the machine spit out a printout. I checked out the room number and name at the top of the sheet, thanked him, and left.

# NINETEEN

The telephone rang as persistently as a bill collector working on commission. Eventually, I gave up trying to smother the sound with my pillow and picked it up. "Hello?"

"Asch, this is Tony Bruenig."

With a little effort, I opened my eyes. "Yeah, Tony."

"I just thought you'd like to know, Dave's car was impounded yesterday."

I sat up. "Where?"

"San Pedro. It was parked on a side street in a street-cleaning zone."

"What about Dave?"

"No sign of him. He hasn't called the impound and he hasn't called me."

"I don't like it."

"Neither do I."

"Has a homicide detective named Hyde from Santa Monica P.D. contacted you?"

"Yeah."

I said he might want to get in touch with Louie, too, and told him about Saffarian. "Jesus Christ, everybody that had anything to do with that case is getting whacked. What the fuck is going on?"

"I wish I knew."

"Whatever it is, I'd be willing to bet that Fox is in the middle of it. I checked with a DEA friend of mine. They've suspected for a long time that he was using that Central American treasure-hunting front to bring in cocaine. Three years ago they were apparently ready to move on him, but he suddenly split the country. They think maybe he got word somehow he was going to be busted."

"They know where he went?"

"I didn't ask them."

I could guess where he had gone—Turkey, where he had linked up with Naci and Papadoupoulous. I told him to let me know if he heard anything more, then forced myself to get up.

After performing my morning ablutions and imbibing my customary four cups of coffee, I went over the hotel computer printout. Arbogast had checked into the Beverly Wilshire ten days ago and since that time he had made twenty-six calls, fourteen of them to the same West L.A. number. I tried it first.

After the second ring, a man's voice answered, "Hello?"

"Is Phil there?"

"Phil who?"

"Phil Sims."

"You must have the wrong number."

"Is this 555-9908?"

"That's right, but there isn't any Phil Sims here."

"That's funny," I said. "That's the number he gave me. Whose residence have I got?"

"The *wrong* one." He hung up.

I called the rest of the numbers. Restaurants. Dry cleaners. The museum. That left the one number. I thought about dialing it again, but I doubted the man would be more cooperative the second time. Up the middle didn't work, so I figured it was time for a little razzle-dazzle, and dug out Pac Bell's C.N.A. service number from my List of Numbers Every Aspiring Detective Should Have.

C.N.A. service numbers are secret numbers kept by various phone companies for settling customer billing disputes. All you have to do is call the C.N.A. number, give the number in question, and the telephone rep will helpfully provide the name and address that goes with the number. Because phone companies don't want their customers to know about these numbers, they are frequently changed. The phone company rep I'd paid $200 guaranteed the one he'd given me would be good through January 1990.

It wasn't any great surprise when the woman recited the Bel Air address Arbogast had visited the previous night. What was a bit of a surprise was the name of the house's owner—C. W. Bryant—although it probably shouldn't have been.

I had read about C. W. Bryant in the papers and seen him interviewed by Barbara Walters and Mike Wallace aboard his private 747. He was the apotheosis of the American dream. From modest beginnings as the son of an Oregon potato farmer, he had made his first million at the age of twenty-two on a patent he acquired for a new vacuum toilet that came to be used on airplanes. With the stake from his fecal triumph, he bought out U.S. West Petroleum, a faltering California oil company, sunk three wells, and hit on two. From then on, it was full steam ahead.

Through ingenuity, imagination, daring, and a seemingly inexhaustible source of energy (all leavened with a good dose of ruthlessness), Bryant parlayed his business successes to the point where today, at the age of sixty-seven, he headed an international conglomerate whose diversified holdings ranged from oil companies to liquor distilleries to insurance companies to department-store chains to phosphate factories to tungsten mines. Hated by environmentalist groups, Bryant had been embroiled in the past year in a vituperative political battle to get off-shore drilling off the coasts of Southern California and Oregon. He had been given the green light by the County Board of Supervisors and the Coastal Commission, and had completed construction of one platform before the EPA had stepped in with a temporary injunction while they reviewed a new Environmental Impact Study. The consensus among reporters who covered the backroom boys was that the decision would stand.

Aside from being a canny businessman Bryant was also an avid art collector, having amassed one of the largest private collections of ancient art in the world. That fit. If I were Arbogast and had something valuable to peddle, Bryant

would definitely be one man I would approach; at least I'd
know his check wouldn't bounce.

What didn't fit was that Bryant was also one of the County
Museum's biggest benefactors, to the extent that he had his
own wing named after him. Why would Bryant compete with
the museum for whatever Arbogast was trying to peddle? It
would have been like competing with himself.

I called the museum, but Gros's secretary said he was out.
I called Louie. He was in, and would be, he said, for the next
two hours.

On the way down town, I stopped off at a coffee shop and
glanced through a paper over a ham omelet. The Saffarian
murder rated about sixteen lines on the back page of Part 2. It
said simply that a man had been found shot to death in a room
at the Mondrian Hotel. Although they were withholding
details of the murder, including the victim's name, a sheriff's
spokesman said that the shooting was believed to have taken
place early Tuesday evening. A motive for the crime was
unknown at this time.

Louie's ensemble today was a gray tweed suit and a
navy-blue beret, which sat at a jaunty angle on his head.
"Good afternoon, Inspector Maigret," I said, pulling up a
chair.

He blinked uncomprehendingly. "Huh?"

"Inspector Maigret. Of the Surete."

"Don't know him." He sounded serious.

"Just a little joke. Because of your fashion statement."

He patted the beret. "Actually, I picked out this one this
morning because I knew I was going to be talking to Paris, and
I wanted to get into the mood. Just got off the phone a little
while ago, in fact. Had a nice little chat with an Inspector
Fragonard from Interpol about Saffarian A K A Deveci
A K A Alkim."

"And?"

"They were unfamiliar with the other two names, but they
have a file—a dossier, as they call it—on Saffarian. The
French have suspected him for some time of being a middleman in a Corsican heroin-smuggling ring. He had an import-
export business, all right—rugs and waterpipes and crapola
like that—and they think he was using it to smuggle dope out
of Turkey, but they could never catch him."

"They couldn't catch Fox, either." I filled him in on the information imparted by Bruenig's DEA source.

"Dope could be the link that joins everything up," he said when I'd finished.

"It could explain what the killer was looking for at Papadoupoulous's place."

He frowned. "If it does, we're either looking for more than one person, or a person with two guns. Papadoupoulous was done with a twenty-two caliber."

"Fox knew both Papadoupoulous and Naci in Turkey," I said, my thoughts speeding up. "We know that from the photograph. If he knew Saffarian, too, it'd make a nice package."

Louie sat back and smiled. "I don't know if he knew him there, but he knew him here. We lifted two of his prints from the bureau in the hotel room."

"You have a warrant out for his arrest?"

"It's in the works."

"No word on Fox's boat?"

"Not yet. We've notified the Coast Guard, and Rothko has called every marina between San Diego and San Francisco. The dipshit has to pull in somewhere."

"Somewhere could be Costa Rica."

He shrugged and smiled. "A little expense-paid extradition might be just the ticket to get the wife off my back. She'd love to go to Costa Rica."

"If that's where Fox went, I hope he didn't take Bick with him." I told him about Bruenig's wake-up call and his expression soured.

"San Pedro," he said thoughtfully. "That's not too far from Redondo."

"I know."

"Forensics gone over the car yet?"

"I don't know."

"I'll check on it." He opened his desk drawer and took out a typed report. "In the meantime, read this. I think it's accurate. If it is, sign it."

It was a statement taken from the facts as I had given them last night about my meetings with Garo Saffarian and the job I had done for him. I signed it and handed it back.

He left it on the desk top and leaned back. "You said Papadoupoulous's girlfriend was young. How young?"

I shrugged. "Twenty-two, maybe."

He pursed his lips. "Dark hair, you say?"

"Black."

"No gray in it?"

"Gray? No, why?"

He picked up a ball-point pen from the desk and clicked the retractable point absent-mindedly while he talked. "At about nine-thirty on the night of the murder, a room-service waiter at the Mondrian was delivering a sandwich down the hall to room seven-six-nine when he passed Deveci's room. A woman was coming out. According to his description, the woman was in her mid-thirties, pale complexion, well-dressed. Dark hair, except for a streak of gray in the front." He watched me closely. "Ring a bell?"

I wondered how much he knew, if he already knew about Heather Piccard and was just trying to get me to commit to a lie so he could trap me. There was only one smart way to play it—spill the whole thing. If he did know about her, I would be off the hook, and if he didn't, there was now plenty reason why he should. "No," I said, trying to sound casual.

"You're sure?"

I nodded. "Yeah. This waiter is positive it was Deveci's room the woman was coming out of?"

He smiled oddly. "Strange you should ask. He thinks it was, but he wouldn't swear to it. The only reason he paid any attention to the woman at all, he said, was that streak of gray in her hair. He said she was too young for it."

"Even if Naci Saffarian had dyed a streak of gray into her hair, the rest of the description doesn't fit."

He didn't say anything. I tried to change the subject. "Did Interpol know if Saffarian had a daughter?"

"No. But even if he didn't, Deveci or Alkim could have. I've sent his prints to the F.B.I. as well as to the Turkish, Egyptian, and Greek authorities to see if we can get some sort of final identification on the guy. Hyde is doing the same thing with the girl's picture and prints. They lifted some at the house in Santa Monica that they think might be hers."

"That could take weeks."

He smiled and shook his head. "We're dealing with govern-ments. Try months."

I told him I would be in touch and wandered down the hall to the cubbyhole Al Herrera called an office, one of the small amenities that came with rank. I knocked and pushed open the door. Al looked up from the pile of reports and folders that covered the top of the scuffed desk and his broad, dark face broke into a grin. "Louie said you might be around today." He pushed out a thick hand. "He told me you've been at it again."

I tossed up my hands helplessly. "Hey, I just find 'em, I don't do 'em."

"Sit," he said, waving at the lone wood chair in front of the desk.

I sat and he leaned back in his chair and linked his hands behind his head. A sign on the wall behind him read: DON'T WASTE GAS—WASTE KHOMEINI.

"How's Rose?"

"Great," he said. "She was just asking about you last week, in fact. Wants to know when you're coming over for dinner."

"The next time she fixes *pollo en mole*." My mouth started to water thinking about it.

"I'll tell her," he said. "We'll set it up for next week. Bring a date. You still seeing that pretty blonde I met with you a couple of months ago?"

I shook my head.

His brow furrowed. "What happened? You two seemed pretty lovey-dovey."

"You'd have to ask her," I said sullenly.

He shook his head. "I'm asking you. You're your own worst enemy when it comes to women. You know what your problem is, Jake—"

Mercifully the phone rang, cutting short the lecture I had heard countless times before. "Homicide, Herrera." His face turned professionally wooden. "Yes, John. Yeah." His eyes rolled toward the ceiling. "I've talked to the D.A., Beamer. He has expressed doubts. I know, but maybe you should talk to him personally. It might carry more weight. Right." He hung up and grunted in disgust.

"Problems?"

"Not for me. For the sheriff." He paused, sighed, and went on. "A couple of nights ago, the lunatic owner of a guard-dog service decided to hijack the truck of a business rival while the guy was making his rounds, dropping off dogs. The business rival sees his truck driving off and starts after it on foot, yelling bloody murder. By coincidence, there happens to be a sheriff's unit on the corner and after the deputy gets the story from the distraught dog owner, he turns on his lights and gives pursuit.

"When he hears the sirens behind him, the lunatic panics. He pulls into an alley, pours gas all over the truck, and torches it with four dogs still inside. Then he barricades himself in his house, which is nearby, and starts screaming that he has a gun and he'll never be taken alive."

"Was he?"

"Yeah, but he's singing a couple of octaves higher now," he said. "Ironically, they sent in one of the K-9 Corps attack dogs." He shook his head thoughtfully. "It's funny, but it was almost as if that dog *knew* what that puke had done to four of his brothers. It went right for his nuts. Tore 'em right off."

I shuddered involuntarily, thinking about it. Suddenly the memory of Fox's field goal didn't seem so horrible. "So if nobody died, why does homicide have the case?"

"The sheriff loves dogs," he explained. "He wants the guy prosecuted for four counts of murder. That's what that call was all about. The D.A. won't file homicide charges. Says dogs aren't covered under One-eighty-seven P.C. The sheriff is pissed."

I shook my head in disbelief. "The life of a homicide lieutenant."

He shrugged his thick shoulders. "Hey, what other job offers this kind of security that's this much fucking fun?"

In the fifteen or so years we had known each other, fun was not part of the job for Albert Herrera. Actually, I was convinced that Al's promotion to lieutenant five years ago had literally saved his life by getting him off the streets. Homicide cops either adopt a hard, cynical crust of black humor, finding comedy in the perversity of the human condition, or they get overwhelmed by the horror. After twelve years of seeing the worst of which man was capable, Al had been on his way to the latter; but since being kicked upstairs, he had gained some perspective by being spared having to confront the horror head-on. His duties were mostly administrative and his dealings were principally with other cops. The frustrations of the system were still part of the job, but sitting in his office, he at least got assaulted by the grief and suffering secondhand. The nervous tic he had developed during his last years as sergeant had even disappeared.

He asked, "So what kind of shit are you mixed up in now?"

I repeated what I had told Louie, feeling a pang of guilt about leaving out the same details. Our friendship went back twenty-odd years and had always been based on mutual trust, but I had painted myself into a corner; there was nothing I could do about it, at least right now.

When I got to Interpol's suspicions about Saffarian, he raised an eyebrow. "Heroin, huh? Think that was a motive for the killings?"

"I don't know. Saffarian hired me to follow the couple. Maybe they had something of his that he wanted back. Maybe he thought they'd lead me to it, then got impatient waiting and tried the more direct approach."

"He kills Papadoupoulous trying to get it back, and Fox decides he'd better get Saffarian before Saffarian gets him."

"It's possible. The four of them were connected in some way, I'm sure of it. What way, I'm not sure. Louie is going to have to sort it out. It's his problem now."

A young, crew-cut-haired man stuck his head through the door and said: "Sorry, Lieutenant, didn't know you were busy."

"That's okay, Jennings," Al told him. "What is it?"

"There's a problem I need to discuss with you." Jennings stepped inside and glanced at me uncertainly.

"It's okay," Al assured him. "What is it?"

"You know that Colombian cocaine kingpin they're holding upstairs? Belasco?"

"What about him?"

"They wired his cell and got him on tape planning a jailbreak with three of his buddies. Somehow Belasco got some rope smuggled in, enough to get from the eighth floor to the ground. But these guys are smart. They know that they'd have to go past some windows and they'd probably be spotted, so they're not going *down*. They've figured out a way they can get through the air-conditioning ducts to the roof."

"Don't tell me. They've arranged for a helicopter to pick them up— "

Jennings shook his head. "No. It's better than that. They're going to drop the rope down to someone waiting with a van down below. Then that wise guy is going to attach the rope to a telephone pole across the street. Now, somehow, they've also had smuggled in these special leather gloves attached to each other by leather straps, which they plan to use to slide down from the roof to the pole, just like in the fucking Marine Corps training films."

Al rubbed his chin. "When is this supposed to take place?"

"Tonight."

"Anybody check this plan out and see if it'll work?"

Jennings nodded. "They brought in this sergeant from Fort Ord who's up on commando shit, and laid it out. He looked it over and said it looked feasible to him. Only according to his calculations there was one problem: by the time they hit the pole, they'll be going a hundred and forty miles an hour."

Al's expression didn't change. "So what's the problem?"

Jennings grinned. "The way I see it, the problem is, once the first guy goes, how do you get the other three to follow? They're gonna hear him screaming all the way down."

Al thought a moment. "Call the K-9 Corps. There's a dog there named Bruno. Take him on the roof. I guarantee *all* of them will go." He turned to me and smiled hugely. "See? What other job could you have so much fucking fun?"

# TWENTY

I stopped at a pay phone and called the museum. Gros was still out and Heather Piccard had just left for the day. I checked with my service and found I'd had one call, from a man who had identified himself only as "the man from the house." He had left a downtown number, saying that he would be there for the next thirty minutes. I dialed the number and the heavily accented voice answered. "Mr. Asch?"

"That's my name," I said testily. "The question is, what's yours?"

"I will tell you that when we meet."

"Who says we are going to meet?"

"It is of the utmost importance that we talk. It is a matter that has international implications."

I thought about it. I wasn't eager to have a gun waved in my face again, but there was little chance of that if the spot was public enough. Unless the man really was an Arab terrorist, which I somehow doubted. "Where are you?"

"At a pay phone near the library, downtown."

"I'll meet you in front of the library steps in ten minutes."

"I will be waiting."

He was pacing in front of the stone steps when I got there. He had on the same wrinkled tan suit and it smelled as if he had slept in it. Maybe being around so many camels had deadened his olfactory senses. It was funny that I didn't remember him smelling that ripe. He bowed his head obsequiously and offered his hand, which I reluctantly took. His handshake was unpleasantly limp. "I am so glad you could come, Mr. Asch. Allow me to introduce myself. My name is Bahadir Bey."

He stuck a hand into his coat and I held up my hands. "I've already seen this performance."

"Eh?" He smiled and shook his head. "Oh, no. This is just my identification, I assure you." He took out a billfold and flipped it open. Inside, encased in clear plastic, was an official-looking identification card with his photograph on it. The writing was in Turkish, so I couldn't understand it, but the seals and all looked pompous enough to be a government I.D. "I am a senior officer with the Turkish Ministry of Antiquities."

"Do all officers with the Ministry of Antiquities carry guns?"

"I must apologize for that," he said. "You caught me at a, uh—how you say?—embarrassing moment."

"I don't know if I'd say it or not." That seemed to confuse him. Before he got serious about trying to figure it out, I asked, "So what did you want to see me about, Mr. Bey?"

He looked around furtively. "Where can we talk?"

Aside from the security angle, there was no way I was going to be in an enclosed area with that much body odor. "Right here."

His expression grew uneasy. "It is very public, no?"

"It is very public, yes. That's why it's here or nowhere."

He sighed and shrugged. "As you wish."

We began walking toward Pershing Square. Several workers from the surrounding office buildings were stretched out on the grass, napping. We passed a bag lady pushing a shopping cart filled with an assortment of garbage, muttering to herself. She gave us the eye and muttered an unintelligible curse. "So what's on your mind, Mr. Bey?"

"I need to know why you were in that house yesterday," he said.

"Why do you need to know?"

"It is not for personal reasons that I ask. I fear you may be unwittingly involved in something you do not understand."

"Why don't you help me understand?"

He shook his head ruefully. "I am not trying to be mysterious, Mr. Asch. But until I know your reasons for being there, I must decline that request."

"I guess we have a Mexican standoff."

He turned toward me. "Mexican—?"

"Standoff," I said. "Like in Western movies, when two guys get the drop on each other." His confusion was deepening. Before it got too deep, I said, "You won't tell me what it's about until I tell you what I know, and I won't tell you what I know until you tell me what it's about."

His eyebrow raised and his head bobbed up and down. "Ah, yes, I see." He scowled and pulled on his lip, then came to a decision. "I will take a chance on you. I hope I am not making a mistake." It took him three more paces to begin. "Three years ago, something of great historical significance was stolen from my country. A collection of artifacts—a burial horde—from the tomb of an ancient king named Tarchundaraus."

"What kind of artifacts?"

"A drinking cup, several statuettes, a dagger, and some jewelry items. Ten objects in all."

"Valuable?"

"To one who collects such things, very. But they are much more valuable in an historical sense."

"Is that what you were looking for at Papadoupoulous's?"

"Actually, I was looking for some clue to where Papadoupoulous had gone. He had the treasure. I did not know at the time that he was dead."

"How did Papadoupoulous get his hands on it?"

He put his hands behind his back and looked down at the sidewalk. "The horde was illegally excavated by a tomb robber from Izmir, named Mehmet Aytal. Three years ago, Mehmet died. We believe that his grand-daughter Naci and Papadoupoulous smuggled the horde out of Turkey with the aid of an American archaeologist who was working in

Turkey, Dr. Benjamin Arbogast. I have been on their trail for three years. I traced them to Switzerland, then to London, and eventually here. I am sure the plan was for the three of them to meet up again and, through Arbogast's contacts, try to sell the treasure to some wealthy collector. I am sure that is why Arbogast is in Los Angeles at this very moment. Once the horde passes from their hands, it will be lost forever."

Always the optimist, I asked, "What makes you think that hasn't happened already?"

He put his hand on my arm and stopped. His dark eyes were intense as they locked onto mine. "Do you know something?"

"Not about any artifacts," I said. "I was just posing the question."

He bit his lip and exhaled. "A man was murdered in Hollywood last night, in the Mondrian Hotel. Perhaps you read about it in the papers?"

I resumed walking, anything to get the wind going. "Perhaps."

"His name was Garo Saffarian. He was also known by the names Deveci and Alkim. He was a smuggler. Of ancient art, narcotics, anything anyone would pay him to smuggle. We believe Arbogast and Papadoupoulous arranged with Saffarian to have the treasure of Tarchundaraus smuggled out of Turkey, and that it was only later, after the publication of an article on the treasure by Professor Arbogast, that he realized what he had let slip through his fingers. I am convinced Saffarian meant to rectify that error. I think he came to Los Angeles to grab the treasure for himself and that he killed Papadoupoulous in that pursuit."

"So who killed him?"

"That, I do not know."

I figured it was time to give him something. "Saffarian hired me to bird-dog Naci."

His eyebrows squirmed. "Bird dog?"

I told him the story, and he said, "I'm afraid Saffarian duped you. Do you have any idea where Naci is now?"

"I think she's in the company of a man named Justin Fox."

His head swiveled around at the mention of the name. "Fox was in Turkey for some time, right around the time the treasure disappeared. He was working for a marine salvage company in the Red Seas as a diver. The company was a front for Saffarian's smuggling operation."

The package now had a bow on it. "Saffarian was Fox's boss?"

"Yes," he said. "Do you know where they are?"

"No, but I'd like to. So would the police. There's a murder warrant out on Fox for Saffarian's murder."

He stared up at the tall buildings that surrounded us, but said nothing.

"Why don't you just go to the cops with all this?"

He cleared his throat. "That would not be practical for me at this time."

"Why not?"

He hesitated, then cleared his throat uncomfortably. "The resources of the ministry are small, as are those of my country. My superiors felt it would not be warranted to allow for the large expense for such an undertaking, without the guarantee of results. So I decided to expend my own resources for the venture. I fully anticipate I will be reimbursed when I return with the treasure, however."

"In other words, you're on your own?"

He pursed his lips. "That is correct."

"And your superiors at the ministry might get ticked off if they found out you'd been conducting a little B and E in a foreign country."

I'd lost him again. "B and E?"

"Breaking and entering."

He smiled sheepishly. "Your assumption, I feel, is correct."

"So what's your angle? Why would you spend your hard-earned cash to come halfway around the world on a dicey treasure hunt?"

His chest swelled with resolve. "Mr. Asch, the artistic heritage of my country has been systematically plundered by the greed of capitalistic collectors for the past two hundred years. I have dedicated my entire life to stopping the illegal trade in antiquities, but it has been like putting one's finger in a dike. But this is no ordinary find. It is of immense archaeological and artistic value, and to the pride of my country. Its rightful place is in Turkey, and I mean to see that it is returned there. Will you help me? I will pay you, of course."

"What do you want me to do?"

"I must locate Arbogast. He is the key to finding the others."

I played dumb. I'd been played a sucker by one of this crowd and I didn't intend for it to happen again. Besides, I'd never met an investigator yet who would spend his own money on a case. "How do you know he's in L.A.?"

"I called the Oriental Institute in Chicago, where he works. They told me he was in Los Angeles, but they do not know where."

"L.A. is a big city."

"That is why I need your help."

"My rate is three hundred dollars a day, Mr. Bey."

His expression dropped. "Three hundred? I do not know if I could afford to pay you that much."

"Is there a reward for the return of this treasure?"

"Only the reward that comes with the knowledge that one is helping the cause of international good will between our two countries."

Great. Before, I was just helping the community. Now I was helping the world. Maybe it would bag me the Nobel Peace Prize. At least there was some money in that. "We'll work something out," I told him. "Where can I get in touch with you?"

"The Mabely Hotel, on Fifth Street," he said, smiling gratefully. "Room three-oh-one."

I took out a piece of paper and jotted it down. "By the way, what kind of a gun was that you were waving around, Mr. Bey?"

"A Beretta."

"What caliber?"

He looked at me suspiciously but replied, "Thirty-two. Why do you ask?"

I shrugged. "I'm interested in guns. I'll be in touch."

I left him standing there and walked across the street to the underground lot where I'd parked my car.

Four blocks away, I pulled into a gas station and used the pay phone to call Louie. "That guy who pulled a gun on me at Papadoupoulous's house is a Turk named Bahadir Bey. He's staying at the Mabely Hotel on Fifth, room three-oh-one. The gun was a thirty-two-caliber Beretta. You might want to check it out."

"I definitely will," he said. "Thanks."

I hung up and drove to Silver Lake.

# TWENTY-ONE

The Dodge was not in the driveway when I pulled up in front of the house. I killed my engine and waited.

The daylight was dimming when she pulled up the street and into the driveway. She got out of the car and lifted a large bag of groceries out of the front seat. She turned, surprised, as I walked up and asked, "Need a hand?"

The surprise left her eyes, replaced by annoyance. "No, thank you. What are you doing here?"

"I want to talk to you. I called the museum, but they said you'd gone for the day."

"I had appointments."

"To buy some potsherds?"

"A doctor's appointment, if you must know," she said coldly. "How did you know where I live?"

"It's my business, remember?"

Her mouth tightened angrily. "Well? What is it?"

"Garo Saffarian."

"I told you, I've never heard of anyone named Garo Saffarian," she said in an exasperated tone.

"How about Ekrem Deveci?"

She looked at me uncertainly and hefted up the grocery bag, which was starting to slip along with her confidence. "Why do you ask?"

"Saffarian and Deveci were the same man."

She caught the tense. "Were?"

"He was shot to death the night before last in his room at the Mondrian Hotel."

Her mouth dropped open but nothing came out. She didn't resist as I lifted the bag out of her arms and said, "Would you like to tell me what you were doing in his room that night?"

Her eyes widened, more startled than afraid. "How did you know—"

"A waiter described you to the police."

Her hand went to her throat. "The police know about me?"

I shook my head. "I haven't told them. Yet."

A thought struck her, and her eyes pleaded with mine. "You can't possibly think I had anything to do with it?"

"Why don't we go inside and I'll get a better idea whether I do or not," I said.

She looked at me warily, then sighed in resignation and started up the walk toward the door.

The living room was small, filled with overstuffed white furniture and plants. The walls were white and unadorned, art being conspicuous by its total absence. She asked me to sit down and I went across the polished wood floor and lowered myself into one of the large, cushy chairs. Through the wood shutters, the lights of the houses glowed like embers that had been scattered over the surrounding hills. Lying open on the couch was a hardback book. *Horned God and Celestial Bull: New Discoveries at Catal Huyuk*, by Graham Lipton, Ph.D. Nothing like a little light reading before bedtime.

She sat down next to the book, her back rigid, her hands clasped together in her lap. "I didn't kill Deveci," she said quietly. "He was alive when I left."

"What time was that?"

"About nine-thirty."

I nodded. That fit with the waiter's statement. "What were you doing there?"

She took a deep breath and let it out. "Deveci called me two days ago at the museum. He told me he had some artifacts he thought I would be interested in and asked me to come to his room at the Mondrian at nine-thirty. I agreed."

"Why would he call you?"

"I'd had some dealings with him in the past."

"What kind of dealings?"

"Two years ago, Deveci came to Los Angeles with some Egyptian pieces he had for sale. Three stone figurines from the time of Ramses III. I looked over the pieces. They were quite good and I recommended we buy them, which we did."

"Deveci was an art dealer?"

"You didn't know that?"

"No, but I probably should have. The man was apparently willing to sell anything, if the price was right."

"You are quite right about that. The man has—had—a reputation in the museum business of being a bit of a scoundrel. A few years ago, he sold the Cleveland Museum two Egyptian cats that turned out to be forgeries. There was quite a stink about it. He claimed that he was innocent in the affair, that he'd bought them from someone else, and that if the museum experts were fooled by the objects how could they expect him not to be. Nobody really believed him, but he did return the museum's money, so nothing much was made of it."

"But you were still willing to do business with him, knowing he was a crook?"

"It's possible he didn't know," she said. "Such things do happen in the antiquities trade. And I know several museums who purchased pieces from Deveci that were of unquestioned authenticity. You just had to be very careful dealing with the man."

"So what did he want to show you at the Mondrian?"

"Nothing," she said angrily. "He'd lied. He had nothing for sale. In fact, he wanted to buy something—me." She stopped and quickly clarified. "I don't mean in any carnal sense. He wanted to bribe me. He said he knew that Dr. Gros was negotiating to make a certain acquisition for the museum. He offered to pay me ten thousand dollars to keep him informed about the progress of the deal. In particular, if terms were agreed upon, he was interested in when and where the final purchase was to be made. I told him that would be betraying my personal and professional ethics, and I walked out. He was very much alive when I left."

"What acquisition was he talking about? The treasure of Tarchundaraus?"

Her eyes went wide again. She was reeling now from the old Asch razzle-dazzle. "How do you know about the treasure?"

"I just spent some time with a man who claimed to be with the Turkish Ministry of Antiquities. At least that's who he said he was. I'm not willing to take anybody's word for anything anymore. He's here on a treasure hunt. He's been trailing Papadoupoulous around the world and he wound up here."

"Does he know that the museum is involved?"

"If he does, he didn't let on. And I didn't tell him."

She shook her head and gazed across the room. "This is getting out of hand." She turned back to me with a decisive look. "How much did he tell you?"

"Not a whole lot."

"Then perhaps I'd better." She took a deep breath. "Three years ago, an article appeared in the *American Journal of Archaeology* by Dr. Benjamin Arbogast. At the time, the article caused quite a stir. Arbogast had made some important Hittite finds in western Anatolia. He was one of the leading experts on Hittite culture." She paused and asked, "You know who the Hittites were?"

"Vaguely," I said. "If they're an integral part of the story, you'd better fill me in a little."

"I'm afraid I can't fill you in much. Nobody can. The Hittites had a powerful political empire that stretched from northern Syria to the west coast of Turkey. They achieved the height of their power from about 1700 to 1200 B.C., five hundred years, but we know very little about them. Their existence was only discovered at the end of the nineteenth century. Unlike the Egyptians, who left monumental architecture and detailed records of their society and history, the Hittites left very little behind. We know a little about their religion, their methods of conducting war, and their language, but that's about all. They are still largely a mystery."

"Go on."

She took another breath. "In the article, Arbogast claimed

that he had been traveling on a train from Istanbul to Izmir, where he had been excavating a Stone Age burial mound, when he noticed a gold bracelet on the wrist of a young girl sitting across the aisle. It looked very old to him and he asked the girl if he could see it. She complied and told him there were many more such things at her house in Izmir and invited him to look at them.

"Arbogast said he was taken to an old house in the city and shown a veritable treasure that had been carelessly stored there. He became convinced the artifacts in his hands had been illegally excavated from a royal tomb. When he deciphered the hieroglyphs on a piece of gold leaf that had once covered a wooden throne, he was sure of it. It said: *Tarchundaraus.*"

She stopped and looked at me with excitement in her eyes. We all got our kicks in various ways, I supposed. "Tarchundaraus was a king who ruled a land called Arzawa around 1400 B.C. We know that because of a stone tablet that was discovered some years ago, a greeting from the Egyptian Pharaoh Amenophis III to king Tarchundaraus, but that's about all we know. What little we know about the Hittites is encyclopedic compared to what we know about Arzawa. We don't even know where it was. Some experts think it was on the south coast, near Kas, others say it was near Melitus in the west. We know that Arzawa was conquered by the Hittites in 1300 B.C., and that it revolted against Hittite rule several times after that. We assume it was overrun and totally destroyed, along with the Hittites, by foreign invaders, around 1200 B.C. No trace of it has ever been found."

"What did this so-called treasure consist of?"

"Ceremonial axeheads, a gold two-handled drinking vessel, the iron hilt of a sword shaped like a leopard's head, figurines of stone and gold. Arbogast spent three days in the house, making detailed drawings of everything. He claimed he forgot his camera and did not want to leave the find to get one, for fear that the girl would change her mind about letting him stay. He said everytime he talked about going out, she started acting skittish. Arbogast's dilemma was that without photographs there was no proof that the treasure actually existed. He expected some skepticism on the part of his colleagues when he decided to go ahead and publish the drawings anyway, but he didn't expect the intensity of the personal attacks upon him or the problems that were to result from the article."

"What problems?"

"When people in the Turkish Ministry of Antiquities read the article, they called Arbogast in and demanded to know where the treasure was, or they would revoke all his permits to dig in Turkey. He accompanied them to Izmir, but the street address he had taken down turned out to be wrong. A search failed to turn up the house or the girl. The treasure was gone."

"It sounds like an Eric Ambler novel."

She nodded. "That's one reason the Turkish government didn't believe Dr. Arbogast's story. They accused him of having helped smuggle the treasure out of the country. They said they had proof he had stolen other artifacts from excavations he had worked on. They revoked his permits to dig and asked him to leave the country.

"By that time he had other problems. He was drawing a lot of fire from colleagues, who accused him of fraud. They said that there wasn't any treasure, that he'd made the whole thing up just to increase his professional reputation."

"Why would they do that?"

She shrugged. "Professional jealousy, in some cases. In others, it was more personal. Arbogast was never much of a diplomat. Over the years, he wrote scathing critiques of the historical theories put forth by several of his colleagues. The study of Near Eastern antiquities is a small, closely knit field. Those whose theories he attacked felt as if their scholarship had been impugned. When the opportunity arose, they attacked back.

"As the years passed and no hint of the treasure surfaced, the fraud theory gained credence. Consensus grew among the experts that the episode was just another Piltdown skeleton in the archaeological closet. I have to admit I was leaning toward that view. Until ten days ago."

"What happened ten days ago?"

"Dr. Arbogast showed up at the museum with a potsherd to be thermoluminescence tested. We do that for a fee. He wouldn't tell me where he was staying, but said he would call back in a few days for the results."

I guessed, "The piece tested out?"

She nodded. "Thirty-four hundred years old. When he called back and I told him, he became quite excited. I asked him where he had gotten it, but he hung up without saying. Two days later, I received a phone call from Papadoupoulous. He said he had in his possession the treasure of Tar-chundaraus and that it was for sale. He said he already had a firm offer of nine million, but that he was still taking bids if the museum was interested."

The sum jarred my senses. "Nine *million? Dollars?*"

She smiled charitably. "Actually, that wouldn't be a great deal of money for a find of that nature. Depending on what kind of shape the other items were in, of course."

"Did he say who made the offer?"

"No." She shifted in her chair. "I agreed to meet him at the motel. He was to bring a potsherd for me to authenticate, plus several other pieces for my inspection, as well as a set of photographs for me to show Dr. Gros."

"Did they?"

She nodded. "I was not all that surprised when I found that the sherd was almost identical to the one Dr. Arbogast had brought in. In fact, it was probably from the same pot."

"What about the other pieces?"

"There were two. A fragment of the sheet gold from the throne. The hieroglyphs on it were identical to those in the Arbogast drawings. The other piece was a five-inch-high gold statue of the sun goddess of Arinna mounted on a lion. She was surrounded by her handmaidens and was holding a set of horns above which was the sun disk, a symbol associated with the Egyptian sun goddess Hathor. The workmanship was magnificent." She envisaged it in her mind and took a deep breath. "On the basis of the two objects, as well as the photographs, I concluded that the treasure was the same that Professor Arbogast had seen in Izmir."

"You authenticated the pieces?"

"Only the sherd. They wouldn't let me take the gold pieces. There is no way to test a metal like gold for age, anyway. There are tests you can make, but I couldn't do them in a motel room. All I could do was examine the pieces carefully under a magnifying glass, but my feeling was that they were genuine. That feeling was strengthened when I got back the test results on the sherd: 1400 B.C., just like Arbogast's piece."

"Where does Arbogast fit into the picture?"

"He isn't here by coincidence, that's for sure. Dr. Gros thinks he was called in. If someone wanted to bring in an expert he would be the logical choice. He is the only person who has actually seen the treasure."

"The man I talked to from the Ministry of Antiquities, Bahadir Bey—do you know him by the way?"

"Bey? No, I've never heard the name."

"He thinks Arbogast is working with the smugglers."

She shook her head. "I can't believe that. Dr. Arbogast is a dedicated scholar. Archaeology is his life. He wouldn't be involved in something like that."

"You think he's working for the mysterious bidder?"

"We don't know that there is only one. These people might have a bidding war going between several potential buyers to drive up the price."

"Why didn't you tell me all this before?"

She winced. "Dr. Gros made me promise not to. He wants the treasure for the museum. He was afraid you would bring in the police, and once that happened the sellers would be scared off."

"So by having me tail Arbogast, he hoped to learn who his competition was and at the same time keep me from going to the cops."

She shrugged helplessly. "Something like that."

"One thing I don't get," I said. "If the treasure was smuggled out of Turkey illegally, how could the museum put it on display? Wouldn't the Turkish government raise a stink?"

"That's one reason I have serious misgivings about its acquisition," she replied, frowning. "The Met is currently embroiled in a legal dispute with Turkey over a Lydian horde that was illegally excavated. The director there had kept the purchase of the horde secret for ten years. The moment it went on display, the Turkish government sued for its return. The same thing undoubtedly would happen with the treasure of Tarchundaraus."

"You say that's one of your misgivings about the treasure. You have others?"

She nodded. "The people we are going to have to deal with to get it." Her brow furrowed worriedly. "Do you really think that's why Papadoupoulous and Deveci were killed? For the treasure?"

"Nine million bucks is one hell of a motive for murder."

"Who did it? That Fox person you were asking about, and Deveci's daughter?"

"They're the two most likely candidates at the moment," I said. "Only she isn't Deveci's daughter. Her name is Naci Aytal, probably the girl on the train in Izmir. Saffarian, or Deveci, was only using me to tail her and Papadoupoulous, hoping they would lead me to the treasure. When you showed up he called off our deal. He probably figured it was getting close to the payoff and he didn't want me to be around when it happened. He must have thought Papadoupoulous was going to cut a deal with the museum and decided to try to work indirectly through you. Has anyone contacted you about the treasure since the motel-room meeting?"

"Just once, a few days after we got the test results. It was the same man who had called before—Papadoupoulous. At least it sounded like him. I told him that the test had come out all right and that Dr. Gros and I wanted to inspect the rest of the treasure. I explained that any bid, of course, would be contingent on approval from the trustees. He said he would give us until the sixteenth—tomorrow—to get approval. If we got it, he said he would arrange for us to look over the treasure. That was the last I heard."

"Did the board approve it?"

She nodded. "Pieter—Dr. Gros—called the trustees individually and sold them on the importance of the acquisition. They approved the purchase, up to fifteen million dollars. Only two voted against it."

Fifteen million. The sums were starting to make me dizzy. "Let me guess. One of them was C. W. Bryant."

She looked at me strangely. "How did you know that?"

"My mother was a gypsy," I said. Before she had a chance to pick at that one, I gave her something more important to deal with. "There's no way to keep the cops out of it now."

"I suppose not."

The phone rang and she went to answer it. "Hello . . . Yes, Pieter." She glanced at me meaningfully. "Mr. Asch is here. . . . That's right. He came to tell me that Deveci has been murdered. It must have happened after I left

him. . . . Yes, he knows that. . . . No, he hasn't told the
police yet. . . . He knows about the treasure. I told him."
She paused and her lips tightened angrily. Her voice picked
up a note of distress. "There wasn't any choice, Pieter. He
already knew some of it. A man from the Turkish Ministry of
Antiquities told him. . . . That's right. They're here in
L.A. . . . Just a minute." She held out the phone to me. "He
wants to talk to you."

I stood up and took the phone. "Yeah?"

"Before you do anything, Mr. Asch, I must talk with you,"
Gros said with a note of desperation.

"Look, Gros, I'm getting tired of being played a chump— "

"I understand your irritation with me, but you must be able
to see my position in this matter."

"There is only one position I can see, Doctor. Mine. It's
called vulnerable—"

"You can always go to the police," he interrupted. "You can
go there directly from here, if you want. Just hear me out
first."

I thought about it. He pounced on my silence. "I'm at my
office at the museum."

I had a feeling I would regret it, but I told him I'd be there.
He asked to speak to Heather Piccard, and she took the
receiver, uttered some "Uh-huhs" and "Yeses," then hung up.

"Are you going, too?" I asked her.

"I think I have a right to sit in," she said. "After all, I *am* the
one the police are looking for."

I couldn't argue with her about that.

# TWENTY-TWO

**W**e took my car. Neither of us talked much during the twenty-minute ride, each lost in our own thoughts. She instructed me to park in the employees' lot on Ogden, and she opened a side door with a key.

The door opened into a long, high-ceilinged corridor lined with narrow wooden crates stacked like books behind locked iron grates. The place was still except for the whirring of the buffer being run over the linoleum floor by a lone janitor. At the end of the corridor, she used another key on the elevator and we went up to the second floor.

The door to Gros's office was open and we went in. He stood behind his desk and smiled tightly. He didn't offer his hand and I didn't offer mine. "Thank you for coming," he said. "Sit down, please." When we had all done that, he said, "Tell me about Deveci."

I told him about Deveci. He listened intently, steepling his fingers in front of his mouth, and when I had finished, he asked, "Are you sure Deveci's murder is tied to the disappearance of the treasure?"

"No, but it stands to reason. He was obviously trying to cut himself in on the deal. That's the reason he hired me to follow Papadoupoulous and called up Ms. Piccard." I paused. "I understand you knew Deveci."

He tilted his head up and sighted me down his nose. "Not socially. My dealings with him were brief and purely business."

"Ms. Piccard said you bought some Egyptian pieces from him."

He tossed a quick, recriminatory glance at her. "That's right."

"Did he say where he got the pieces?"

He shrugged. "He said they came from the collection of a dealer he knew in Zurich. I assumed he was lying."

I raised an eyebrow and he responded in a condescending tone. "Any valuable piece of ancient art that has crossed an international boundary has broken at least two laws: one of the country it left and the other of the country it came into. Only a fool would think otherwise."

I tried not to sound like too much of a fool and said, "Art wasn't the only thing Deveci smuggled. Did you know he was also a suspected heroin smuggler?"

His brows lowered and he said in an indignant tone, "Of course not."

"You didn't tell me that," Heather Piccard said, sounding slightly miffed.

Gros's face assumed a thoughtful expression. "Then his death might not have been related to the treasure at all. It might have been the result of his other criminal activities."

"It's possible," I admitted, "but I wouldn't say likely, considering the timing."

He crossed his arms. "So what *is* your opinion?"

"Unlike Angela Lansbury, I'm a sucker for the obvious. I think Fox and Naci liked the split two ways instead of three and got rid of Papadoupoulous. I think that Deveci tried to cut himself in, but the idea of a three-way split didn't look any better to them by that time, so they did him, too. But that's just an educated guess."

"What about this man from the Turkish Ministry of Antiquities?"

"His name is Bahadir Bey. Ever heard of him?"

"No," he said. "He doesn't know the museum is involved in the bidding?"

"Not that I know of."

"What does he want with you?"

"He wants me to help him get the treasure back for Turkey."

He frowned gravely. "How did he find you?"

"We ran into each other at Papadoupoulous's."

The frown deepened and he took a deep breath. "What would it take to induce you to continue to work for us?" I shook my head, but he plunged ahead. "How about double your daily rate? Say, six hundred dollars?"

Even if I'd had Parkinson's, the mention of that kind of money would have stopped my head from shaking.

He seemed encouraged by that. "If and when Fox calls back and we come to terms, I would like you along when the exchange is made, to insure the safety of Heather and myself. We are not used to dealing with people like this. You are."

"The police are more used to it than I am."

He shook his head. "The moment the police step in, any possibility of recovering the treasure for the museum will be lost. If the people who have it were to find out, they would automatically sell it to whomever else they're dealing with."

"They wouldn't have to know. The cops could set up a trap and pinch them when the buy is made—"

"I can't take the chance that they wouldn't botch it. Anyway, even if they were successful and recovered the treasure, they would probably impound it as evidence. The Turkish government would undoubtedly take steps to recover it by claiming it had been illegally smuggled out of the country."

"And they would be right," I added.

He made an abrupt, annoyed motion with his hand. "Of course they would be right. So what?"

"The Turkish government is going to find out about the treasure anyway, the minute you put it on display—"

"That's for me to worry about."

I bit my lip and tried to look as if I were thinking it over. "You haven't been contacted since that first time. How do you know Fox and the girl haven't already made a deal with your competition?"

"I don't. But I have no choice but to assume they haven't."

"You're going to pay me six hundred bucks a day to sit around on my butt and wait?"

"No. I'm going to pay you six hundred dollars a day to do what you've been doing—find out who Dr. Arbogast is working for. When and if they call back, we'll get in touch with you and let you know about the arrangements."

I inspected the fingernails of my right hand. "Like I said, you'll be paying me to sit around and wait." I looked up at him. "I already know who Arbogast is working for."

His back straightened. "Who?"

"C. W. Bryant."

His lips compressed and he slammed a hand down on the desk top. "I should have guessed!"

"Why?"

"Bryant has been at odds with the trustees for some time," he said, "ever since the Board voted to house other collections in the wing he donated to the museum. He insists that only *his* collection be there. Lately, he has been talking about yanking his support entirely and building his own museum."

"That's why you wanted to know if Bryant voted against the acquisition," Heather Piccard said in a revelatory tone.

I looked at her but said nothing. Gros continued to rant, more to himself than to anyone else. "Bryant likes this kind of atmosphere. He thrives on intrigue and deceit. He is one of those men with whom the process of collecting is like an illicit love affair. The more secretive and dirty, the more attractive it is to him."

"You think he's trying to get the treasure for himself?" I asked.

He nodded. "I'm sure of it. After I made the calls to the other board members trying to get the go-ahead for the purchase, I found out that Bryant had called several of them and tried to get them to vote against its acquisition. He cited the international implications. I thought that sounded a bit funny, coming from him—especially after Mexico City—but it makes perfect sense now. He doesn't want us to have it because he wants it for himself."

I looked from one to the other. "What about Mexico City?"

Heather Piccard answered. "A little over a year ago, the National Museum in Mexico City was robbed of some priceless Aztec and Olmec artifacts. It was one of the biggest museum burglaries in history. It was believed by investigators that most of the pieces wound up in the hands of a wealthy collector in Texas, but that some of them went to Bryant. He flatly denied it when questioned, of course, and they couldn't do anything about it, but he has them, all right. In a secret basement vault in his house."

"You know that for sure?"

"I have it on good authority," Gros replied. "And that's just where the treasure of Tarchundaraus will wind up if Bryant gets his hands on it. It will disappear for who knows how long. Perhaps forever. And nobody will be able to do anything about it."

"Perhaps Mr. Asch is right," Heather Piccard broke in. "Perhaps the police should be brought in, if only to make sure that won't happen. Even if Turkey wound up with the treasure, it would be better than its being lost to the world."

Gros waved his hand in a choppy, impatient gesture. "Don't you see? Involving the police at this stage would not guarantee the recovery of the treasure. It would in all likelihood guarantee just the opposite. In order for the police to set any trap to recover the treasure, they would have to have Bryant's cooperation, as well as ours, and they'd never get it, not if he has his mind made up about going after it. I know the man. Once he has his mind set on an object, he will stop at nothing to get it. If the police approached him, he would only deny any knowledge of the whole affair, as he did with the Mexico City artifacts. Then, when the dealers got in touch with him, he would tell them that we are in league with the police, insuring they would sell to him."

I had to admit that made sense. The police wouldn't dare attempt to bully a man with Bryant's economic and political clout. Not on the say-so of a lowly private eye.

Gros's eyes grew fiery as he continued. "The museum *must* have the treasure. It is not just art, but a piece missing from history. We would be the sole owners of a piece of mankind. We can't let it get away! The Getty beat us on that kouros two years ago. I'm not going to be beaten on this!"

He had made a believer out of me. I sat back and thought

over my options. If Gros was right about Bryant, and Fox was allowed to wander into the sunset with fifteen million bucks, my chances of finding out what happened to Bick would be slim indeed. It would definitely be easier working from the inside than the outside. "I assume the museum retains legal counsel."

"Best, Nicholson, and Katelbaum."

"I'll want to talk with someone in the firm who is familiar with criminal law," I said. "If I'm going to hold out on the police, I'm going to need some insulation."

"Then you agree?" Gros asked eagerly.

"I'll let you know after I talk to the attorney."

"Of course," he said with a satisfied smile.

We stood up, and this time he offered his hand.

# TWENTY-THREE

**M**y stomach started growling as Heather Piccard and I pulled out of the museum parking lot. "Are you hungry, perchance?"

"Starved," she said without hesitation.

"Would you like to join me for dinner?"

"That would be nice."

I thought so, too, which was why I had suggested it. I'd been eating alone too much lately.

I drove down to the Rio Bravo Grille on Beverly Boulevard. It was one of those California yuppie restaurants where the waiters and waitresses insist on going through adjective-laden verbal recitations of every dish on the menu, including the geographic point of origin of each of the ingredients. In spite of that, the food was pretty good.

It wasn't crowded and we didn't have to wait for a table, which was unusual for this time of night. We were seated at a small table near the pastel-colored wall lined with prints from various art exhibits. We both ordered glasses of Chardonnay, and after listening to the young, ponytailed waitress deliver her spiel, I ordered the wild Alaska salmon with lemon and

Maui butter, and Heather Piccard ordered the range chicken with shittake mushrooms and Iowa onions.

After the waitress had departed, I wondered out loud if they had "pet," as opposed to "wild," salmon in Alaska, and we jokingly debated the merits of "Maui" versus "California" butter.

"Have you eaten here before?" Heather asked.

I nodded. "We're through the pretentious part. The rest of it is just the eating which, in spite of the pre-meal hype, is surprisingly good."

We finished our wine and I ordered two more glasses. Maybe it was too much wine on an empty stomach, or the candlelight from the table, but my companion looked extremely attractive, especially her eyes.

I asked her, "Did you mean what you said to Gros about it being better that the Turks wind up with the treasure than it being lost to the world?"

"Of course. Why?"

"Just wondering. I don't think your boss shares your sentiments."

"I'm sure he doesn't. The competition is everything to Pieter. When he wants something, he lets little stand in his way."

"Including the law."

"Including the law," she repeated. "But he's not alone in that respect. You have to understand, Mr. Asch—"

"Jake."

She smiled and corrected herself. "Jake. The American art-museum world is the last true bastion of Yankee imperialism, the one institutional form in which the credo of Manifest Destiny is still firmly entrenched. Directors like Dr. Gros see themselves as morally superior beings representing a higher good—the cause of art. They view their mission as messianic. They feel that they have been given a spiritual mandate, to save the world's art from destruction. That means the divine right to write checks for whatever they deem necessary. To them, national boundaries are nothing but a mere inconvenience."

There was an undertone of asperity in her voice. "You don't sound as if you're too fond of Gros."

"I respect him," she hedged. "And I owe him a lot."

"How is that?"

She peered into her wineglass thoughtfully. "He took me under his wing and groomed me to be head of the department. It's more than that, though. He taught me how not to just look at a work of art, but how to peel away its outer layers, to get at its very essence. I will never be able to pay that back."

I had to wonder if the passion went beyond her work. "That was a very skillful evasion of my question."

Her demeanor cooled again, and she looked away. "In order to be fond of someone, you have to first be able to get close to him. Dr. Gros's passion for his work keeps anyone from getting close to him. I admire him and respect him. Let's leave it at that."

I left it at that. For the time being. "How did you get into this racket, anyway?"

She shrugged. "I got my Ph.D. in art history from the University of Pennsylvania, then came west, having no idea what I wanted to do with it. All I knew was what I didn't want to do with it—be locked up in the confines of academia teaching it. I got a job at the Getty, photographing their artifacts. Pieter found me there, wooed me away, and the rest is history."

"Tell me about Bryant. You've met him?"

"Many times. He has frequently asked my opinion of some of his purchases."

"What's he like?"

"An addict."

"*Drugs?*" I asked, surprised.

She smiled amusedly. "To collecting. But that can be an addiction as hard to break as drugs. It isn't the art that is the passion for C. W. Bryant, but the act of collecting itself."

"He could collect beer cans," I commented. "It'd be cheaper."

"That's the *point*," she said emphatically. "A big part of the attraction of collecting antiquities for a man like Bryant is that they are so expensive and so unique. The artists who made them are not going to be making any more. And the escalation in prices over the past few years has made the acquisition of truly great pieces of art impossible, except for the incredibly rich or for institutions using O.P.M."

"O.P.M.?"

"Museum lingo," she explained, her eyes twinkling with amusement. "Other People's Money."

"The Golden Rule of Arts and Sciences," I mused.

"Pardon me?"

"Whoever has the gold makes the rules."

"That's one way of putting it, I suppose." She twirled the stem of her wineglass between two fingers. "C. W. Bryant's interest in art is solely for his own self-ennoblement. He grew up poor and never overcame his feelings of inadequacy over the fact. Unfortunately, there are a lot of other collectors around like him. They try to use their art collections to compensate for their own ego deficiencies."

Her expression was animated again. Looking at her was like staring at one of those geometrical patterns in a psychology text that changes on you, then changes back, as you stare at it. All the changes were pleasant. "You must have no ego deficiencies."

She cocked her head to one side curiously and took a sip of wine. "Why do you say that?"

"You don't collect anything. I thought for sure your house would be full of pieces of classical art—"

"A curator never collects his or her specialty," she apprised me. "It would be a conflict of interest. I know some curators of ancient art who collect old English sporting prints, or 1950s furniture, but never antiquities." She leaned back. "Anyway, I do enough collecting at work. I don't need to bring my job home."

"So what is your ambition?" I asked. "To be director of a big metropolitan museum some day?"

She smiled at that. "God, no. I lack the primary Machiavellian skills necessary for that. I could never work people like Pieter. He's a master of manipulation. That's how he became director."

"How?"

She looked away and bit her lip. "I've already said too much."

"I promise it will never go beyond this table."

She looked at me earnestly. "For some reason, I believe you." She hesitated, then said, "It happened before I came on the scene. Dr. Gros was at that time the museum's expert on Renaissance art. He was contacted by a collector in France who had a Goya for sale. Pieter went over and saw it and was impressed. He tried to get the owner to bring the painting to L.A. so that the museum conservation team could inspect it, but the man refused, saying that the sale had to be made immediately, and that if the museum was not interested, there were others that were. Pieter had no choice, or so he says. He recommended its immediate purchase to the then-director, Kenneth Schneck, who flew over to look at the painting. Schneck liked what he saw. He told Pieter to stay in France and monitor things while he flew back to L.A. to present the purchase at an emergency meeting of the trustees. Schneck sold it to the trustees, the museum wound up paying four million dollars for an eighteenth-century forgery, Schneck was fired as director, and Pieter was voted in."

"I don't get it," I said, shaking my head. "Why would they make Gros director? He was the expert. He was the one who touted the painting all along—"

"Not toward the end. He claims he began to have second thoughts after Schneck left Paris. He called up several of the trustees warning caution, saying that in his opinion, the painting was questionable, but they took Schneck's more seasoned advice against his, and voted the money for the purchase."

"Gros didn't call Schneck and voice his doubts?"

She smiled strangely. "He says he did, Schneck says he didn't."

"You think Gros knew all along that the painting was a forgery?"

She took a sip of wine and shrugged. "I don't know. What he did know was that Schneck was an egomaniac and a glory grabber. If he liked you, like he liked Pieter, he would advance your career rapidly, but he would always make sure he took credit for your successes. Pieter also knew that Schneck was on shaky ground at that time with some of the bigger trustees because of some mediocre acquisitions he had made, and he guessed rightly that Schneck would try to take full credit for the acquisition of the Goya, to try to score points. Pieter dropped into the background while poor Schneck got up in front of the trustees and pitched the painting as his own find."

"I never realized there was so much skulduggery in the museum trade," I remarked.

She frowned unhappily. "That's one reason I've been thinking of getting out of it."

"What would you do?"

"Oh, I don't know. I've been seriously thinking about going into the commercial end of the trade. The only problem there is that you can never go back. Museum directors will not hire anyone who comes from a commercial background. Laughingly, they consider it an ethical conflict."

"Would that bother you very much, not being able to go back to it?"

She sighed. "I don't know, really. Giving up the security of any job you've been doing for ten years is scary, I suppose. Especially going into a field as competitive as the antiquities trade, although it probably isn't any more competitive or cutthroat than the museum business. That's what is so disenchanting to me. The acquisition has supplanted the art in importance. The deal has become the art form. You would expect that in the commercial world, but not in the museum. This treasure is a perfect example."

"How so?"

She leaned toward me. "I don't feel the museum should be dealing with criminals. The police should be brought into this. But there is no way in hell Pieter is going to do that. He is a driven man and he's going after the treasure, no matter what. The problem is, his ego is going to defeat his purposes."

"How is that?"

She shrugged. "If he really wanted the treasure for the museum and not to stroke his ego, he would be cooperating with Bryant, not fighting him. The treasure is a priceless piece of mankind's history. They should be working together to make sure that it doesn't disappear again, but all they can both think about is their own selfish motives. The only thing their petty bickering is going to do is drive the price up. At least I hope that's all they do."

"What do you mean by that?"

She said somberly, "Through their squabbling, they could succeed in losing it altogether."

"How would you handle it?"

She leaned forward as if getting ready to share a conspiratorial secret and her eyes came alive. "A joint deal. It's not done often, but it is done. The museum and Bryant would purchase the treasure together, with the understanding that Bryant would keep the treasure as long as he was alive. The museum couldn't display it for years, anyway. Upon his death, the treasure would become the property of the museum."

"Sounds logical," I admitted. "Have you brought it up to Gros?"

She smiled slightly and shook her head. "Pieter would never go for it. It would mean splitting the glory." Her passion drained, and she said in a lighter tone, "Enough museum talk. Tell me about you."

"There's not that much to tell, I'm afraid."

"Is it true what Pieter said, about your going to jail on a matter of principle?"

"Yeah, it's true."

"I'm impressed."

"That was a different time, a different profession."

She raised an eyebrow. "And a different man?"

"Sometimes I wonder," I said honestly.

"So what kind of a profession is the private-eye business?" she asked with what sounded like honest curiosity.

"About like the museum business, except the intrigue is usually at a much more petty level."

"Do you like it?"

"Not really."

That seemed to surprise her. "Then why do you do it?"

I gave her the result of twelve years of pondering that same question. "Because I'm good at it."

"That's the only reason?"

I smiled. "The only one that makes any sense at all."

Dinner arrived and as we ate we lapsed into small talk, mostly about the food, which was exceptionally tasty that night. By the end of the meal, we had decided that Maui butter tasted about like any other kind, and we had stumped the waitress on what part of the country the parsley garnish had come from. Heather made a token offer to pick up half the check, which I rebuffed with a slight shake of the head and a wave of the credit card. She didn't know it, but it would be going on her boss's bill, anyway.

I drove her home feeling a nice warm glow from the wine.

I walked her to her door and she stopped outside and said, "Thank you for dinner."

"Would you like to do it again sometime?"

She smiled demurely. "That would be nice."

She tilted her head up at the perfect angle and her eyes softened. I put my arms around her and we kissed. After ten seconds or so, the kiss turned into something a little heavier than a good-night kiss and she pushed away and looked up at me with a coquettish grin. "I think maybe we'd better call it a night."

I stepped back and nodded. I could still smell her hair, her skin.

"I like you," she said.

"I like you, too."

"I'm afraid I talked too much tonight. Maybe it was all the wine. Please don't repeat anything I said to anyone. Especially Pieter."

"Don't worry about it," I assured her.

Her brow relaxed relievedly. "Thank you. Good night."

I drove home thinking about Hugo von Castiglioni, a nineteenth-century Italian industrialist. "There are men that are proud of their poverty," von Castiglioni had once said. "These are the poets. There are women who are proud of their ugliness. These are the intellectuals. Avoid both like the plague."

I never had. I liked intellectual women, which may have been one reason I was still living alone at the age of forty-one.

I knew what von Castiglioni had been talking about. Some intellectual women I had known wore austerity like a badge of courage, a statement of identity. I'd come to the conclusion that that was not the case with Heather Piccard. She simply seemed like a woman comfortable with the way she looked and felt no need to dress it up. From that standpoint, she did not fit von Castiglioni's bill. And even though a few cosmetic touches here and there probably wouldn't have hurt, the woman was far from ugly.

Not that it mattered. Avoid them, not avoid them, the result was the same: I was still living like a plague victim.

# TWENTY-FOUR

When I got home, I made myself a see-through and worked on it while I checked with the service. Tony Bruenig had called and left his home number. His wife answered and I gave her my name and waited while she went to get him. After what seemed like a long time, he picked up the phone. "Sorry it took so long, Asch. I was on the can."

"That's okay. What's up?"

"Nothing good. Forensics went over the car. They got some prints, but none of them Fox's. I've filed a missing persons report, but that's about all I can do at this stage."

"Santa Monica P.D. has an APB out on Fox and the girl and the S.O. has a murder warrant on Fox as of this afternoon. They are definitely a hot ticket."

"A ticket I'd like to punch. They seem to have disappeared into thin air. I've checked every marina up the coast. They haven't put in anywhere. Either they've blown the country, or they've scuttled the boat and are holed up somewhere."

I thought it unlikely that Fox would have scuttled his boat, but with nine million bucks at stake it was a possibility.

"Could they have put in at a cove somewhere?"

"Not on this coast," he said.

"What about *off* the coast?" I threw out.

"The Channel Islands?"

"It's a thought."

"Not a bad one, either. I'll get on it in the morning."

I hung up feeling good and morose. I turned on the tube to get the latest installment of the Saga of Tent City, but there was nothing on the ten o'clock news except a couple of murders, which I was not in the mood to hear about. I switched channels until I landed on a 1950s classic, *Attack of the 50-Foot Woman*, starring Allison Hayes. I made myself another drink and was in the process of burying my thoughts in some gloriously bad filmmaking, when the phone rang.

I said hello and a man's voice I didn't recognize said, "Jacob Asch, please."

"Speaking," I said, cautiously. I have a tendency to speak that way when unfamiliar voices call on my unlisted number at ten o'clock at night.

"My name is Maynard Tarcher, Mr. Asch. I'm personal assistant to Mr. C. W. Bryant."

"Yes?"

"Mr. Bryant would like to speak with you."

"Okay," I said. "Put him on."

"He would like to speak with you in person. He would like you to come to his home."

"When?"

"This evening, if it would be convenient."

"I wouldn't say it would be convenient, but I can make it. Half an hour?"

"That will be fine," he said. "I believe you know where it is."

I thought there might have been a touch of irony in that last part, but I wasn't sure. Irony was one of those little subtleties in life that often escaped me. "I know where it is. By the way, how did you get this number?"

"It wasn't difficult," he said casually.

I pulled up in front of the metal gates with three minutes to spare and pushed the intercom button. A voice asked who I was and I told it and there was an electronic buzz and the gates swung open.

The driveway wound up a wooded hillside through stands of oak and toyon and cottonwood and ended in the brightly floodlit front of a huge medieval-style English manor house, with masonry walls and diamond-paned windows, and dormers jutting from its multiplicity of steeply pointed roofs. The Mark VII and the Cutlass were both parked out front and I parked behind them.

I started up the stone walkway toward the front door, which must have been nine feet high. It opened before I got to it and the square-jawed All-American from the Lincoln stepped out. He was either wearing the same dark suit, or he had more than one. Probably the latter, I decided, unless he had the one pressed every day.

"Tarcher?" I asked.

"That's right." His tone was coldly hostile. He took a step back and waved me into the house.

As I passed him, I said, "Tsk, tsk. You lied to me."

"About what?"

"Burt and Loni don't live on Roxbury."

His jaw clenched.

"Where's Leroy? Watching the street through the video monitors?" Maynard and Leroy. It sounded like a city council from Tupelo, Mississippi.

"This way," was all he said.

He led the way through an enormous marble-floored entryway past a huge red-carpeted staircase and into a wide high-ceilinged study, the oak-paneled walls of which were crowded with old dark oil paintings in gilt frames. A fire blazed in the huge stone fireplace at the other end of the room, and Arbogast stood beside it, watching me. In a large high-backed leather chair a few yards away from him, also watching me, was C. W. Bryant.

He wore a pale blue shirt, gray slacks with suspenders, a red and blue polka-dot bow tie, gray socks, and black bedroom slippers. His head, which was bald except for a sparse fringe of white, looked too big for the small, fragile-looking body. He had a turned-down owl-beak of a nose, a small, almost lipless mouth, and small, dark eyes, which were watchful behind a pair of tortoise-shell glasses. His clawlike hands, with bluish nails, gripped the wooden arms of the chair tightly. Perhaps it was an illusion created by the oversized chair in which he seemed almost lost, but he looked older, more insubstantial than he did in the television interviews I'd seen of him. He looked like a shriveled little gnome.

"Thank you for coming," Bryant said in a surprisingly strong voice. He made no attempt to stand or to shake hands. "This is Dr. Benjamin Arbogast. But I believe you already know that."

Arbogast eyed me coldly. "You came to my room at the hotel."

I nodded and returned his stare without saying anything.

Bryant waved at a chair. The hand remained clawlike in the air, the fingers arthritically bent. "Sit down, Mr. Asch. May I offer you something? I have some excellent hundred-year-old brandy."

"Fine."

He waved the claw at Maynard, who unhappily walked over to an antique burl table and poured a snifter of brandy from a cut-glass decanter. I sank into the leather twin of the chair in which Bryant was sitting. Tarcher came over and handed the brandy to me grudgingly before moving around behind his boss's chair. He remained standing—there was no sense getting too comfortable, in case Bryant waved his hand again—his eyes fastened on me. They were the eyes of a man conscious of security.

I held up the snifter. "Nobody else is going to join me?"

"Dr. Arbogast doesn't drink," Bryant said. "And I've already had my one for the evening." He seemed proud of his self-discipline.

I took a sip of the brandy. He was right, it was excellent, and I said so. He smiled appreciatively. "Brandy is one thing that gets better with age. Like good art. Time is the greatest regulator of quality control that we have. If a work of art is truly great, it must stand the test of time. Don't you agree?"

"I'll let you know in about twenty years."

He looked puzzled. "What happens then?"

"If Jackie Collins is still in print then, I'll have to give you an argument."

He chortled halfheartedly. "A sense of humor. I like that."

I didn't think he particularly liked it or disliked it. I don't think he cared about it at all. The chortle had been nothing more than a polite gesture, to show me that he could be magnanimous with power.

I swirled the brandy around in the snifter before taking another sip. That was what they did in the movies, and it seemed as good an idea as anything else. "So what am I doing here, Mr. Bryant?"

He said unflinchingly, "You are working for Pieter Gros."

I blinked dumbly. "Pieter who?"

Bryant let out a breath and leaned forward. "Okay. Just to save time, we'll play it that way. I'll tell *you*; that way there won't be any doubt. You are working for Gros, who is trying to acquire for the L.A. County Museum of Art a certain collection of artifacts known as the treasure of Tarchundaraus. I am currently negotiating to purchase the same artifacts, which is why you have been following Professor Arbogast."

I said nothing. The flames of the fire were reflected in his glasses, eclipsing his eyes. I tried to keep my face blank as we exchanged gazes, but there was something disconcerting about the round circles of flame, as if I were looking into his empty eye sockets and seeing a fire that was his brain. A tolerant smile spread across his bloodless lips. "You know anything about me, Mr. Asch?"

"What I read in the papers."

"That's enough to know I usually get what I want."

That I believed. Never underestimate a gnome. Look at Yoda. He had the power of the Force behind him. I felt the power of some Force behind Bryant, too. Part of it was the money and the power that came with it. But part of it was how he had gotten the money, a little bit of which he had just let me see. He sat back and the fire went out of his eyes. "Pieter knows I'm after the treasure, doesn't he?"

He already knew the answer to that. He only wanted me to answer it as a positive affirmation on my part as to who was in charge. "You seem to be supplying the answers."

He nodded and smiled and ran a hand across his skull. "When he called me up to get my approval for the purchase, I was frankly surprised. Even if Pieter managed to acquire it for the museum, he couldn't exhibit it. The Turkish government would immediately file suit. He has to see that."

"You'll have to ask him that," I told him. "I'm just a hired hand. But he might ask you the same question."

"I don't intend to put the treasure out on display," he said.

"It doesn't bother you that you're robbing these countries of their artistic heritage?"

His smile turned indulgent. "Art is mankind's heritage, Mr. Asch. It belongs to no nation. It has historically been a form of plunder. It was for Sulla when he sacked Athens and for Napoleon when he conquered Egypt. Art has always been one of the spoils of war."

"What war are you in, Mr. Bryant?"

His tone became chagrined. "You miss the point."

"Just what is the point?"

"The art wound up in the hands of those who loved it. If Napoleon hadn't taken those pieces out of Egypt and put them in the Louvre, they would have been lost to the world. They would have been broken up and defaced, covered with graffiti spray-painted by submoronic delinquents.

"You don't think the countries from which the art has been taken know that? Why do you think their laws are so lax? Hell, if the officials who were doing all the squawking were serious, they'd execute the smugglers when they caught them, instead of giving them a slap on the wrist like they do." He rested his hands on his knees and went on. "The fact is, son, they don't care. They don't care because they don't want to commit the resources necessary to preserve and protect mankind's precious artistic heritage. And because half the politicians doing the squawking are taking a slice of the pie under the table."

He waited for me to say something and when I didn't, he wet his lips and said in a tone that was slightly recriminating, "You look on it as exploitation. What it really is is economic democracy in action. In the antiquities trade, everybody profits: from the collector who gets what he wants, to the lowest tomb robber who gets what he wants, to the middlemen with itchy palms who get what they want. So where is the harm? These people may get up and scream about disguised colonialism and the economic plundering of the Third World, but if they really wanted the trade stopped, they'd stop it. It's as simple as that."

I waited for the lecture on the "white man's burden," but thankfully it didn't come. I asked casually, "You still haven't answered my question. What am I doing here?"

"Right now, you are only a mild nuisance, but you could possibly become a major problem in the very near future."

"You mean when the deal goes down."

He nodded, pleased that I'd gotten it. "Precisely. I asked you here to see if we could reach some sort of amicable accord. How much do you want to butt out of this business?"

I rubbed my chin. "I'd have to give that some thought."

"Why don't you do that now?"

I tried to look pensive. I wondered if he knew just what he was getting mixed up in, that his original contact was dead, and that Fox and Naci were wanted for questioning about that murder and perhaps two more. Probably not. Otherwise, he would have certainly used that to sway the other museum trustees into turning down Gros's appeal for funding. "How did you learn about the treasure?"

He thought about it and shrugged. "I don't see what harm there would be in telling you that. I received a set of photographs in the mail at my corporate headquarters downtown. Along with the photographs was a note that said that if I was interested I should be in the office at noon, two days later. I was. In the meantime, I had sent copies of the photographs to Dr. Arbogast at the Oriental Institute. We talked on the phone, and he said it was very possible that the treasure was the same one he had seen in Turkey." He paused. "You know the background of the treasure?"

"Sketchily," I said, glancing at Arbogast, who was still standing by the fireplace.

"I flew Professor Arbogast out here. I wanted him to be on hand when the man called back. That was on a Thursday. The man arranged for a meeting that night at a motel on La Cienega. He was to bring three pieces for my inspection, along with a sample to be thermoluminescence tested. Unfortunately, I had to be out of town that night. There was an important business deal I had to close in Dallas and I'd put it off so that I'd be there when the phone call came. I told the man that Arbogast would be coming in my place. He said that was fine with him."

I turned to Arbogast. "What pieces did they bring?"

He described the same three pieces they had shown Heather Piccard. "You're sure they were the same pieces you saw in Izmir?"

"Not only the pieces," he said. "The girl, too."

I scratched my cheek. A few points about this story still bothered me. "Did this mystery girl ever say how she was supposed to have come by this treasure?"

He shrugged. "She said her grandfather had found it. In the chest with the treasure in Izmir were several photographs. They were yellowed and charred, and one of them had a date written on it in pen: December 4, 1922. The photographs were of some opened graves in which were skeletons, surrounded by the objects in the chest. I'm convinced the girl's grandfather had stumbled on the gravesite during the Greco-Turko war. Perhaps the entrance to the tomb had been opened by an explosion or something."

"And you never found the house in Izmir again?"

He made a frustrated gesture. "No. When I went back, I was told they changed the street names every couple of months in Izmir. The address I'd taken down simply didn't exist anymore, neither did any record as to where it had been.

"The Turkish government made a big issue out of that. They claimed that I had conspired with the girl to help smuggle the treasure out of the country. That was absurd, of course. If I'd wanted to smuggle the treasure out of Turkey, why would I call attention to it by writing an article about it?"

I didn't have an answer for him, so I didn't try to give him one. He went on, his face becoming angrily flushed as he reminisced. "At the same time the treasure disappeared, the senior officer of the Ministry of Antiquities resigned his government post to become director of the Izmir trade fair. The timing was too coincidental. The man was a crook, a middleman between tomb robbers and dealers in illicit art. I'm sure he had a hand in helping smuggle the treasure out of the country."

"And the government decided to make a scapegoat out of you to cover it up," I postulated.

"Exactly," he said emphatically.

"This man's name wouldn't happen to be Bahadir Bey, would it?"

His eyes narrowed. My mind-reading act was right-on tonight. "Yes. How did you know?"

"I talked to him. He's in L.A. now."

"What is he doing here?" Bryant asked.

I shrugged. "He says he's trying to recover the treasure for Turkey."

"He's lying," Arbogast said. "He hasn't worked for the Turkish government for years. He's trying to grab it for himself."

"That's pretty much what he says about you," I told him. "He says you are in league with the sellers and are using your connections to set up a buyer."

"That's ridiculous," Bryant cut in. "Dr. Arbogast knew nothing of the treasure being in L.A. until I called him."

I turned to Arbogast. "While you were in Turkey, did you ever run into a man named Garo Saffarian?"

"I met him once. He represented himself as a dealer in antiquities, but he was a reputed smuggler. He had a shop in the bazaar in Istanbul. He invited me over to take a look at some of the artifacts he was selling. They were mostly forgeries."

"Bahadir claims you contacted Saffarian to smuggle the treasure out of Turkey."

His face reddened. "Preposterous! The man is nothing but a foul-mouthed liar!"

His reaction looked genuine, and for the moment I was willing to believe him. I turned to Bryant. "So what's the deal?"

"That's for you to tell me," he said. "You were going to name a price."

I shook my head and smiled as if I pitied him. Actually, pity was the last thing I was feeling. "Sorry, Mr. Bryant, but no can do."

"You would be much better advised to work for me than for Gros," he said steadily. "With Gros, this one job will be the end of it. In my many businesses, the need often arises for an investigator. Cases of industrial espionage, all sorts of matters—"

I had never before had so many people want to pay me to work the same case differently. "You wouldn't be able to use a man who said yes to an offer like that, and you know it. How could you trust me not to sell out your secrets to the next guy who came along waving some green in front of my face?"

He nodded sadly. "I talked to some people about you. Frankly, I'm disappointed to find that you live up to your reputation for honesty. I'm warning you for your own good, Mr. Asch, stay out of my way on this." His tone was not threatening, but the meaning was clear enough.

I thought about what Heather Piccard had said at dinner. I decided to try it out. I doubted he would go for it, but what the hell. "From what I can see, Mr. Bryant, you and Gros are only going to succeed in driving the price of the treasure out of sight. That isn't going to be advantageous for either of you. All you're going to do is screw each other. Why don't you try working together for a change?"

He grunted deprecatingly. "And just how do you propose we do that? Split the expense and divide the spoils?"

I laid out the bare bones of Heather's plan. He listened and when I'd finished, he sneered, "I've seen how they handle my donations while I'm alive, I can imagine how they would do it once I was dead and not around to raise hell about it. Forget it. I couldn't deal with Gros. The man is impossible."

"Because he wounded your ego?"

He leaned forward and stared at me intently. I could see his eyes just fine and they were burning as hot as the flames had been. "What I go after, I get, Mr. Asch. Gros knows that. If you stick with him, you'll find it out. I'm going to have the treasure of Tarchundaraus."

I didn't say anything.

"Stay out of the way, or I promise you, you're going to get steam-rolled."

I drained the rest of the hundred-year-old brandy in one gulp and stood up. I handed the snifter to Maynard Tarcher, who took it, albeit resentfully. "Ever hear of the Collyer brothers, Mr. Bryant?"

He grasped the arms of his chair and frowned up at me. "No."

"Homer and Langley," I said. "They were the sons of a New York doctor. Back in 1909, they shut themselves up in their Fifth Avenue townhouse and devoted their lives to collecting. When the cops finally broke down their doors in 1947 because of a complaint by one of the next-door neighbors about the smell, they had to chop their way through a solid mass of newspapers and junk that the brothers had accumulated. They found fourteen pianos, a dismantled Model T, hundreds of toys, and everything else the pair had ever bought. They also found the brothers. Homer's body had been partially eaten by rats. Langley had been crushed to death under a mass of newspapers, a trap the two had rigged up to fall on any burglars who might have wanted to come in and steal their prized collection."

"I fail to see the point," Bryant said, scowling. "I don't collect newspapers."

"Langley was killed by the weight of his own collection, Mr. Bryant. Call it a metaphor."

"I'm not much of a poet, I'm afraid." His tone was unregretful.

"It doesn't bother you that there could be blood on the treasure?"

He emitted a dry cackle that sounded like dead twigs snapping. "You want to talk about blood, Mr. Asch? Try putting in an off-shore oil platform. Good night."

I turned and walked out with Maynard on my heels, my snifter still in his hand. At the front door, I stopped and smiled at him. "What else does a personal assistant do beside fetching drinks?"

The skin seemed to grow tauter across his face. "Who knows? Someday you might find out. Someday soon."

"Don't tell me. Let me guess. Ex-Secret Service, right?"

He might have smiled then, but then again maybe not. It was hard to tell. He pulled open the door and walked me out to the car. He wasn't being polite. He just wanted to make sure I left.

# TWENTY-FIVE

I woke up the next morning at seven, unrested and bleary-eyed. I sat at the breakfast table and drank coffee until the pattern on the wallpaper cleared up, after which I showered and shaved and dressed to kill, in charcoal slacks and socks, a yellow button-down shirt, and the new gray tweed sports jacket I'd bought on sale the previous month.

I always tried to look at least semi-prosperous when I talked with attorneys. As a breed of humanity I didn't have much use for them, but they were my bread and butter; you never knew when a new one might throw some business your way. Checking myself over in the mirror, I decided I looked pretty spiffy except for my brown loafers, which had sustained a few uncosmeticizable scuff marks while making the rounds. I figured that was okay. It would show Morris Katelbaum he would be getting a lot of legwork for a buck.

Gros had left the message with my service that my appointment with Katelbaum was set for eight-thirty in the lawyer's Westwood office, which turned out to be on the twelfth floor of a glass and steel skyscraper overlooking Wilshire. I arrived on time and was ushered immediately through the already-busy offices by a blond secretary to a door at the end of a plushly carpeted hallway.

The office behind the door was a spacious, paneled affair, typical of those of the most affluent attorneys, replete with the obligatory stacks of legal briefs on the desk. Katelbaum was a small, gray-haired man with a rubbery clown's nose and a strongly cleft chin. His dark blue tailored Brioni suit said quietly that he was very good at what he did. We shook hands and sat down.

"Pieter filled me in briefly on your problem" he began, tapping all of his fingers together repeatedly. "Just to make sure I have all the facts straight, why don't you tell me in your own words?"

I did. When I had finished, he cleared his throat and said, "The question here is whether as a private citizen it is legally your affirmative duty to do the police's job for them. It is my opinion that it is not." He thought for a moment, then inquired, "Did they ask you any specific direct questions concerning the woman at the Mondrian Hotel?"

"They asked if the description sounded like anybody I knew."

He frowned unhappily. "You told them no."

"Yes."

He put his hands on the desk. "You could have a problem there. Again, I don't think legally. There are probably hundreds of women in this city with gray streaks in their hair. At the time you were asked, you could have had a lapse of memory. As far as your license is concerned, that is another problem. If they wanted to go hard on you they could probably go after it, and maybe get it. How are your relations generally with the police?"

"Good, I'd say."

He shrugged. "The odds are, then, that they probably wouldn't go that far."

"What about your firm hiring me?"

"Frankly, in a case like this, I don't know how much that would shield you. Our firm does not handle criminal matters. Anyway, Ms. Piccard has not been charged with a crime. The police only wish to talk with her in regards to the homicide."

"What if Ms. Piccard and I went to the police and she told her story?"

He turned up a palm. "That, of course, would solve everybody's problem. If she has nothing to hide, she has nothing to worry about."

I knew Gros would never go for that, not as long as the treasure was at stake. "What if we went to the police after the purchase was made?"

"Again, it would depend on the attitude of the police. If the suspects get away because of your conscious failure to report your dealings with them, they could give you—and the museum—trouble. I have informed Pieter that. The question is what kind of trouble. In this country a person, at least in theory, is innocent until proven guilty. For all you know, these two people the police are looking for could have had nothing to do with either crime."

"Okay," I said, nodding. "Say Gros came to you and said he thought it was possible that the museum could be embroiled in a scandal involving the murder at the Mondrian, and you hired me to investigate Heather Piccard's involvement. Would the confidentiality rules between lawyer and client give me any protection?"

He thought about that and concluded, "I frankly don't know. It probably wouldn't hurt."

That was good enough for me. "Let's do it."

The phone buzzed and he picked it up. "Yes? All right, put him on. And Miss Stans, fill in a retainer agreement with Mr. Asch. Date it—" He looked the question at me.

"The day before yesterday."

"The nineteenth. That's right." He punched one of the rotary lines and said, "Hello? Yes, he's here now. Just a minute." He handed me the receiver.

"Asch?" Gros asked. "How are things going with Katelbaum?"

"Okay."

"Are you still working for us?"

"For six hundred dollars a day," I said.

Katelbaum looked shocked by the mention of the sum.

"Yes, yes," Gros said impatiently. "I want you to come to my office as soon as you finish up there. C. W. Bryant is going to be here at ten."

"Bryant?" I asked, somewhat surprised.

"That's right," he said gruffly. "He called me this morning at home. He wants to meet to discuss the treasure. He said you were over at his place last night."

"I was summoned. What does he want to talk about?"

"That's what I want to talk to *you* about. Before he gets here."

I glanced at my watch. It was going to be tight, but I assured him I would make it over there as quickly as possible. Katelbaum was staring at me incredulously as I hung up the phone. "Six hundred dollars a day? No investigator gets six hundred dollars a day."

I smiled at him and shrugged. "When you're hot, you're hot."

I took the elevator downstairs and used the pay phone to call Louie. "You pick up Bey?"

"We picked him up. We couldn't find any gun, though, on him or in his room. He denies there ever was a gun. He says you made it all up."

"Why would I do that?"

"He doesn't know."

"Did he admit being in Santa Monica?"

"Yeah, but he says the door was open, like you said, and he wandered in looking for his good buddy Papadoupoulous. You came in and ran him out. Hyde has him now."

"You didn't hold on to him?"

"Nothing to hold him with. He has a watertight alibi for the time Saffarian was killed. And the gun business is your word against his."

"Did you check him out with the Turkish authorities?"

"Yeah. The consulate says Bey used to work for the Ministry of Antiquities but resigned three years ago."

"Did he tell you what he was doing in the United States?"

"Sure. He's here to see Disneyland."

I hung up and called Hyde. "What's up, Asch?"

"Are you holding Bahadir Bey?"

"Not as of an hour ago."

"Why'd you cut him loose?"

"No reason to hold him," he said. "The guy only arrived in the States three days ago. That means he couldn't have possibly killed Papadoupoulous."

"Did he tell you any cockamamie stories about a treasure?"

"A treasure? What kind of treasure?"

"Never mind," I said quickly, and hung up.

# TWENTY-SIX

---

Gros and Heather were waiting in his office when I arrived at 9:50. She was dressed sedately in a black knit dress cinched at the waist with a wide black belt; he had on a gray gabardine suit, white shirt, and a blue and gray paisley tie.

Extra chairs had been brought in. I sat in one of them and proceeded to hit on the high points of last night's conversation with Bryant. When I got around to my suggestion of a joint purchase, Gros interrupted angrily. "Where in the world would you come up with such a harebrained idea?"

Out of his line of vision, Heather caught my eye and shook her head, almost imperceptibly. "It just struck me that it might be to your benefit to join forces with Bryant, instead of trying to fight him—"

"It struck *you?*" he said, tight-lipped. "Just who the hell are you to decide what is to my benefit?"

Heather jumped in quickly. "You have to admit, it's a novel proposal. One that could solve everybody's problem—"

"It isn't going to solve anything," Gros snapped at her. "There is no way in hell Bryant would enter into a joint deal. He is not the kind of man to share anything. All it succeeded in doing was tipping off Bryant that we knew about him." He turned back to me and said sternly, "You should never have gone to see Bryant without my permission."

I waited for him to tell me I was grounded. "What would have been the purpose in turning him down? I thought you'd want to know what's on his mind."

He grunted. "Nobody ever knows what's on C. W. Bryant's mind except C. W. Bryant." He exhaled and pulled distractedly on his cheek. "I wonder what's on his mind."

We were soon to find out. The intercom buzzed and Gros picked up the phone. "Yes? Send him in."

Gros's expression changed instantly as the political demon inside him took over. His frown turned into a gracious smile and he stood to greet the diminutive billionaire, who came in trailed by Arbogast and Tarcher. Bryant and Tarcher looked neat and pressed in dark blue suits, Bryant wearing a yellow and gray polka-dot bow tie today. By contrast, Arbogast's appearance was rumpled and unkempt. His hair was frazzled, the knot in his green tie was askew, and his cheap brown corduroy jacket was badly wrinkled.

"C. W.," Gros said in an oily voice and thrust out his hand. "How are you?"

Bryant grunted something and unenthusiastically offered his own hand. "You know my personal assistant, Maynard Tarcher. And, of course, Dr. Arbogast."

"We have not formally met," Gros said, pumping the professor's hand. "But I feel as if we have. I've read almost everything you've written. It is an honor."

Arbogast smiled, apparently taken in by the flattery.

Everyone sat down except for Tarcher, of course, who gave away his true calling by walking to the window and peering out suspiciously.

Bryant looked around and cleared his throat. "I'm assuming there is nobody in this room that shouldn't be here."

Gros looked at Heather, then at me. "Not unless you object to somebody's presence."

Bryant shook his head. "If everybody here has your confidence, Pieter, that's good enough for me. I assume Asch here told you all about our meeting last night."

"Yes," Gros said.

"I have to admit that at first I flatly rejected the idea of a

joint venture in going after the treasure of Tarchundaraus. All
I could see were the difficulties involved and the unresolved
conflicts we've had in the past. But the more I thought about
it, the more I thought the idea to be viable. I saw it as a way
to work out our differences and get the museum back on the
right track, to inject some vitality back into this institution."

Gros was trying hard not to look stunned. "You are in favor
of the idea?"

"Yes, I am. If the details can be worked out." Bryant paused
and eyed Gros shrewdly. "You look surprised, Pieter. I'm
assuming Asch was acting as your emissary in bringing up the
proposal?"

Gros tried to regain his balance. "Yes, certainly. I just never
thought you would go for it."

"I've looked at it from a lot of different perspectives,"
Bryant said, "and from what I can see, the down side is
minimal. The museum could not display the treasure for
years, anyway. No matter when it is displayed, the Turkish
government will raise holy hell, but by then there will be
enough time for a sequence of alleged owners to be laid down.
I will arrange on paper to purchase the treasure from a
European dealer, who bought it from a family who had owned
it for years." He paused, then dropped the bombshell. "After
all, we don't want it to get around that it was acquired from a
couple of fugitives wanted for murder. That kind of publicity
wouldn't do anyone any good."

Gros flushed and looked at me angrily.

"Don't look at me," I said defensively.

"Asch didn't tell me," Bryant told Gros.

"Who did?" I asked.

Bryant smiled enigmatically. "I have my sources." He
continued as if unaware of the effect the revelation was having
on Gros, who was pale. "The Turks will protest, of course,
but the chain of ownership can be clouded enough so that
their legal claim to it will be questionable. In the interim, I
will retain possession of it. Upon my death, the treasure,
along with all of my other pieces, will be bequeathed to the
museum, to be housed in the C. W. Bryant wing. To the
exclusion of all other exhibits, of course."

Gros said irascibly, "You can't be serious. We've been all
through this for the past year—"

"With a little difference," Bryant cut him off. "We're not just talking about what is on exhibit in the museum now. We're talking about my private collection, too. Seventy million dollars worth."

"Some of that private collection the museum could not possibly exhibit, even in 2025," Gros insisted. "The Toltec pieces were not just smuggled out of Mexico, they were from a burglary, for God's sake—"

Bryant pooh-poohed that with a wave of his hand. "So give them back to Mexico. You can be a hero. Hold a press conference and say they were donated to the museum by an anonymous donor and you want to return them to their rightful home. You can score points with UNESCO and the international community to offset the screaming of the Turkish government when the treasure goes on display."

Gros fixed Bryant with a suspicious stare. "What brought you to this decision, C. W.?"

Bryant said quietly, "I have a legacy to leave. A legacy to mankind. It's either going to be left to an institution like the County Museum, or I'm going to have to build my own museum. I'm not really anxious to take on a project of that magnitude at this time. I have enough problems right now with environmental groups and the Coastal Commission and the County Board of Supervisors without having to deal with architects and bitchy-fag interior designers."

Gros's expression remained skeptical. Bryant didn't seem to notice. "We've had our difference in the past, Pieter, but we both love this museum. There are only a couple of institutions in the country big enough to handle my collection properly. You and I both know that. I don't want to leave my collection to the Met or the National Gallery. I'm a Western boy. This is where my roots are, this is where I've made my money. I want my collection here. And I want the treasure of Tarchundaraus to be part of that collection."

Gros rubbed his chin thoughtfully, then nodded, apparently satisfied. "All right."

"We're agreed?"

"Yes," Gros said. "You're right about one thing, C. W. For all our differences, we are the standard bearers of humanity. We owe it to the world to bury our past bitterness and make sure this treasure does not elude us."

I half expected them to stand up, pick up flags, and march around the room singing "The Battle Hymn of the Museum."

"I'll have my attorneys get in touch with Katelbaum immediately to begin working out the details," Bryant said. "When did the dealers arrange to call you about the purchase?"

"Today at noon."

Bryant nodded. "They are supposed to call me at twelve-thirty. That will give us time to discuss the arrangements for the payoff."

Worry momentarily darkened Gros's expression. "I wonder how they'll take the news that we're working together?"

Bryant shrugged. "Where else are they going to go? There are no other private collectors of antiquities in L.A. big enough to handle this kind of a deal. And I personally know the reserves of the only other local museum that could possibly swing the deal—the Getty—are depleted. They made several large acquisitions this year which used up a lot of their funding. They could possibly raise the needed funds by calling an emergency meeting of the trustees, but it would take too long. Besides the money, we offer these people one commodity nobody else can—time."

"What are we going to set as a ceiling?" Gros asked.

"We're splitting the bill," Bryant said casually. "How about the amount approved by the trustees? Fifteen million?"

Gros considered it and said, "Seven and a half apiece. That sounds all right to me."

"We should be able to get it for considerably less than that figure," Bryant said. "You have your part of the payment ready?"

"DeBeers has assured me they will be here at two o'clock," Gros said.

"Diamonds?" I chimed in.

Bryant nodded. "That was how they insisted payment be made. Blue-white, flawless, between one to two-and-a-half carats. Nothing smaller."

I tried to imagine what fifteen million in diamonds looked like. "I hope you realize we're talking major security problems, guarding that much ice."

"Security problems are Maynard's specialty," Bryant said

confidently. "He was with the Secret Service for eleven years before he came to work for me."

I gave Tarcher my best I-knew-it smile. He didn't smile back.

"Maynard?" Bryant cued him.

Tarcher turned his back to the window, carelessly opening himself up to sniper fire from the nearby skyscrapers. "The key to controlling the buy is to control the location. The location we pick has to meet certain requirements. It has to be secure for us and easily monitored, in case they decide to get cute and try a rip-off, and it has to satisfy them it isn't a police trap. It has to be a place where they're not likely to run into the cops. These people have both the Sheriff's Office and the P.D. looking for them. We don't want an arrest screwing up the deal. And it's going to have to be somewhere quiet and private where Dr. Arbogast can spend at least an hour with the treasure, to insure its authenticity."

"Why not here?" I suggested. "That way we'll only have to transport the diamonds once."

Tarcher shook his head. "Too risky. Aside from running the risk of them being picked up before or after the deal, there are too many ways in and out of this building. We'd have to bring more people into it. Then, if something did go wrong, the museum would be directly implicated."

Gros reacted to that. "That would be disastrous. It has to be somewhere else."

"You have somewhere in mind?" I asked Tarcher.

"The U.S. West platform off Malibu," he said. "It's perfect. It's beyond the twelve-mile limit, so it's out of the jurisdiction of the local law enforcement agencies. Fox can approach it by boat at night, to reduce the chance of his being spotted—"

I instantly latched on to that. "How do you know Fox is on a boat?"

It was his turn to smile. "Like Mr. Bryant says, we have our sources."

They were beginning to impress me more all the time.

Tarcher went on. "There is only one way they can get from the boat up to the platform, and that's by a narrow staircase on the north face. The climb up to the second level production platform is a good ninety-foot climb, so we can observe them coming up, to make sure they don't show up with any extra troops. With perimeter access controlled by us, the area will be easy to secure. The set-up is perfect. The deal can go down in one of the offices and we can have a backup in the next room monitoring everything, just in case something does start to go wrong."

"What about the rig's crew?"

"Since the EPA's injunction, there's only a skeleton crew. They can be sent ashore for the time we need."

He seemed to have thought of everything. "What if the dealers don't go for it?"

"We'll just have to stand firm," Tarcher said evenly. "They're getting the diamonds, like they wanted. They can't expect to have everything their way."

Gros looked at me questioningly. "Asch?"

I shrugged. "Sounds all right to me."

Gros nodded and checked his watch. "An hour and a half to go. Are you going to wait here for the call, C. W.?"

"I figured that would give them a definite message that we are solidly together on this thing, as well as making it easier to coordinate the arrangements," Bryant said. "Where is a private line I can use?"

"Right out here."

Bryant and Tarcher followed Gros out into the outer office, and I said to Heather, "Glory-grabbing seems to be a universal trait with museum directors. Why didn't you want me to tell Gros that the joint venture was your idea?"

She shrugged diffidently. "He would have seen it as a backdoor move on my part. He tends to see conspiracies everywhere."

"It seems to have worked out fine," I said.

"We'll see. I don't know how Pieter expects to be able to sell it to the trustees. It will mean expecting them to swallow all the demands Bryant has been making on them all year."

"How are they going to handle the fact that the museum has been involved in a deal with wanted criminals?"

"If they ever find that out," she said gravely, "it'll be Pieter's head."

"That's one thing I can't understand," I said.

"What?"

"Why Bryant didn't sabotage Gros's pitch to the trustees if he wanted to grab the treasure for himself? All he would've had to do was let the word get out that the museum was dealing with wanted criminals, and they would have turned him down flat."

She turned up her hands. "Why should he? This way, he's got everything he's wanted, and he's only laying out half the money for it."

That made sense, but it did little to allay the bothersome thoughts tugging at the corners of my mind.

# TWENTY-SEVEN

---

**C**offee and croissants were imported for the wait—a museum director's idea of stakeout fare—but I turned out to be the only one indulging. Bryant and Gros spent the hour and a half on and off the telephones to their respective attorneys, Heather and Arbogast babbled excitedly about "Egyptian and Cycladic influences," and Tarcher alternated between staring warily out at the Tar Pits and standing around looking like an aging chorus boy from *G-Men on Parade*.

As the hands on my watch crept toward noon, an expectant hush fell over the office, and everyone began to involuntarily eye the phone on the desk. I had to admit, the thought of parting with that kind of money was making me tense too, and it wasn't even my money.

At one minute past twelve the phone rang much louder than it should have, and Gros snatched it up. "Pieter Gros here."

There was a pause, then a voice that could have been Fox's sounded accusingly through the speakerbox on the desk: "You're on a speakerbox."

Gros looked around. "Uh, yes, that's right."

The voice quivered with paranoia. "Who else is there with you? Who's listening in?"

"C. W. Bryant, Heather Piccard, Dr. Benjamin Arbogast, and Maynard Tarcher, Mr. Bryant's personal assistant."

I felt slighted that he had omitted me, but only slightly.

"*Bryant?*" the man asked, startled.

"That's right," Gros said. "Mr. Bryant and the museum have decided to purchase the treasure jointly. So you can forget any thought you had of driving up the price by getting us to bid against one another."

"What kind of a bullshit trick is this?" the caller demanded angrily.

Bryant leaned toward the speaker on the desk. "This is C. W. Bryant. I can assure you it's no trick. What Dr. Gros just told you is correct. If you don't believe it, call my private number, the one you contacted me on last time you called. The man who will answer is named Phillips. He will tell you where I am."

There was a long, confused silence. "Well, if that's the case, you've got twice as much money to spend—"

"It doesn't work that way," Bryant told him. "The bid is nine million. Take it or leave it."

"This is bullshit," the man snarled. "The treasure is priceless—"

"The price of anything is determined by the market demand," Bryant explained calmly. "In this case, the market demand dictates that it's worth nine million."

That only seemed to agitate the man more. "I'll go elsewhere. There are other buyers."

Bryant shook his head sadly. "Not a lot of them who would be willing to cough up nine million dollars in diamonds. And the number would shrink considerably when word got around that the treasure had the blood of at least two men on it."

There was a pause. "What do you mean by that?"

"Papadoupoulous and a smuggler named Saffarian. At least that was one of the names he went by."

"The cops know about our deal?" he asked urgently.

"Take it easy. They don't know anything." Bryant sat listening to the silence singing through the box. "You still there, son?"

"I'm here."

The bald head bobbed, once. "The art world isn't that big. News spreads very fast. After the word got out that there were a couple of murders attached to the treasure, no major institution would touch it. That would leave individual collectors. But then, they'd know about the treasure's history too, and they'd most likely use that to try to grind the price down. Hell, son, that's how half of them got the money in the first place. There's a chance you might even wind up with less than nine million, and even before that happened, you might wind up in jail."

"We didn't kill anybody," the man insisted.

"That's between you and the police," Bryant said in a bored tone. "As far as I'm concerned, it doesn't have anything to do with our transaction. Except to sort of limit your options, of course. Now, I could try to grind you down myself, but that isn't the way I do business. I made an offer and I'm ready to make good on it. We have the diamonds ready and we're ready to deal. So let's cut out the crap and get this show on the road."

There was a muffled sound as the caller put his hand over the receiver. After a few seconds, he got back on and said, "It has to happen tonight."

"I told you, we're ready," Bryant said. "The next voice you hear will be Maynard Tarcher. He is my personal assistant. He will give you instructions when and where the purchase will be made."

"Look, man, this is gonna go down like I say, or the deal is off," the man said, but the bluster in the voice was hollow. Bryant had seized control of the situation, and they both knew it.

Tarcher took the phone. "You don't think I'm going to agree to show up at some unknown location with nine million bucks in cash. You say you didn't kill anybody. That's fine, but you can't expect us to just take your word for it. We don't know who you are or who your friends are—"

"I don't have any friends," the man said.

That I believed.

Tarcher braced his hands on the edge of the desk next to Bryant and leaned forward. "You pick the time, but we pick the place. It's a spot we think will be acceptable to both you and us. You have access to a boat?"

"Why?" The voice quivered with paranoia. He had to think he was dealing with Kreskin.

"Because the location is fourteen miles due west from Malibu," Tarcher told him. "A U.S. West Petroleum drilling rig. Latitude thirty-four-oh-three north, longitude one-nineteen-point-fourteen west. It has the minimum amount of risk for both of us. We can insure our physical security, and since it's beyond the twelve-mile limit, the police agencies that are looking for you will have no jurisdiction."

I could almost hear him thinking through the box on the desk. "Go on."

"You will approach by the sea and moor alongside the north face. You'll see a set of stairs there, with some long knotted ropes hanging down from the top of the rig. The ropes are to help you steady yourself getting onto the platform. We will meet you at the second level. The diamonds will be there for your inspection. Professor Arbogast will need approximately one hour to verify the authenticity of the treasure. If everything checks out, you will be given the stones and nobody will ever know the transaction took place."

"What about the crew?"

"There won't be any. Just you and us."

He thought it over for what seemed to be a long time. "Okay. Arbogast and one other person. We'll be watching. If we see more than two people on that platform, we sail with the treasure. You got that?"

"We got it."

He thought it over and said, "If I see one cop there— "

"You won't, don't worry."

"Give me those coordinates again."

Tarcher recited them and the caller said, "Eleven o'clock." The voice assumed a threatening tone: "This better be on the up and up."

Tarcher responded to the voice by hardening his own. "We'll keep our end of the bargain, you just be sure you keep yours. If you have any ideas about pulling any funny stuff, better forget them. You're dealing with an international corporation now, not the L.A.P.D. We don't recognize twelve-mile limits. We'll find you, wherever you go."

"What's your name again?" the caller asked.

"Tarcher."

"You gonna be there tonight, Tarcher?"

"I don't know. Why?"

"I'm just kind of curious what you look like. You sound like a real fucking dickhead." The man laughed and a dial tone sounded through the speaker.

Tarcher handed the phone over to Gros, who positively beamed as he hung it up. "That was brilliant, C. W.! What a coup! It's an absolute steal at nine million! For a moment there, I had to admit, I was a little nervous. I thought you were playing it a little too hard-nosed, but it worked out marvelously—"

"So far," I interjected. "Who's going to be the second man?"

"I will," Tarcher volunteered.

I wanted some answers from Fox, and this could be my last chance of getting them. I decided to play on Gros's suspicions about Bryant's motives. "Don't you think someone from our side should be represented at this buy?"

Bryant looked at me sharply. "We're all on the *same* side, remember?"

But Gros caught my drift and picked up the cue. "Asch is right. Somebody from the museum should be there. After all, it's half our money. And Dr. Arbogast is working for you."

"Are you trying to imply that I would compromise myself in some way for Mr. Bryant?" Arbogast asked, insulted.

Gros offered him a placatory smile. "Of course not. All I'm saying is that this is a joint venture and it should be handled as such."

"The second man is going to have to be someone who can handle the situation in case something goes wrong," Tarcher said.

I turned up my palms. "I guess I'm elected."

"This isn't time to be playing *Star Search*," Tarcher protested. "We're going to need a professional on this job."

"I'm not exactly an amateur," I told him.

Tarcher looked at me levelly. "You've been involved in a buy situation like this before?"

"Not exactly like this, but close enough."

Tarcher ignored that. "You have a weapon?"

"Yeah."

"What kind?"

"Colt Commander."

"How good are you with it?"

"Good enough."

"You fire at least one hundred rounds a month with it?"

"Yeah."

"What is all this?" Gros asked restlessly.

Tarcher turned to him and blinked slowly. "We don't even know for sure these people have the treasure. They could be setting this thing up just to get the diamonds."

"But I've *seen* the treasure," Arbogast interjected.

"You were shown three pieces of it by Papadoupoulous," Tarcher countered. "Papadoupoulous is dead." He turned back to me. "I want to be sure, in case something happens, that there aren't any fuck-ups. Normally, I'd take Asch over to a range and test his marksmanship, but there isn't time for that now. I'm willing to take his word for his competence with a handgun."

"I'm good enough to handle the job."

His eyes grew steely as they peered into mine. "Shooting at targets is a lot different than shooting at a man. You ever shoot anybody before?"

I stared back levelly. "Yeah."

"How long ago was that?"

"Ten years."

His expression remained blank. "Why did you do it?"

"He was trying to kill me."

"Did he die?"

"Yeah."

"How do you feel about that?"

"Better now than I did then," I said truthfully.

"Under the same circumstances, would you hesitate to do the same thing again?"

"No," I said. "I like myself too much."

Arbogast shifted nervously in his chair. "All this talk of violence is beginning to frighten me. I didn't realize it was going to be dangerous."

"It probably won't be," I tried to assure him. "If they have the treasure, there's no reason for them to try a rip-off. Why should they? It's like Mr. Bryant said, they'd never be able to dump it anywhere else. All they're interested in is the diamonds."

"Asch is probably right," Tarcher said. "But it's necessary to plan for every contingency. Don't worry, professor, we'll make sure nothing happens to you."

Arbogast frowned, apparently not appeased by Tarcher's confident pronouncements, but said nothing. I glanced over at Heather, who also looked troubled.

Bryant said, "We'll meet at the U.S. West building downtown at five o'clock with the diamonds. A company helicopter will fly Asch and Professor Arbogast out to the rig at that time, while it's still light. That will give you a good five hours to go over the final arrangements. Maynard will already be out there, setting things up."

Bryant rose and he and Gros congratulated each other again before the billionaire and his entourage exited. When he had gone, Heather looked at Gros and said with obvious misgiving, "I hope you know what you're doing."

"I do."

"It sounds more like an F.B.I. operation than a purchase of art."

"It will be all right," Gros said, frowning.

"I hope so," she said. "For everybody's sake."

Gros raised an eyebrow. "Don't you have an appointment with Hermann at one-thirty about the Etruscan Venus?"

"Yes," she said and stood up. She turned to me with a concerned look, and said, "Good luck tonight. Be careful."

I assured her I would. As I watched her go out, Gros asked, "What do you think?"

I turned back distractedly. "About what?"

"The arrangements for the purchase."

I shrugged. "Tarcher is the expert. I have no reason to doubt his judgment."

"I want you to keep a close eye on things, just the same."

"You think Bryant is up to something?"

"I don't know. I don't trust this suddenly acquired spirit of cooperation."

"You said the diamonds will be here at two?"

"Yes."

"You've made arrangements for security while they are going to be here?"

"Yes."

I nodded and pushed myself out of the chair. "I'll be back in a couple of hours," I told him. "I have to pick up some things for tonight."

A black stretch Lincoln limo was parked on the far side of the lot with its engine idling when I walked outside. The blacked-out windows eclipsed any view of the interior, giving the car an ominous appearance. Cars with that kind of windows always made me feel vaguely unsettled, as if someone was watching me from inside. I shook off the feeling and walked to my Mustang.

The limo was still sitting there, its engine purring softly, as I got in and put my key in my ignition. Curious, I didn't turn the key, but sat there and watched.

Half a minute later, the back door of the limo opened and Heather Piccard stepped out. She closed the door, the limo pulled away, and she turned and started toward her own car, which was parked in a space nearby. I waited until she had pulled out of the lot before I started up the Mustang and left.

# TWENTY-EIGHT

The cardboard mattress was still under the stairs when I checked on my way up to the office, but all the cooking utensils and household items were gone, and I figured the building's boarder had taken the hint and vacated the premises. When I got upstairs, I found he had left payment for his stay outside my door. If I hadn't been looking down at the keys in my hand, I probably would have stepped in it. It looked like the guy had no sense of humor, after all.

The string of curses seemed to come of their own volition as I went downstairs and ripped two pieces of cardboard from the abandoned bed. I used the cardboard pieces as a pooper-scooper and tried to keep from gagging as I carried the disgusting pile down to the trash, then went up to the bathroom. I pulled out a dozen paper towels, soaked them with liquid soap and water, swabbed down the cursed spot, then washed my hands three times with water as hot as I could take before going back to the office.

I had plenty of time to kill, so I sorted through the mail. Most of it was junk mail and bills, but there was one intriguing letter that I took time out to answer. It was from a

Herman T. Warnes of Alhambra, who wrote (in an almost illegible forehand scrawl) to request my help in a "most urgent matter." Herman, it seemed, was being pursued by the "Danny Thomas Gang out of Seattle," the members of which were "Danny Thomas, Frank Sinatra, Connie Stevens, and Mickey Rooney." The vicious desperadoes knew where Herman was because they had implanted an electronic tracking device in his skull, and he wanted me to use my expertise in "electronic survalence" [sic] to jam the device's signals. I wrote a brief note to Mr. Warnes explaining that the case was too big for me, and gave him Jim Gordon's office number at the Los Angles D.A.'s Organized Crime Division. I smiled as I sealed the envelope, mentally invoking Jim's response when he found out who had referred the call. It couldn't be any worse than shit on my doorstep. Anyway, if you couldn't have a little fun with your friends, who could you have fun with?

I stamped it and set it to one side, then worked the combination on the Diebold. I opened the door and pulled out the Colt Commander and the Seecamp LWS-25 auto. I laid them on the top of the desk and closed the safe. The snub-nosed Seecamp looked ridiculously small next to the big .45, like a toy, which was precisely why I liked it as a backup gun. It was superconcealable and its double-action capacity made it more reliable and more versatile than most other .25s. And although it didn't have the all-out stopping power of the Colt, it would get the job done if the shot was good.

I sat down at the desk and pulled open the bottom drawer. I removed the shoulder holster rig for the Colt, along with two clips and a box of ammo for each gun. I pulled back the slide of the .45, tested its action, then did the same with the Seecamp. Satisfied everything was in working order, I loaded the clips, stuck one in each gun, and laid them back out on the desk.

From beneath the desk I pulled out my Spy vs. Spy Model MC1 briefcase recorder. I set it on the desk and pushed the handle to the left to activate the microcassette recorder, then went to the other side of the room and held a short conversation with myself. I returned to the recorder and my voice played back loud and clear. I rewound the tape in the back file to the beginning—to get the full three hours of recording time—loaded the guns, holster, and spare clips into the case, and then locked up the office.

As I pulled out of the lot, I noticed a dark blue Chevy sedan pull out from the alley that ran behind the office. The car stayed six or seven car lengths back as it followed me down Washington. I signaled left on Pacific and watched as the Chevy made the turn. I turned into my street and kept my eyes glued to the mirror. The Chevy passed, heading straight down Pacific, and I let out a breath and pulled into my driveway.

In my apartment I shed my suit and donned a pale blue turtleneck sweater, a pair of loose-fitting brown slacks, gym socks, and running shoes. From the top shelf of the closet I pulled down the ankle holster for the Seecamp, sheathed the tiny auto and strapped it on my shin, then slipped into the .45-stuffed shoulder holster. For bulk as well as warmth I selected a sheepskin-lined rawhide coat, and stood in front of the mirror on the bedroom door.

The guy staring back at me was not only looking old, he was looking worn out. I could have exchanged coats with the bum under my office stairs and moved right into Tent City, no problem. Perhaps that was how close we all were, I thought momentarily. I shook off the mood, getting back to the business at hand.

After satisfying myself that my coat showed no unsightly bulges, I practiced a few quick-draws with both guns. The butt of the Colt slanted down under my left armpit and it was a fairly easy cross-draw with the buttons of the coat undone, but the ankle holster was more troublesome. After five minutes of hopping up and down like a one-legged aerobics instructor, I finally managed to get the gun out of the holster, and after three more successes, I told myself I had it down. If things deteriorated to the stage where I would have to resort to the damned thing, I'd better have it down, or I would be one dead one-legged aerobics instructor.

I left on the empty ankle holster and loaded everything else into the attaché case, then sat down with the phone to practice my other specialty—ass-covering.

Hyde and Bruenig were both out and I left messages with both departments that I'd called. Louie was in. "What's up?" he said.

"Anything new on Fox?"

"No."

"Here's something for you. Naci Saffarian's real name is possibly Naci Aytal. They met in Turkey three years ago. Fox was living there, working for a marine salvage outfit owned by Saffarian."

"Where'd you get this?"

"My foreign bureau," I said. "Fox was also suspected of smuggling heroin for Saffarian."

"That's the link."

"Maybe. How would you like to ask him about it?"

"Speak to me, brother."

"I have it on good authority that Fox and Naci will be at the U.S. West Petroleum drilling platform off Malibu at eleven-thirty tonight." That gave me half an hour, just in case he decided to show up for the party. If I hadn't found out what I wanted to know by that time, I figured I wasn't going to find out at all.

"Drilling platform? What the hell are they going to be doing out there?"

"Meeting some people."

"What people?"

"I'm not at liberty to say."

"What's the purpose of this meeting?"

"It's some sort of deal," I said.

"Drugs?"

"I don't know. Maybe."

"You're not saying U.S. West is involved in drug traffic?" he asked doubtfully.

"No."

"Then what are you saying? Why would they be dicking around with a slimeball like Fox?"

"Maybe it isn't the company," I said cryptically. "Maybe it's some of the company employees."

"You're going to have to do better than that," he told me. "Before we go sticking our nose into an operation as big as U.S. West, I'd need more details. A lot more."

"Sorry, but at this time, I can't give them to you." I tried to sound peeved. "Jesus Christ, I thought you wanted to grab the guy—"

"I *do* want to grab the guy, and if you gave me an address

where you thought he might be, I could do something about it. *A street address.* But for this, I'd have to get approval for a copter. You have any idea what that takes? You know what those things cost the county *a minute?*"

"I'm just giving you the information," I snapped. "What you do with it is your business."

"Where did you happen to come by this information?"

"I can't say. But the source is good."

"This source have a name?"

"Yeah, but I can't give it to you. And it didn't come from me, either."

He sighed in exasperation. "You're not giving me a lot I can sell."

"I'm giving you all I can."

"Your source know where Fox is going to go after this meeting?"

"No. But my guess is south. *Way* south."

He sighed. "I'll notify the Coast Guard, but I wouldn't count too much on anything coming of that. Before they're going to get off their asses, they're going to want the same answers."

I gave him the map coordinates of the platform and said, "Just in case they do send a boat, tell them not before eleven-thirty. It'll screw everything up."

I had anticipated his response. We lived in a society in which *everything* was bureaucratized—especially justice. I had only bothered because I wanted to be covered when the fingers started pointing, which they inevitably would. I hung up and toted everything down to the car.

My stomach went pitty-pat when I stopped at the entrance to the driveway and spotted the blue Chevy parked at the curb four cars down. I backed up and parked, then unsnapped the lid of the carrying case and brought out the .45. I went through the back alley and circled around the block, coming up behind the car in a crouch.

Bahadir Bey sat behind the wheel of the rental, his eyes fixed on the driveway entrance. I stuck the gun barrel through the window and pressed it against the back of his neck. He froze.

"Why are you following me?" I asked.

"Mr. Asch," he said. "You startled me."

"Why are you following me?" I repeated.

His mouth twisted into a nervous smile. "Is there a law in your country about following someone?" He looked at the gun and licked his lips. "Please. There is no need for that."

"What?"

"The gun."

I looked down at the .45. "What gun? I don't see any gun."

He nodded, regaining a bit of his lost composure. "Ah, yes, I see. You are referring to my story to the police. That was necessary, in light of your betrayal. I was deeply disappointed in you, Mr. Asch."

"Life is a long string of disappointments," I said. "Who are you working for, Bey? You're not with the Ministry of Antiquities."

He licked his lips. "Not at the present time."

"So who?"

"I am presently what you would call 'free-lancing,' I believe. Frankly, I was hoping I could convince you to join forces with me—"

"You were the one who was working with Saffarian, weren't you? You helped him get the treasure out of the country, only realizing later what it was worth. You followed him to L.A., thinking you could cut yourself in for a piece, but he refused, so you killed him—"

"That is not true," he cried. "I did not kill Garo. I have proven that satisfactorily to the police."

I smiled. "Maybe I can unprove it. When I get the time. Right now, I don't."

I glanced up and down the street, then cocked the gun and took a step back. Bey covered his head with his arms and dove sideways on the seat as I fired into the sidewall of the tire. By the time I was heading out of the lot he had worked up enough nerve to leave the car and was in the middle of the street shaking his fist at me as I drove past.

It was a little past two-thirty and since I had no idea when I was going to get the chance to eat again, I stopped at the Penguin coffee shop on Olympic, bought copies of the *Times*, the *Chronicle*, and the *Outlook*, and skimmed them over a club sandwich and coffee.

There wasn't anything more about the killings, but one story in the *Chronicle*, on page two, caught my attention. The

banner read, TENT CITY ORGANIZER ACCUSED OF POLITICAL
PROFITEERING. According to the article, an ex-Tent City staff
member had revealed to the *Chronicle* that Lyle Cummings,
champion of the homeless and "mayor" of Tent City, had been
diverting funds from his nonprofit corporation, Homeless
International, for his personal use. A subsequent investigation
by the *Chronicle* had discovered that a seven-unit apartment
building in Encino and another two-bedroom townhouse in
West L.A. had recently been purchased by Early Ann Reeves,
Cumming's sister. When contacted for comment, Cummings,
who claimed to be homeless himself, denied allegations that he
had misused Tent City contributions to finance the two
properties, saying, "It's my sister's money. What she does
with it is her business." County and state officials apparently
thought otherwise, however. Since Ms. Reeves had been on
the welfare rolls for the past three years, they wanted to know
just where the $180,000 in down payments for the two
buildings had come from, and were promising an immediate
investigation.

I couldn't help but smile. "Bick, you old fucking gypsy."
The thought of Bick reminded me of what was ahead and
turned my mind instantly gloomy. I left half of my sandwich
and drove to the museum.

Two uniformed guards stood outside Gros's office door
when I arrived, attaché case in hand. After the secretary
verified my identity they let me in without checking inside the
case or under the coat of my arm. That was what five dollars
an hour bought these days.

Gros sat alone at his desk, looking rather nervous.

"I take it the stones arrived?"

He nodded somberly. "An hour ago, by armed guard."

"Where are they?"

"In the wall safe."

"Are those two guys outside going to ride with us over to
U.S. West?"

"Yes."

They were better than nothing, I guessed, although probably not much. "Do they know what they're guarding?"

"No. Not even my secretary knows."

"What about Heather? Is she coming?"

"No."

I debated whether to tell him what I had seen in the parking lot earlier and decided not to. Actually, I was not sure just what I had seen. Gros already had enough suspicions; he didn't need mine, too.

Gros watched curiously as I swung the attaché case up onto the desk top and flipped open the locks. I brought out the holstered .45 and slipped it on, then lifted my pants leg and sheathed the Seecamp. I put on the sheepskin coat, dropped the Uwara stick into one side pocket, and the extra clips into the other. I caught Gros's surprised expression and said, "I like to be prepared." I checked my watch. "We'd better start. Traffic is going to be a bitch."

Gros nodded and went to a wood cabinet behind the desk. He opened the doors across its front and unlatched a false front that was made to look like book bindings, revealing a heavy safe door. He worked the combination, opened the door, and brought out a black soft-leather pouch, perhaps eighteen inches square.

"May I see them?" I asked.

He shrugged and unzipped the pouch, pulled out four small manila envelopes and laid them on the desk top. He selected one marked VVS 1, 2-CARATS, 38, opened it, and spilled the contents out into his palm. The diamonds seemed to catch all light in the room and concentrate it in his hand. I found myself mesmerized by their cold, smoldering fire.

"Each one of those stones is worth ten thousand dollars," Gros said, jarring me out of my trance. I did a rapid calculation and figured I was staring at about $300,000. "The stones have been separated into the different envelopes according to carats. Nothing is below VVS One quality. Altogether, there are five hundred and sixty-one stones."

Gros put the diamonds back into the envelopes, zipped up all of the envelopes in the pouch, and tucked it under his arm. He opened the door and said to his secretary, "We're ready. Arrange for the limo to be brought to the back entrance. And call Bryant's office and tell them we're on our way."

# TWENTY-NINE

The two guards went ahead to the elevator while I took up the rear. We made it to the ground floor without encountering any bandits. At the back entrance, I took point and cracked the door. A dark-suited driver stood outside the gray Caddy limo, holding the back door open. After Gros verified that he knew the man, we all piled into the car, one of the guards in the front seat, the rest of us in back.

I keep a paranoid eye on all passing cars as we drove down Wilshire. Gros looked cool and unruffled, as if he did this sort of thing all the time. When I thought about it, he probably did. It didn't matter whether you walked around with a Greek crater in your hands or a bag full of diamonds, I supposed; either way, it was four million bucks. Actually, the diamonds were probably less nerve-racking; if you dropped them, at least they wouldn't break.

Traffic on Wilshire was heavy and it took twenty-five minutes to get downtown. The driver made a left on Olive and pulled into the underground lot of the twenty-story U.S. West building. Tarcher's crewcut-haired partner, Leroy, was waiting for us by the pay booth. His long gray overcoat was unbuttoned, revealing a dark suit beneath. I rolled down the back window and he stuck his head in and surveyed our faces. "No problems?"

"No," I said.

He nodded. "The helicopter is waiting. Follow me."

He walked ahead of the limo, his hand inside the jacket of his pin-striped suit as his eyes searched the shadows for pop-up targets. He stopped in front of an elevator door, inserted a key, and the door slid open.

We got out of the car and Leroy said to the two guards, "We'll be all right from here."

Gros told them to wait with the driver, and the three of us got into the elevator. Leroy hit the top button on the panel and we began to ascend swiftly.

The door opened onto the roof, where Bryant and Arbogast stood watching the chopper warm up on the helipad. The only addition Arbogast had made to his rumpled ensemble of the morning was the black leather doctor's satchel in his hand. He was perspiring and his eyes looked jumpy.

"All set?!" Bryant shouted, trying to make himself heard over the whine of the rotors.

I nodded, figuring I would save my voice for when I needed it. Bryant handed Leroy a gray attaché case, which Leroy handcuffed to his left wrist. I needed my voice now. "Leroy is going too?!"

"Extra security!" Bryant yelled. "Maynard has it all worked out! He'll explain it when you get out there!"

I didn't particularly care for it—it was just going to be one more person getting in the way of Q and A—but there wasn't time for debate and we couldn't have conducted one out there, anyway. Gros handed me the diamond pouch and I put it into the attaché case and the three of us ran in a crouch through the artificial windstorm to the chopper. It was a four-seater and Arbogast and Leroy climbed into the back. The pilot waited for me to get strapped in next to him, then lifted off.

I had a strange, queasy feeling in the pit of my stomach as the nose of the copter dipped and the edge of the building dropped away. We passed through the canyon of downtown skyscrapers and then the buildings flattened out into the seemingly limitless urban sprawl that spread out in all directions and disappeared into a greasy haze of smog. The pilot locked in on the Santa Monica freeway and began following it toward the coast.

The city was in dire need of some serious bypass surgery. All the freeways were clogged to a standstill. L.A. may have been the glamour capital of the world, but from up here it looked about as glamorous as a sweatshirt from Thrifty's. It felt good to be above it all, above the smog-choked congestion, the blare of horns, the wail of police sirens. I thought about all those poor chumps down there in their air-conditioned cubicles, radios tuned to their easy-listening stations, heading home to the wife and kids or to lonely studio apartments. Then I thought about where I was headed and my feelings of superiority quickly faded.

We passed over miles and miles of stucco houses and mangy palm-lined streets, over swimming pools like inlaid chips of blue tile, over neighborhoods of the overly possessed to those of the dispossessed, where the language on the signs in corner-market windows changes from block to block.

We flew over Santa Monica, over the Pacific Coast Highway, jammed with the cars of beach-goers calling it a ray-day, and the land was gone. Below, a few surfers paddled their boards out toward the sunset to wait for one last chance to unite with the rhythm of the tide, and then there was only the dying sun playing on the surface of the sea.

Less than ten minutes later I saw it dead ahead, squatting on the horizon like some monstrous black water-striding spider, its proboscis poised to suck the blood out of the earth. As the structure grew in the windows of the copter I was awed by its staggering size. How they got anything that big to float was a complete mystery to me, and one I wasn't particularly interested in solving. The world was going to run out of oil in a few years, anyway. It struck me as foolish that instead of spending the billions developing alternate technologies, we were willing to risk the ecology of the world's oceans to prolong the agony an extra year or two.

We circled the drilling derrick that rose two hundred feet from the middle of the platform, and set down on the helipad. We climbed out and when we had cleared the whirling blades, the pilot lifted off, leaving the three of us standing in the middle of the large heliport.

Leroy waved a hand to our right and led the way to a metal

stairway at the edge of the elevated pad. Tarcher was waiting at the bottom, smiling. "You made it, I see." He eyed both attaché cases. "The diamonds?"

"The diamonds."

He nodded and said, "This way."

We followed him between two large metal shedlike buildings, past a series of large bulk storage tanks, to another stairway that dropped through the deck and zigzagged down the side of the platform. It was only then that I got the full impact of how high up we were and I felt slightly giddy looking straight down the 150 feet to the water's surface. Two switchbacks and 70 feet below, we arrived at the door of a solid aluminum structure and went inside.

We were in a long, narrow, windowless hallway, with a series of doors along one wall. The first doorway was open and I peeked in as I went by. It was full of sophisticated-looking computer equipment and control boards. Tarcher stopped at the second door and opened it. "This is the pusher's quarters. This is where you'll bring Fox."

"Pusher?" I asked. Maybe I'd been closer than I'd thought when I'd talked to Louie.

"It's a slang term for drilling contractor."

We went in. The room was a plain-walled office, perhaps thirty by forty, with a desk, two filing cabinets, and a couple of chairs. There was an IBM computer on the desk along with neat stacks of technical-looking paperwork. Tarcher turned to Arbogast. "Will this be enough room for you to do your tests?"

Arbogast surveyed the desk top and said, "Yes, this will do nicely, thank you."

Tarcher stepped around the desk to the door on the far side of the room and pushed it open. The room beyond was considerably smaller, with just enough room for the bed and bureau that were its only furnishings. "If you want to rest, Professor, you can lie down in here."

"Thank you," Arbogast said.

Tarcher pointed at the telephone on the desk and said to me, "There is a microphone and transmitting device planted in the phone. I'll be right next door, listening to everything that goes down in here. If I hear trouble, I'll be in. If you see or hear something you don't like, just say, 'Did this thing just rock?' and I'll be in. You armed?"

I nodded and pulled back the sports jacket to reveal the butt of the .45.

"That all?"

"No. There's you." I wasn't sure why I didn't tell him about the Seecamp. What the hell. What he didn't know wouldn't hurt him.

"I think you're right," he said. "I don't think you're going to need it anyway."

He went out and we followed him next door. The setup was similar to the pusher's quarters, but bigger. A large geological map was tacked on one wall. Laid out on the desk next to the computer were two Motorola HT-220 radio units with ear-plug attachments and wrist microphones, two Starlite infrared scopes for night vision, and a double-barreled Holland and Holland 12-gauge sawed off to twelve inches, with a pistol grip. I pointed to the shotgun. "Is that what you're going to be coming in with if there's trouble?"

"Yeah."

"Remind me to get out of the way." I hooked a thumb at Leroy. "Where's he going to be?"

"Outside, watching the stairway in case anybody else tries to sneak up while you're occupied. He and I will be in communication with these." He picked up one of the HTs. "I'll be receiving on the same RH frequency as the transmitting unit in your room."

"You buy these or lift them from the Secret Service when you left?"

He obviously didn't see the humor in that. He glowered at me and put the unit back on the desk. "Any more questions?"

"A couple," I said. "What if Fox or whoever shows up wants to take a look in here?"

"The door will be locked," Tarcher said. "You won't have a key. The only way they'll be able to get in is to kick it in. They won't do that."

"Is there coffee anywhere around here?"

"In the galley next door. There are sandwiches, too, if you're hungry."

"Perhaps later," Arbogast said, and went out.

Leroy opened the door to the bedroom and went in. Laid out on the bed were two Ithaca Model 37 pump-action shotguns and two boxes of shells. He unlocked the handcuffs and put the attaché case beside the bed, then sat down on the bed and began loading one of the shotguns.

"You guys came loaded for bear," I said.

"With nine million bucks in diamonds lying around, I'm not taking any chances," Tarcher said. "It's better to have the stuff and not need it than find out later you should have brought it."

Leroy stood up. "I'll take the first watch." He scowled at me and went out. When he'd gone, I commented to Tarcher, "Friendly guy."

"He isn't paid to be friendly, just efficient."

"I take it he is that."

"You take it right. Goddamned efficient. Leroy and I had our asses in some pretty tight squeezes. There's nobody I would rather have with me when the shit comes down."

"The Secret Service was his alma mater, too?"

"We were partners."

"You both quit at the same time?"

"I quit two months before he did."

"Why?"

He lifted an eyebrow and shrugged. "Money. Mr. Bryant offered me a hell of a lot more of it than I was getting working for the government. And I'd had it with the bureaucratic bullshit that went with the job."

"You got Leroy the job with Bryant?"

"That's right." His eyes became veiled as he realized he was being almost friendly, and he turned his back on me. "If you don't mind, I've got some work to do."

I went next door, where Arbogast was removing the contents of his black bag and laying them neatly on the desk. There was a small flashlight, a magnifying glass with three power lenses, a Swiss Army knife, a small bottle of some sort of liquid, a box of Q-Tips, and a miniature UV lamp. "Tools of the trade?"

He looked up distractedly. "Hmmm? Oh. Yes."

I picked up the bottle. "What's this?"

"Xylene," he said. "It's a solvent for removing varnishes."

I put it back down on the desk. "You can tell if the treasure is bogus with just this stuff?"

"I can get a pretty good idea," he said. "Of course, to do a thorough analysis, more sophisticated equipment would be needed. Other tests would have to be run— "

"Like thermoluminescence testing?"

He looked at me curiously. "You know about thermoluminescence testing?"

"Only what I've learned on this case," I said, "but it has made me want to learn more. I find the whole field fascinating."

His head bobbed up and down excitedly as the irrepressible teacher in him came out. "Actually, for most of the treasure of Tarchundaraus, thermoluminescence testing would not be applicable. That test is only for clays. You can't thermo-luminescence-test metals or stone, and those two materials are what most of the artifacts that make up the treasure are made of."

"So what kind of tests would you use?"

He leaned forward intently. He had a live one. "X-ray analysis would be able to show if a metal object had been hammered from an ingot or rolled, for instance. If it had been rolled, it would be a fake. If the object is gold, an elemental analysis would determine what the alloying elements were. If it was only silver or copper, it would be highly suspicious. Usually craftsmen at that time, in that part of the world, used both. An analysis would also tell if it had been made out of mined or panned gold. The composition of the two is quite different, you know."

I nodded as if I did, and that seemed to be enough, because he went on. "You would look for the carat content of the gold. Eighteen to twenty-two carats would be the acceptable range. Anything more or less would be suspect. Twenty-point-two carats, for instance, would be okay. If any repairs had been done to the object, or if any solders had been used, we could analyze the solder to determine its chemical composition. Certain cultures used certain kinds of solder—"

He would have gone on forever if I hadn't cut him off. "But you can't run those kinds of tests here. How do you tell if the stuff is legit or not with just this stuff?"

He smiled knowingly and tapped the corner of his eye with a forefinger. "It boils down to this—the eye. And experience. You must look at the object, examine the craftsmanship, and compare it to how similar objects were made by artisans of the time—"

"I thought there was nothing to compare this with. I thought Arzawa was an unknown commodity?"

His eyes widened and he held up the finger he had touched his eye with. "That's right, it is. But we can make certain deductions from what we know about the artistic styles of the cultures surrounding Arzawa, the Hittites and the Egyptians, for example, and from the techniques employed by artisans of the period. The best craftsmen, for example, would hammer an object from one piece. If there are seams, the object is undoubtedly a forgery. Another thing to examine closely is the surface of the object."

He picked up the magnifying glass. "That's what this is for. Any work of art that has been buried for three thousand years will have scratches on its surface."

"Did the objects in Izmir?"

"Of course. That is another reason I am so sure the artifacts I was shown in the motel room were the same ones I saw in Izmir. I will also closely examine the objects for a patina—"

"Patina?"

"A surface layer of oxidation," he said. "All metals oxidize, except gold, which is one reason it has been valued above all others. But no gold is pure and the metals used to alloy it do oxidize. During ancient times, certain alloys were used, as I've said, and they have a distinctive oxidation pattern. Bronze, for example, turns green on top and beneath that is a layer of brown, due to the patinas of cupric oxide and cupric chloride. Silver turns a bluish-purple, etc."

"There isn't any way to fake all that?"

He shrugged. "You could put a gold object in a tumbler with sawdust to bump and scratch it. To accelerate the development of a patina, you could bury it in some organic material, such as humus. In Turkey, I heard of fishermen who made money on the side working for forgers by keeping artifacts submerged in their nets while they fished. But all these methods are imperfect, and detectable to the trained eye."

I barely heard the last of what he said. I was still locked into three sentences ago. "Humus? You mean, like fertilizer?"

"Yes."

I buried my thoughts and shook my head in admiration. "You really know your stuff, Professor."

He frowned and his voice turned suddenly bitter. "Not if you listen to some of the so-called experts in my profession."

"This treasure hasn't been too lucky for you, has it?"

His gaze wandered away and fixed on a spot across the room. "It has been a curse," he said, then smiled strangely. "But the curse will soon be lifted."

He might have known a lot about Hittite pottery, but he didn't know much about curses. I had a feeling it was going to take a hell of a lot more than nine million bucks to make this one go away.

# THIRTY

I was alone at the long table in the galley, munching on a ham sandwich and silently commiserating with all the Orthodox Jews, Moslems, and other religious fanatics who had cut themselves off from the joys of pig, when Leroy came in, the Ithaca cradled in his arms like a baby. He leaned the shotgun in the corner, took off his heavy overcoat, and shivered. A wire ran from the earplug in his ear and disappeared under the collar of his shirt.

"Cold out there?"

"Not that bad," he said as if talking were a chore. "Just wet."

He poured himself a cup of coffee and sat down.

Just to be making conversation, I asked, "How long you been working for Bryant?"

"Three years."

"How is it?"

"Better than working for the G."

"That's what Tarcher said. I understand you two were partners."

He didn't look at me, but stared straight ahead as he sipped his coffee. He didn't say anything. I took a bite of sandwich.

"You married?" I asked.

"Not anymore."

"Sorry."

He shrugged.

"Any kids?"

"Two."

"How old?"

He turned and looked at me then. His eyes were flat, expressionless. "You ask a lot of fucking questions." He had a personality like #9 sandpaper.

"Force of habit, I guess," I said.

"A habit you should break, maybe."

Obviously I had touched on a sore spot. "I didn't mean to get personal. I was just trying to be friendly—"

He stood up and looked down at me. "I don't need any more friends. I'm a hired hand, here to do a job. So are you. Let's just keep it that way."

"You got something against me, Leroy?"

The question seemed to surprise him. "Why should I have anything against you? I don't know you."

He picked up the shotgun and went out.

Ten minutes later, I picked up my attaché case and went by the operator's quarters. Through the open door I could see Leroy stretched out on the bed, the shotgun by his side like a lover. Arbogast was sacked out in his room, too. I went outside.

The platform was lighted up like a miniature city, but the immense inky blackness that surrounded it reminded me uncomfortably of its fragile and isolated impermanence. In the distance the lights of the real city glowed faintly, like a phosphorescent toxic tide washed up on the land.

The night was clear and black and the stars burned with a terrible clarity. A cold, wet breeze blew off the ocean, chilling me, and I turned the lapels of my coat over my ears. I must have leaned on the railing like that for ten minutes or so, staring out at the darkness and listening to the water slap the hull columns below, when someone coughed behind me. I turned but could see nobody. "Tarcher?"

He stepped out of the darkness. The shotgun was slung

over his shoulder and he held one of the Starlite scopes in his other hand. "What are you doing out here?"

"Just came out to get some air." I looked down at the black ocean and said, "I wouldn't want to be on one of these things during a blowout. I don't know if I'd have the nerve to jump."

"You'd jump," he said. "It'd either be that or be french fried in boiling oil."

After a moment I said, "I was talking to your partner a little while ago. I think I hit a nerve."

"Why?" he asked sharply. "What'd you say?"

"I asked him about his kids."

He seemed to relax, and nodded. "It's a touchy subject with Leroy. He went through a bad divorce a few years ago."

"Are there any good ones?"

"Mine was," he said, smiling. "I thoroughly enjoyed the entire process of getting rid of that bitch. But my situation was different from Leroy's. There were no kids involved. When Leroy lost his kids, it really fucked him up. His kids were his life."

"Doesn't he have visitation rights?"

He shrugged. "She lives in Texas. Got remarried to a dentist. With Mr. Bryant moving around so much, Leroy doesn't get down there very often. The last time he did, four months ago, he heard his little girl call the dentist 'daddy.' When he got back he stayed drunk for two days."

"And you stayed drunk with him."

He smiled. "I'm his partner." He was becoming almost human. He checked his watch. "Nine-ten. I'd better get out of the light in case they're out there, watching."

He melted back into the shadows and I went back inside. An hour and forty minutes and four cups of coffee later, Tarcher stuck his head through the galley door. "Boat coming. Let's go."

He went into his room and locked the door from the inside and I went back outside, to the head of the landing. I could hear the boat, its cut throttle tapping like a cane as it felt its way through the darkness. I leaned over the railing, my eyes fixed on the landing below as the boat slid into the circle of light.

Naci was standing on the bow, making ready with the bow lines as the pilot maneuvered the boat toward the landing.

There was some chop, but she handled the rope expertly and moored the boat without much difficulty.

"Hello!" I called down.

She looked up. Fox stepped out of the cabin of the boat holding a large suitcase. They eyed me apprehensively, then the climb that lay ahead of them.

"There are just the two of you?"

"Yeah!" Fox shouted. "You alone?"

"Dr. Arbogast is inside. Come on up. There are some knotted ropes hanging down there to help you steady yourselves while you get on the landing."

He swung the suitcase onto the landing, then grabbed one of the ropes and stepped aboard. He helped her aboard and they started up the stairs. I watched them carefully as they trudged up the stairs. At the first switchback they stopped to rest for a moment, and Fox moved the suitcase to his other hand for the last leg. By the time they got to the top they were moving slowly and breathing hard.

Fox collapsed against the railing, then his eyes widened in surprise as he recognized me. *"You."*

"People have called me that my whole life," I said, looking them over. If they were packing, their pea jackets did a good job of hiding it. "That the treasure?" I asked, pointing at the canvas suitcase.

"Yeah." His head bobbed warily at my attaché case. "Those the diamonds?"

"Half of them. The other half is inside."

We stood sizing each other up like two alley cats getting ready to scrap, and I said, "Shall we get this over with?"

I opened the door and led the way down the corridor to the pusher's office, where Arbogast was seated at the desk, eagerly awaiting the treasure's arrival. His eyes were riveted on the suitcase; he seemed oblivious to anything else. "Open it," he said excitedly.

Fox eyeballed the room, then stuck his head in the bedroom. "The diamonds."

"Yes, yes," Arbogast said, and pulled a large manila envelope out of his satchel. I opened the attaché case and pulled out the leather pouch, then closed up the case and set it on the floor, pushing the handle to activate the recorder.

Arbogast and I placed the two parcels side by side on the

desk, and Fox put the suitcase on the floor and unzipped it. Arbogast's excitement grew visibly as he watched Fox rummage through the excelsior-filled case and come up with one newspaper-wrapped bundle after another. When he had finished, there were thirteen bundles on the desk, varying from small to bowling-ball size. Arbogast started with the largest, tearing away the newspaper to reveal a tarnished bronze helmet, pointed at the crown.

Arbogast stared at it in awed silence for a few moments, rotating it to get a look at it from all angles. "I hadn't seen this helmet before. You see that pointed crown? Definitely Hittite."

He busied himself, completely absorbed by the task of tearing away the paper wrappings, and within a few minutes all of the objects were lined up on the desk. There was the gold goddess Heather had described, astride two lions and holding a set of horns; a neck pendant of gold chains inset with garnets; a brooch of two golden bees hovering around a honeycomb, three golden droplets hanging from their wings; a piece of what looked like a scepter of green marble; a golden sword hilt shaped like back-to-back leopard heads; a gold two-handled drinking vessel; a ceremonial ax head made of iron; a dagger with a pitted iron blade and an ornate silver handle; some broken strips of gold sheeting covered with what looked like Egyptian hieroglyphs; a patched-up two-handled clay pot adorned with primitive pointy-headed figures; a pair of golden earrings with pendants shaped like horns; and a six-inch-high marble statue of a bare-breasted goddess in a tall conical hat, a serpent entwined around each of her outstretched arms.

Arbogast seemed mesmerized by each of the objects in turn, mumbling things to himself like "magnificent" and "incredible workmanship" and "definite Cycladic influence," as he went over them with his magnifying glass. Fox, in the meantime, was doing an inspection of his own, picking diamonds from packages at random and staring at them through the jeweler's loupe stuck in his eye.

I glanced over at Naci, who remained standing by the door with her hands in the pockets of her coat. Her black hair was pulled back and fastened, and the patina of sweat on her perfect skin gave her the appearance of having been crafted from polished gold herself. But I knew that either Fox or Arbogast would have traded her for any of the objects on the desk. I wondered if she knew it, too.

Despite the fact that both she and Fox were perspiring from the climb, neither of them had made any move to remove their coats, maybe for the same reason I hadn't removed mine.

Fox held up a two-carat diamond in the light and clucked in approval. "Good stones."

I nodded and looked down at him. "The deal has changed."

His head snapped up. "What?"

"The deal has changed," I repeated. "The diamonds for the treasure *plus* the story of what happened to Bick."

His brow lowered. "Who?"

"That friend of mine I asked you about the other day. Remember?"

He licked his lips. "I told you then and I'll tell you now: I don't know anything about it."

I shook my head. "You're going to have to do better than that."

"I don't have to do shit," he said angrily, and started to stand up. I put a hand on his shoulder and roughly pushed him back down in the chair with one hand and brought out the Colt with the other. I had the .45 cocked and pointed against Fox's head before Naci could level the nickel-plated .38 automatic that had materialized from her pocket. I heard Arbogast gasp, but I didn't look his way. There was already too much in the room to keep my eyes on. "I think you'd better put that down before your boyfriend's brains are all over the wall."

Fox was frozen in his chair. "Do what he says, Naci."

She kept her eyes riveted on mine as she bent down and set the gun on the floor.

"Now push it over here with your foot and step back."

She did what I told her. I told Fox to stand up, slowly, and I stepped behind him, keeping the .45 against his spine while I patted him down. His right-hand coat pocket was weighed down and I pulled out what was doing the weighing—a Walther PPK. I ejected the clip and nosed out one of the bullets with my thumb. A Winchester Silvertip.

I dropped the Walther into my own coat pocket, then bent

down, picked up the .38 on the floor, and deposited it in my other pocket.

"What in God's name are you doing, Asch?" Arbogast demanded to know.

"Don't worry, Professor, the deal will still go through. You'll get your treasure. And they'll get their diamonds. I just want a couple of answers, that's all." I told Fox and Naci, "Sit down."

Fox asked belligerently, "What are you going to do?"

"Just what I said. All I want are some straight answers, and you can take the diamonds and be on your way."

Fox licked his lips. "Straight goods?"

"Straight goods."

Thoughts moved furtively behind his eyes. He turned up his palms. "I don't know what answers you expect me to give you. I told you, I don't know anything about your buddy— "

"I know what you told me, and I think you're a lying sack of shit. What'd he do, see you kill Papadoupoulous?"

His head wagged vehemently. He looked sick. "I didn't kill Dimitrios, man. We were partners."

"Some partners," I said scoffingly. "Part of the deal with him was that you got to pork his old lady?"

"Pig," Naci spat.

I ignored her. "Why did you off him? Did he find out the two of you intended to double-cross him?"

He came forward in his chair. His face was lathered with sweat now. "No, no, I swear. We'd never do anything like that. Naci came home and found him like that. It was horrible. His face was all sliced up—" He stopped and shivered at the memory. "She called me up, panicked. We figured somebody was after the treasure and they'd tortured Dimitrios to find out where it was. He hadn't told them, though. The stuff was right where we'd hidden it. We figured we'd better get the hell out of there before whoever did it came back and shredded our faces, so we buried him in the backyard and took the treasure to the boat. Whoever killed Dimitrios had been there while we were gone. The boat was all torn up. Your friend was there, dead. I swear, that's the truth."

I took a breath and held it. The news was not unexpected,

but hearing it still made me slightly nauseous. "How had he been killed?"

He dropped his eyes. "Shot in the back of the head."

"What'd you do with the body?"

"Took it out to sea and dumped it." He looked up at me pleadingly. "That's the honest to God's truth."

"Why did you tee off on me when I came around?"

"I was fucking scared, man. I didn't know who you were. You could have been one of them."

I thought he was probably telling the truth, or at least a good part of it. "One of who? Who else knew about the treasure?"

He bit his lip and looked away. "I don't know."

"Saffarian knew," I said. "That's who you figured did it, didn't you?"

He squirmed in his chair. "Not him personally. I figured he sent some guys."

"You knew he was in town," I said.

He nodded and wiped some perspiration from his brow with two fingers. "He called me up two days before Dimitrios got it. He wanted to be cut in on the deal. Otherwise, he said, he would go to the Turkish authorities and spill the works. I told him to take a hike."

"Why did Saffarian go to you?"

"I worked for him in Turkey."

"Doing what?"

"Diving. He had a marine salvage business."

"And maybe a little heroin smuggling on the side?" I asked. He said nothing.

"What did Saffarian do when you told him to take a hike?"

"He got pissed off. *Real* pissed off. Told me we'd all be sorry."

"Did he say what he meant by that?"

"No. He must have figured Dimitrios's face would convey the message, loud and clear."

"So you went to his hotel room and shot him with this," I said, holding up the Silvertip. "You were careless. You left the shell casing behind, along with a fingerprint or two."

"I didn't go there to kill him," he said. "I just wanted him to lay off Naci and me. He tried to grab for the gun and it went off. It was an accident. I didn't mean to kill him."

I nodded understandingly. "I think you went there to kill him, all right. You went to kill him because he knew that the treasure of Tarchundaraus was a complete fraud. That was his bargaining chip, wasn't it, not any threat to go to the Turkish authorities?"

There was a hiss from Naci's side of the room. Fox shook his head, but his eyes told another story.

"A fraud?" Arbogast blurted out in astonishment. "What the devil are you talking about?"

"I've wondered about it for a while, but you said something earlier that tipped it for me, Professor. When these two buried Papadoupoulous, they buried him in the same spot they'd been keeping the treasure—in a fertilizer pit in the backyard. The pit served a two-fold purpose: as a hiding place and as an aging chamber."

"You're nuts," Fox said weakly.

"It's impossible," Arbogast sputtered.

"You were set up from day one, Doc," I said. "Papadoupoulous was an expert forger. Some of those forgeries he made for Saffarian, which is probably how he got wind of the deal, and which is also probably how he originally joined up with Fox. The three of them—Fox, Saffarian, and Naci—decided to utilize Papadoupoulous's talent to make a real killing. It's just speculation on my part, but they probably used the money Fox had made running dope for Saffarian to finance the raw materials for the treasure. Papadoupoulous picked the treasure of Tarchundaraus because nobody knew anything about Arzawa, therefore it would be harder for experts to prove it a phony. But because it was an unknown quantity, they needed an expert to authenticate it. That was where you came in.

"They found out what train you were going to be on and Naci made sure she was in the same compartment flashing her bracelet. Like a trout rising to a shiny lure, you went for it. When you left the house in Izmir, convinced of the importance of your find, they pulled up stakes and split. Your article, in the meantime, caused the value of the treasure to skyrocket. Unfortunately for you, your own fortunes plummeted because of it."

"Pig," Naci spat again. I realized suddenly that those were the only two words I had ever heard her speak.

"Didn't you ever wonder why, if the treasure was dug up in 1922, they didn't try to sell it until now?"

Arbogast remained silent.

"They smuggled the artifacts out of Turkey and laid low for a couple of years to let things cool down and the mystery build. In the meantime, Papadoupoulous was making more items to add to the treasure to increase its value. They even added a genuine Hittite potsherd to provide a date for the treasure and add further proof of its authenticity."

Arbogast shook his head, dazed, and slumped back in his chair. "It's impossible. I couldn't have made such a mistake."

"Experts make mistakes all the time," I said. "You can't blame yourself too much. The atmosphere of intrigue they set up, the reluctance on the part of the girl, all helped convince you. You probably would have found out they were fakes eventually, but by that time these two would be nowhere around." I took a breath and went on. "They would have gotten away with a lot more, but they didn't count on Bryant and the museum cooperating and shutting down the bidding. And they didn't count on a couple of murders, which also threw a monkey wrench into the works. But nine million wasn't a bad haul for a couple of years' work—if they could have gotten away with it."

The door opened and Tarcher came into the room, his sawed-off shotgun in hand. "Nice to see you, Maynard," I said, smiling. "You've heard everything, I presume."

"I heard," he said, frowning.

"Don't look so glum," I told him. "You just saved your employer four and a half million bucks."

He said into his microphone, "Leroy, where are you?" After a couple of seconds, he nodded and said, "Okay. Get up here. We have a problem."

Tarcher walked over to Fox and looked down at him with a pathetic look. "Don't feel too bad about it, Fox. You wouldn't have gotten away with it, anyway." He turned and stuck the shotgun under my chin and said, "I'll take that, Asch."

I was too shocked to do anything but let go of the gun in my hand. Even if I hadn't been shocked, there wouldn't have been much I could do. "Gee," I said, my jaw working against the cold barrels, "just when I thought we were getting to be pals."

He kept the gun at my throat while he yanked the

automatics from my pockets and stuck them in his belt. He
pulled out the Uwara stick and looked at it curiously. "What's
this?"

"A little persuader I brought along, in case Fox was
reluctant to answer questions," I said.

He smiled and dropped it into his own pocket. "Well, bright
boy, you got your answers. Now sit down."

I pulled up a chair and sat down sideways, wrapping my
right foot behind the chair leg, out of his line of sight. He
turned to Naci and said, "You, too. On the floor over here. I
want everybody together."

Naci moved around him and sat on her knees in front of
Fox.

"Economizing on buckshot?" I asked.

He shook his head sorrowfully. "You had to go and play
detective and fuck everything up. It was going to be so
simple— "

"Let me guess," I said. "We make the swap and Fox and
Naci sail off into the sunset. Or at least everybody thinks so.
Only they don't go anywhere except the bottom of the ocean.
That's why you insisted on this location for the deal, and why
Leroy's along."

"You aren't bad," he said with what sounded like real
respect.

"Leroy is waiting for them on the boat when they go
aboard. He kills them, sails off a little ways and scuttles the
boat, then comes back here in a dinghy. You two split up the
diamonds and nobody is the wiser. Bryant has his treasure, so
he doesn't care, Fox and the girl stay in the police files as
wanted fugitives."

"Beautiful, huh?" he asked, grinning.

"Professor Arbogast and I aren't going to be that easy to
dispose of. How are you going to arrange that?"

"We'll think of something," he assured me.

Arbogast looked from one of us to the other, blinking in
bewilderment. "I don't understand. What is going on?"

It was my turn to lecture him. "Maynard and Leroy are
murderers and thieves, Professor. Because we know that, they
intend to kill us." I turned back to Tarcher. "That was a nice
job you did on Papadoupoulous."

He shrugged and said icily, "He was stubborn. He should have talked. It would have been easier on him."

"How did you know where to find him?"

"It wasn't any great feat of detective work," he said amusedly. "We trailed him from the motel where he met Arbogast."

Slowly, I tugged my right pant leg up from the knee. He didn't seem to notice. "Why did you kill Bick?"

"Papadoupoulous lied to us and said the treasure was on Fox's boat. We went over there and I tossed the place while Leroy kept lookout. Your friend was a little too curious. Leroy spotted him sitting on the place."

"So he killed him?"

"Leroy overreacted."

I knew I had to do something before Leroy got up here and overreacted again. I wished I had spent more time practicing, but there was nothing left to do now but go for it.

Fox started to whimper. "Look, man, take the fucking diamonds. I won't say anything to anybody. I can't. Hell, I'm wanted for murder myself. Just let us go. I swear we won't say a word—"

Tarcher looked down at him and snarled, "Shut the fuck up, asshole. I can't stand whiners."

I touched my forehead with my left hand and turned a little bit more away from him. "I don't feel so good," I groaned and doubled over as if I were going to be sick.

He stepped over to the door and started to open it for Leroy. To do that, he had to turn his head away from us for an instant, the instant I was waiting for. I prayed as I pulled out the Seecamp and brought it up to fire. He caught the motion out of the corner of his eye and wheeled around. The double barrels of the shotgun looked like Carlsbad Caverns as they made the ninety-degree arc and swung toward me, and I cut loose with the .25.

The first bullet caught him just above the left kneecap. He screamed and started to topple sideways and there was an ear-shattering explosion as the shotgun cut loose. Fox had jumped up when I had made my move, which turned out to be a mistake. The shotgun blast caught him in the chest and sent him hurling backward over the chair. I kept pulling the trigger as Tarcher fell, and then I realized the hammer was clicking on nothing.

Naci scrambled on all fours over to Tarcher, who had crumpled into a heap on the floor, and was trying to roll him over to get at the guns in his belt, which he had fallen on. I reached her in two giant steps, grabbed her by the hair, and yanked. She screamed as her head came up and I slugged her on the side of the jaw; the side of her face opened up and she collapsed on top of Tarcher. I looked down at my hand and realized then that the Seecamp was still in it. Those sorts of oversights are bound to happen in the heat of battle.

I pushed her off Tarcher and rolled him over. The front of his shirt was soaked with blood. He had taken at least three slugs beside the one in the leg, one in the gut and two in the chest. He was dead. I tried not to think about it as I pulled out the Detonics .38 auto, the Walther, and my Colt.

I pocketed the Detonics and moved over to where Fox had fallen. He was lying against the blood-splattered wall, his head propped up at an awkward angle. There was a hole the size of a softball in the center of his chest. I didn't bother to feel for a pulse.

Arbogast was still sitting like a statue at the desk, whites showing around the irises of his eyes. His face was freckled with Fox's blood. I shoved the Walther into his hand and said sharply, "Listen to me. She'll probably be out for a while, but in case she comes to, keep her covered. I'm going to close that door. When I come back, I'll knock and identify myself. If anybody tries to come through that door without knocking, shoot him. You understand me?"

He looked up at me, dazed, and nodded.

I pointed to the phone. "Call the L.A. Sheriff's Department. Tell them to get some help out here, that there's been a shooting. You got that?"

"Yes," he said, nodding again. "Police."

"Right."

I was not sure he was in shape to handle the job, but I couldn't wait around to find out. I ran to the door, closing it behind me, and sprinted down the hallway. The cold air outside hit me in the face like a wet washcloth. I looked over the railing. Leroy was at the switchback, huffing up the last flight of steps with the Ithaca. Bless Tarcher. He had picked his location well.

I went to the head of the stairs, dropped into a prone position, and took aim at the middle of his torso with the Commander. "The pursuit of happiness can be exhausting, can't it, Leroy?"

He stopped and looked up, his eyes wide.

"It's over, Leroy. Maynard is dead. Drop the shotgun."

His eyes narrowed calculatingly and he looked behind him. He was a trapped base runner, thirty steps below me and a dozen beyond the switchback landing. His head snapped back and forth, his eyes measuring the distances. I could see the decision in his body as he made it. He brought the shotgun up to firing position and pulled the trigger. The blast had a very personal sound to it and I ducked as buckshot rebounded off the metal around me.

When I raised my head, he had turned and was taking two steps at a time back down to the landing. I squeezed off three shots and he grunted and grabbed his left hip and stumbled. The shotgun clattered down the metal stairs as he took the landing with his face and kept going through the railing and disappeared.

I don't know why in the movies they always shriek like women; Leroy didn't make a sound except the splash when he hit the water. I went down the stairs to the bottom landing where the boat was tied up, but couldn't spot him in the black water. By the time I got back up top, I knew why all of them had been breathing hard.

My hand was on the door handle when I remembered. I knocked and called out, "Professor Arbogast, it's me! Asch! Don't shoot!"

I opened the door cautiously and, when no bullets whistled at me, stepped inside. Arbogast was standing by the desk, staring at the figure of the snake-goddess he held in his hand. Nobody else in the room had moved.

The room was humid, suffocatingly close, filled with the smells of death and cordite. Events were beginning to catch up with me, and I was feeling shaky. My knees turned rubbery and I sank gratefully into one of the chairs. My face was covered with a clammy sweat. I laid the .45 down on the floor, leaned forward, and put my head in my hands. "Have you called the cops?"

He didn't say anything.

I looked up. He had put the statue back on the desk and was aiming the Walther at my midsection. I waved the gun away from me and snapped at him, "Would you mind pointing that gun somewhere else, Professor? It could accidentally go off."

"Yes, it could." His voice was calm, but there was something wrong with his eyes. They looked glazed, out of focus.

"Put the gun down on the desk," I said as forcefully as I could.

He shook his head, slowly. "I'm afraid I can't do that, Mr. Asch. I can't allow you to tell the world."

I blinked at him, trying to make sense of what he was saying. "Tell the world what?"

"That I was duped. That these people made a fool out of me. All these years of struggling with the stigma that came with this treasure, the lies, the innuendo. I won't be made a laughingstock—"

"You won't be a laughingstock," I said. "You can be the one who exposes the treasure as a fraud— "

"I said it was *real*," he whined. "You don't understand. I staked my professional reputation that it was real. Now, even that will be gone."

I was tired of having guns pointed at me, and my voice reflected that as I snapped, "Put the gun down, Professor, before you hurt somebody."

His eyes glistened with tears and he shook his head. "I'm sorry."

I had come through a battle with three cold-blooded killers only to be shot to death by some wigged-out, dipshit archaeologist. My mind reeled from the irony of it, and this time the irony didn't escape me.

I stood slowly and said in a soothing tone, "But, Professor, don't you know? *This* treasure was phony, sure. But the treasure you saw in Turkey was *real*."

He seemed to reel a bit. He blinked, and his face contorted in confusion. *"Real?"*

I moved toward him slowly, holding out my hands in a nonthreatening manner. "Sure. The real treasure is still in

Izmir. Papadoupoulous duplicated it, thinking they could sell it secretly two or three times."

He seemed stunned by the revelation. I was arm's length from him now. He hesitated, then lowered the gun about twenty degrees, which was all I needed. I stepped into the right with everything I had. The automatic flew out of Arbogast's hand and clattered against the wall, and his eyes were all whites as his head snapped back and he fell straight down like a dynamited building.

I looked down at his unconscious form. "Dumb fuck. You've been hanging around academia too long."

I called Louie. This time, he said he thought he could get somebody to spring for a helicopter.

# THIRTY-ONE

The Coast Guard couldn't find any trace of Leroy, but they thought he would probably pop up in a couple of days, as soon as the gases started to bloat the body.

Louie and Company took Arbogast away somewhere and installed me in the galley, where they spent three hours matching up what I told them to the recording of the evening's events. Bryant was contacted at the U.S. West building, but upon hearing the news of what had happened, refused to answer questions until he could confer with his attorney.

I was flown downtown to the Hall of Justice, where I was grilled for another five hours by a battery of detectives and a red-faced deputy D.A. named Tarkenton, who, while openly expressing his contempt for me as a person and a professional, eventually decided (especially in view of my earlier call to Louie) that it would not be worth the county's time and money to prosecute me for any crime. He said he would make up his mind later whether or not to initiate proceedings with the state to try to get my license revoked.

Louie wasn't overjoyed when I asked for a ride to the museum, but he arranged for a black-and-white to drive me

there. It was a little after ten when I stepped through the door
of Heather Piccard's office. She was standing in front of her
desk, transferring the contents of her drawers into a large
cardboard box. She looked up and jumped. "You startled me."
She caught her breath and said, "It's good to see you're alive.
That must have been horrible."

"I've had better times."

"Is it true that Tarcher murdered Papadoupoulous and your
friend?"

"Yeah, it's true."

She lowered her eyes. "I'm very sorry."

"So am I," I said. I pointed at the box. "Are you leaving?"

"This office," she replied. "The board of trustees held an
emergency meeting this morning. They fired Pieter as director as soon as they heard about the scandal."

"It didn't take long for them to get the word."

"News travels fast around here." She went on packing.

"You're the new director?"

She looked up. "Temporarily, until the board can consider
other candidates."

I shrugged. "Don't worry. If Bryant has anything to say
about it, and I'm sure he will, you'll get the job permanently.
That was the plan, wasn't it?"

Her gray eyes were as cold as they were the first day I had
met her. "What do you mean?"

"You were Bryant's inside source," I said. "You and Bryant
had the partnership idea with the museum already worked out
way before you and I had dinner. You used me to suggest the
alliance so you could distance yourself from the whole affair.
That way, I would be acting as Gros's hireling when I brought
it up. That number you sang over dinner about the museum
business being too Machiavellian for you was a crock. You
wanted the director's job all along."

Her expression stiffened, but she remained silent.

I continued. "Bryant and you would have come out winners
either way. If things had gone smoothly, Bryant would have
owned the treasure for half-price, plus gotten what he wanted
with the museum. In the meantime, Bryant would have been
pushing behind the scenes for Gros's dismissal and your
replacing him. The fact that it all blew up in his face only
speeded things up. Gros was finished as soon as the facts came

out, and Bryant still gained. He didn't lose his diamonds and
he still got his way with the trustees."

"You can't prove any of that," she said in a hard tone.

"I don't intend to," I said, and pulled out the bill for $1,200
I had written up on the way over. "I only came over to give
Gros this. I wanted to make sure Katelbaum pays it. I guess
you're the one who takes care of it now."

She gave the bill a cursory glance and put it down on the
desk. "I'll call him and okay it."

I was sure she would have approved it, no matter what the
amount. That money had a lot to cover. I turned and started
to leave but was stopped at the door by her voice. "What about
that dinner we talked about?"

"I don't think so," I said. "When I paid the check, I'd be
wondering if it was my idea or yours."

Her eyes thawed. "We could go dutch. I meant it when I
said I liked you."

I shook my head. "You don't like fakes. Neither do I."

Three days later, high winds and a record surf moved onto
Venice beach, leveling Tent City and exiling its residents back
to the sidewalks and alleys of the inner city. Residents were
calling it an act of God, which seemed to indicate that they did
not buy the propaganda about the downtrodden being His
favorite people. Personally, I didn't see it as part of any divine
plan, but of a lack of one. It was all a big cosmic crapshoot.
Some people had all the luck, others had none. Most of us had
it dished out in dribs and drabs, like winning five dollars in
the lottery.

I went down to the beach a lot for the next few weeks, to
watch the gradual, straggling return of the joggers and the
roller-skating beach bunnies and to stare out at the ocean and
wonder where Bick and Oscar the Movie Penguin were now
that I needed them.